Mark Akenside, Jeremiah Dyson

The Poems of Mark Akenside, M.D.

Mark Akenside, Jeremiah Dyson

The Poems of Mark Akenside, M.D.

ISBN/EAN: 9783337406998

Printed in Europe, USA, Canada, Australia, Japan

Cover: Foto ©Andreas Hilbeck / pixelio.de

More available books at **www.hansebooks.com**

P O E M S

OF

MARK AKENSIDE, M.D.

L O N D O N,

PRINTED BY W. BOWYER AND J. NICHOLS:

AND SOLD BY J. DODSLEY, IN PALL MALL.

MDCCLXXII.

ADVERTISEMENT.

THIS Volume contains a complete Collection of the poems of the late Dr. Akenside, either reprinted from the original Editions, or faithfully published from Copies which had been prepared by himself for publication.

That the principal Poem should appear in so disadvantageous a state, may require some explanation. The first publication of it was at a very early part of the Author's life. That it wanted Revision and Correction, he was sufficiently sensible; but so quick was the demand for several successive republications, that in any of the intervals to have completed the whole of his Corrections was utterly impossible; and yet to have gone on from time to time making farther Improvements in every new Edition would (he thought) have had the appearance at least of abusing the favor of the Public. He chose therefore to continue for some time reprinting it without alteration, and to forbear publishing any Corrections or Improvements until he should be able at once to give them to the Public complete. And

a 3

with

with this view, he went on for feveral years to review and correct the Poem at his leifure; till at length he found the task grow fo much upon his hands, that, defpairing of ever being able to execute it fufficiently to his own fatisfaction, he abandoned the purpofe of correcting, and refolved to write the Poem over anew upon a fomewhat different and an enlarged Plan. And in the execution of this Defign he had made a confiderable Progrefs. What Reafon there may be to regret that he did not live to execute the whole of it, will beft appear from the perufal of the Plan itfelf, as ftated in the General Argument, and of the Parts which he had executed, and which are here publifhed. For the Perfon, to whom he intrufted the Difpofal of his Papers, would have thought himfelf wanting, as well to the Service of the Public, as to the Fame of his Friend, if he had not produced as much of the Work as appeared to have been prepared for publication. In this light he confidered the intire firft and fecond Books, of which a few Copies had been printed for the ufe only of the Author and certain Friends: alfo a very confiderable part of the third Book, which had been tranfcribed in order to its being printed in the fame manner: and to thefe is added the Introduction to a fubfequent Book, which in the Manufcript is called the Fourth, and which appears to have been compofed at the time when the Author intended to comprize

the

the whole in Four Books; but which, as he had afterwards determined to diftribute the Poem into more Books, might perhaps more properly be called the Laft Book. And this is all that is executed of the new work, which although it appeared to the Editor too valuable, even in its imperfect State, to be withholden from the Public, yet (he conceives) takes in by much too fmall a part of the original Poem to fupply its place, and to fuperfede the re-publication of it. For which reafon both the Poems are inferted in this collection.

Of Odes the Author had defigned to make up Two Books, confifting of twenty Odes each, including the feveral Odes which he had before publifhed at different times.

The Hymn to the Naiads is reprinted from the fixth Volume of Dodfley's Mifcellanies, with a few Corrections and the addition of fome Notes. To the Infcriptions taken from the fame Volume three new Infcriptions are added; the laft of which is the only inftance wherein a liberty has been taken of inferting any thing in this Collection, which did not appear to have been intended by the Author for publication; among whofe papers no Copy of thiswas found, but it is

printed

printed from a Copy which he had many years fince given to the Editor.

The Author of thefe Poems was born at Newcaftle upon Tyne, on the 9th Day of November 1721. He was educated at the Grammar School at Newcaftle, and at the Univerfities of Edinburgh and Leyden, at the latter of which he took his Degree of Doctor in Phyfic. He was afterwards admitted by Mandamus to the Degree of Doctor in Phyfic in the Univerfity of Cambridge: elected a Fellow of the Royal College of Phyficians, and one of the Phyficians of St. Thomas's Hofpital: and upon the Eftablifhment of the Queen's Houfehold, appointed one of the Phyficians to Her Majefty. He died of a putrid Fever, on the 23d Day of June 1770, and is buried in the Parifh Church of St. James, Weftminfter.

CONTENTS.

THE

PLEASURES

OF

MAGINATION.

A

POEM.

IN THREE BOOKS.

Ἀσεβὲς μέν ἐςιν ἀνθρώπῳ τὰς παρὰ τῦ θεῦ χάριτας ἀτιμάζειν.

EPICT. apud Arrian. II. 23.

Published in the Year MDCCXLIV.

B

THE

DESIGN.

T H E R E are certain powers in human nature which seem to hold a middle place between the organs of bodily sense and the faculties of moral perception: They have been called by a very general name, *The Powers of Imagination*. Like the external senses, they relate to matter and motion; and, at the same time, give the mind ideas analogous to those of moral approbation and dislike. As they are the inlets of some of the most exquisite pleasures with which we are acquainted, it has naturally happened that men of warm and sensible tempers have sought means to recall the delightful perceptions which they afford, independent of the objects which originally produced them. This gave rise to the imitative or designing arts; some of which, as painting and sculpture, directly copy the external appearances which were admired in nature; others, as music and poetry, bring them back to remembrance by signs universally established and understood.

But these arts, as they grew more correct and deliberate, were of course led to extend their imitation beyond the peculiar objects of the imaginative powers; especially poetry, which, making use of language as the instrument by which it imitates, is consequently become an unlimited representative of every species and mode of being. Yet as

their

their intention was only to exprefs the objects of imagination, and as they ftill abound chiefly in ideas of that clafs, they of courfe retain their original character; and all the different pleafures which they excite, are termed, in general, *Pleafures of Imagination.*

The defign of the following poem is to give a view of *thefe* in the largeft acceptation of the term; *fo that whatever our imagination feels from the agreeable appearances of nature, and all the various entertainment we meet with either in poetry, painting, mufic, or any of the elegant arts, might be deducible from one or other of thofe principles in the conftitution of the human mind, which are here eftablifhed and explained.*

In executing this general plan, it was neceffary firft of all to diftinguifh the Imagination from our other faculties; and in the next place to characterize thofe original forms or properties of being, about which it is converfant, and which are by nature adapted to it, as light is to the eyes, or truth to the underftanding. Thefe properties Mr. *Addifon* had reduced to the three general claffes of greatnefs, novelty, and beauty; and into thefe we may analyfe every object, however complex, which, properly fpeaking, is delightful to the imagination. But fuch an object may alfo include many other fources of pleafure; and its beauty, or novelty, or grandeur, will make a ftronger impreffion by reafon of this concurrence. Befides which, the imitative arts, efpecially poetry, owe much of their effect to a *fimilar* exhibition of properties quite *foreign* to the imagination, infomuch that in every line of the moft applauded poems, we meet with either ideas drawn from the external fenfes, or truths difcovered to the underftanding, or illuftrations of contrivance and final caufes, or, above all the reft, with circumftances proper to awaken and ingage the paffions. It was therefore neceffary to enumerate and exemplify thefe different fpecies of pleafure; efpecially that

from

from the paffions, which, as it is fupreme in the nobleft work of human genius, fo being in fome particulars not a little furprizing, gave an opportunity to enliven the didactic turn of the poem, by introducing an allegory to account for the appearance.

After thefe parts of the fubject which hold chiefly of admiration, or naturally warm and intereft the mind, a pleafure of a very different nature, that which arifes from ridicule, came next to be confidered. As this is the foundation of the comic manner in all the arts, and has been but very imperfectly treated by moral writers, it was thought proper to give it a particular illuftration, and to diftinguifh the general fources from which the ridicule of characters is derived. Here too a change of ftile became neceffary; fuch a one as might yet be confiftent, if poffible, with the general tafte of compofition in the ferious parts of the fubject: nor is it an eafy tafk to give any tolerable force to images of this kind, without running either into the gigantic expreffions of the mock heroic, or the familiar and poetical raillery of profeffed fatire; neither of which would have been proper here. .

The materials of all imitation being thus laid open, nothing now remained but to illuftrate fome particular pleafures which arife either from the relations of different objects one to another, or from the nature of imitation itfelf. Of the firft kind is that various and complicated refemblance exifting between feveral parts of the material and immaterial worlds, which is the foundation of metaphor and wit. As it feems in a great meafure to depend on the early affociation of our ideas, and as this habit of affociating is the fource of many pleafures and pains in life, and on that account bears a great fhare in the influence of poetry and the other arts, it is therefore mentioned here and its effects defcribed. Then follows a general account of the production of thefe elegant arts,

and

and of the fecondary pleafure, as it is called, arifing from the refemblance of their imitations to the original appearances of nature. After which, the work concludes with fome reflexions on the general conduct of the powers of imagination, and on their natural and moral ufefulnefs in life.

Concerning the manner or turn of compofition which prevails in this piece, little can be faid with propriety by the author. He had two models; that antient and fimple one of the firft *Græcian* poets, as it is refined by *Virgil* in the *Georgics*, and the familiar epiftolary way of *Horace*. This latter has feveral advantages. It admits of a greater variety of ftile; it more readily ingages the generality of readers, as partaking more of the air of converfation; and, efpecially with the affiftance of rhyme, leads to a clofer and more concife expreffion. Add to this the example of the moft perfect of modern poets, who has fo happily applied this manner to the nobleft parts of philofophy, that the public tafte is in a great meafure formed to it alone. Yet, after all, the fubject before us, tending almoft conftantly to admiration and enthufiafm, feemed rather to demand a more open, pathetic and figured ftile. This too appeared more natural, as the author's aim was not fo much to give formal precepts, or enter into the way of direct argumentation, as, by exhibiting the moft ingaging profpects of nature, to enlarge and harmonize the imagination, and by that means infenfibly difpofe the minds of men to a fimilar tafte and habit of thinking in religion, morals, and civil life. 'Tis on this account that he is fo careful to point out the benevolent intention of the Author of nature in every principle of the human conftitution here infifted on; and alfo to unite the moral excellencies of life in the fame point of view with the meer external objects of good tafte; thus recommending them in common to our natural propenfity for admiring what is beautiful and lovely. The fame views have

have alfo led him to introduce fome fentiments which may perhaps be looked upon as not quite direct to the fubject ; but, fince they bear an obvious relation to it, the authority of *Virgil*, the faultlefs model of didactic poetry, will beft fupport him in this particular. For the fentiments themfelves, he makes no apology..

[ix]

C O N T E N T S.

THE PLEASURES OF IMAGINATION.

[As firſt publiſhed.]

THE PLEASURES OF THE IMAGINATION.

[On an enlarged Plan.]

ODES ON SEVERAL SUBJECTS.

BOOK THE FIRST.

BOOK THE SECOND.

Ode

H Y M N   T O   T H E   N A I A D S.

I N S C R I P T I O N S.

THE

THE

PLEASURES

OF

MAGINATION.

BOOK THE FIRST.

C

ARGUMENT

OF

THE FIRST BOOK.

THE subject proposed. Difficulty of treating it poetically. The ideas of the divine mind, the origin of every quality pleasing to the imagination. The natural variety of constitution in the minds of men; with its final cause. The idea of a fine imagination, and the state of the mind in the enjoyment of those pleasures which it affords. All the primary pleasures of the imagination result from the perception of greatness, or wonderfulness, or beauty in objects. The pleasure from greatness, with its final cause. Pleasure from novelty or wonderfulness, with its final cause. Pleasure from beauty, with its final cause. The connexion of beauty with truth and good, applied to the conduct of life. Invitation to the study of moral philosophy. The different degrees of beauty in different species of objects: colour; shape; natural concretes; vegetables; animals; the mind. The sublime, the fair, the wonderful of the mind. The connexion of the imagination and the moral faculty. Conclusion.

THE

THE

PLEASURES

OF

IMAGINATION.

BOOK THE FIRST.

WITH what attractive charms this goodly frame
Of nature touches the confenting hearts
Of mortal men ; and what the pleafing ftores
Which beauteous imitation thence derives
To deck the poet's, or the painter's toil ;   5.
My verfe unfolds.   Attend, ye gentle powers
Of mufical delight! and while i fing
Your gifts, your honours, dance around my ftrain.
Thou, fmiling queen of every tuneful breaft,
Indulgent Fancy! from the fruitful banks   10
Of Avon, whence thy rofy fingers cull
Frefh flowers and dews to fprinkle on the turf
Where Shakefpeare lies, be prefent: and with thee
Let Fiction come, upon her vagrant wings
Wafting ten thoufand colours through the air,   15

C 2

Which,

Which, by the glances of her magic eye,
She blends and shifts at will, through countless forms,
Her wild creation.   Goddess of the lyre,.
Which rules the accents of the moving sphere,
Wilt thou, eternal Harmony! descend   20
And join this festive train ? for with thee comes
The guide, the guardian of their lovely sports,
Majestic Truth ; and where Truth deigns to come,
Her sister Liberty will not be far.
Be present all ye Genii, who conduct   25
The wandering footsteps of the youthful bard,
New to your springs and shades : who touch his ear
With finer sounds : who heighten to his eye
The bloom of nature, and before him turn
The gayest, happiest attitude of things.   30

     Oft have the laws of each poetic strain
The critic-verse imployed ; yet still unsung
Lay this prime subject, though importing most
A poet's name : for fruitless is the attempt,
By dull obedience and by creeping toil   35
Obscure to conquer the severe ascent
Of high Parnassus.   Nature's kindling breath
Must fire the chosen genius ; nature's hand
Must string his nerves, and imp his eagle-wings
Impatient of the painful steep, to soar   40

                                              High

High as the fummit; there to breathe at large
Æthereal air : with bards and fages old,
Immortal fons of praife.   Thefe flattering fcenes
To this neglected labour court my fong ;
Yet not unconfcious what a doubtful tafk   45
To paint the fineft features of the mind,
And to moft fubtle and myfterious things
Give colour, ftrength, and motion.   But the love
Of nature and the mufes bids explore,
Through fecret paths erewhile untrod by man,   50
The fair poetic region, to detect
Untafted fprings, to drink infpiring draughts,
And fhade my temples with unfading flowers
Cull'd from the laureate vale's profound recefs,
Where never poet gain'd a wreath before.   55

From heaven my ftrains begin ; from heaven defcends
The flame of genius to the human breaft,
And love and beauty, and poetic joy
And infpiration.   Ere the radiant fun
Sprang from the eaft, or 'mid the vault of night   60
The moon fufpended her ferener lamp ;
Ere mountains, woods, or ftreams adorn'd the globe,
Or wifdom taught the fons of men her lore ;
Then liv'd the almighty One : then, deep-retir'd
In his unfathom'd effence, view'd the forms,   65

The

The forms eternal of created things;
The radiant fun, the moon's nocturnal lamp,
The mountains, woods and ftreams, the rowling globe,
And wifdom's mien celeftial.   From the firft
Of days, on them his love divine he fix'd,   70
His admiration : till in time compleat,
What he admir'd and lov'd, his vital fmile
Unfolded into being.   Hence the breath
Of life informing each organic frame,
Hence the green earth, and wild refounding waves;   75
Hence light and fhade alternate; warmth and cold;
And clear autumnal fkies and vernal fhowers,
And all the fair variety of things.

    But not alike to every mortal eye
Is this great fcene unveil'd.   For fince the claims   80
Of focial life, to different labours urge
The active powers of man; with wife intent
The hand of nature on peculiar minds
Imprints a different byafs, and to each
Decrees its province in the common toil.   85
To fome fhe taught the fabric of the fphere,
The changeful moon, the circuit of the ftars,
The golden zones of heaven: to fome fhe gave
To weigh the moment of eternal things,
Of time, and fpace, and fate's unbroken chain,   90

                                                         And

And will's quick impulſe: others by the hand
She led o'er vales and mountains, to explore
What healing virtue ſwells the tender veins
Of herbs and flowers; or what the beams of morn
Draw forth, diſtilling from the clifted rind   95
In balmy tears.   But ſome, to higher hopes
Were deſtin'd; ſome within a finer mould
She wrought, and temper'd with a purer flame.
To theſe the ſire omnipotent unfolds
The world's harmonious volume, there to read   100
The tranſcript of himſelf.   On every part
They trace the bright impreſſions of his hand:
In earth or air, the meadow's purple ſtores,
The moon's mild radiance, or the virgin's form
Blooming with roſy ſmiles, they ſee portray'd   105
That uncreated beauty, which delights
The mind ſupreme.   They alſo feel her charms,
Enamour'd; they partake the eternal joy.

    For as old Memnon's image, long renown'd
By fabling Nilus, to the quivering touch   110
Of Titan's ray, with each repulſive-ſtring
Conſenting, ſounded through the warbling air
Unbidden ſtrains; even ſo did nature's hand
To certain ſpecies of external things
Attune the finer organs of the mind: 115

So

So the glad impulſe of congenial powers,
Or of ſweet ſound, or fair proportion'd form,
The grace of motion, or the bloom of light,
Thrills through imagination's tender frame,
From nerve to nerve: all naked and alive   120
They catch the ſpreading rays: till now the ſoul
At length diſcloſes every tuneful ſpring,
To that harmonious movement from without
Reſponſive.   Then the inexpreſſive ſtrain
Diffuſes its inchantment: fancy dreams   125
Of ſacred fountains and Elyſian groves,
And vales of bliſs: the intellectual power
Bends from his awful throne a wondering ear,
And ſmiles: the paſſions, gently ſooth'd away,
Sink to divine repoſe, and love and joy   130
Alone are waking; love and joy, ſerene
As airs that fan the ſummer.   O! attend,
Whoe'er thou art, whom theſe delights can touch,
Whoſe candid boſom the refining love
Of nature warms, o! liſten to my ſong;   135
And i will guide thee to her favourite walks,
And teach thy ſolitude her voice to hear,
And point her lovelieſt features to thy view.

    Know then, whate'er of nature's pregnant ſtores,
Whate'er of mimic art's reflected forms   140

With

With love and admiration thus inflame
The powers of fancy, her delighted sons
To three illustrious orders have referr'd ;
Three sister-graces, whom the painter's hand.
The poet's tongue confesses ; the sublime,   145
The wonderful, the fair.   I see them dawn !
I see the radiant visions, where they rise,
More lovely than when Lucifer displays
His beaming forehead through the gates of morn,
To lead the train of Phœbus and the spring.   150

    Say, why was man so eminently rais'd
Amid the vast creation ; why ordain'd
Through life and death to dart his piercing eye,
With thoughts beyond the limit of his frame ;
But that the omnipotent might send him forth   155
In sight of mortal and immortal powers,
As on a boundless theatre, to run
The great career of justice ; to exalt
His generous aim to all diviner deeds ;
To chase each partial purpose from his breast ;   160
And through the mists of passion and of sense,
And through the tossing tide of chance and pain,
To hold his course unfaultering, while the voice
Of truth and virtue, up the steep ascent.
Of nature, calls him to his high reward,   165

D

The

The applauding ſmile of heaven?   Elſe wherefore burns
In mortal boſoms this unquenched hope,
That breathes from day to day ſublimer things,
And mocks poſſeſſion? wherefore darts the mind,
With ſuch reſiſtleſs ardour to embrace   170
Majeſtic forms; impatient to be free,
Spurning the groſs controul of wilful might;
Proud of the ſtrong contention of her toils;
Proud to be daring?   Who but rather turns
To heaven's broad fire his unconſtrained view,   175
Than to the glimmering of a waxen flame?
Who that, from Alpine heights, his labouring eye
Shoots round the wide horizon, to ſurvey
Nilus or Ganges rowling his bright wave.
Through mountains, plains, through empires black with ſhade
And continents of ſand; will turn his gaze
To mark the windings of a ſcanty rill
That murmurs at his feet?   The high-born ſoul
Diſdains to reſt her heaven-aſpiring wing
Beneath its native quarry.   Tir'd of earth   185
And this diurnal ſcene, ſhe ſprings aloft
Through fields of air; purſues the flying ſtorm;
Rides on the rollied lightning through the heavens;
Or, yok'd with whirlwinds and the northern blaſt,
Sweeps the long tract of day.   Then high ſhe ſoars   190
The blue profound, and hovering round the ſun

Beholds

Beholds him pouring the redundant stream
Of light; beholds his unrelenting sway
Bend the reluctant planets to absolve
The fated rounds of time.   Thence far effus'd   195
She darts her swiftness up the long career
Of devious comets; through its burning signs
Exulting measures the perennial wheel
Of nature, and looks back on all the stars,
Whose blended light, as with a milky zone,   200
Invests the orient.   Now amaz'd the views
The empyreal waste, where happy spirits hold,
Beyond this concave heaven, their calm abode;
And fields of radiance, whose unfading light
Has travell'd the profound six thousand years,   205
Nor yet arrives in sight of mortal things.
Even on the barriers of the world untir'd
She meditates the eternal depth below;
Till half recoiling, down the headlong steep
She plunges; soon o'erwhelm'd and swallow'd up   210
In that immense of being.   There her hopes
Rest at the fated goal.   For from the birth
Of mortal man, the sovran maker said,
That not in humble nor in brief delight,
Not in the fading echoes of renown,   215
Power's purple robes, nor pleasure's flowery lap,
The soul should find enjoyment: but from these

Turning difdainful to an equal good,
Through all the afcent of things inlarge her view,
Till every bound at length fhould difappear,   220
And infinite perfection clofe the fcene.

    Call now to mind what high capacious powers
Lie folded up in man; how far beyond
The praife of mortals, may the eternal growth
Of nature to perfection half divine,   225
Expand the blooming foul? What pity then
Should floth's unkindly fogs deprefs to earth
Her tender bloffom; choak the ftreams of life,
And blaft her fpring! Far otherwife defign'd
Almighty wifdom; nature's happy cares   230
The obedient heart far otherwife incline.
Witnefs the fprightly joy when aught unknown
Strikes the quick fenfe, and wakes each active power
To brifker meafures: witnefs the neglect
Of all familiar profpects, though beheld   235
With tranfport once; the fond attentive gaze
Of young aftonifhment; the fober zeal
Of age, commenting on prodigious things.
For fuch the bounteous providence of heaven,
In every breaft implanting this defire   240
Of objects new and ftrange, to urge us on
With unremitted labour to purfue

Thofe facred ftores that wait the ripening foul,
In Truth's exhauftlefs bofom.   What need words
To paint its power?   For this the daring youth   245
Breaks from his weeping mother's anxious arms,
In foreign climes to rove: the penfive fage,
Heedlefs of fleep, or midnight's harmful damp,
Hangs o'er the fickly taper; and untir'd
The virgin follows, with inchanted ftep,   250
The mazes of fome wild and wondrous tale,
From morn to eve; unmindful of her form, .
Unmindful of the happy drefs that ftole
The wifhes of the youth, when every maid
With envy pin'd.   Hence, finally, by night   255
The village-matron, round the blazing hearth,
Sufpends the infant-audience with her tales,
Breathing aftonifhment! of witching rhimes,
And evil fpirits; of the death-bed call
Of him who robb'd the widow, and devour'd   260
The orphan's portion; of unquiet fouls
Rifen from the grave to eafe the heavy guilt
Of deeds in life conceal'd; of fhapes that walk
At dead of night, and clank their chains, and wave
The torch of hell around the murderer's bed.   265
At every folemn paufe the croud recoil
Gazing each other fpeechlefs, and congeal'd
With fhivering fighs: till eager for the event,

Around

Around the beldame all arrect they hang,
Each trembling heart with grateful terrors quell'd.   270

  But lo! difclos'd in all her fmiling pomp,
Where Beauty onward moving claims the verfe
Her charms infpire: the freely-flowing verfe
In thy immortal praife, o form divine,
Smooths her mellifluent ftream. Thee, Beauty, thee   275
The regal dome, and thy enlivening ray
The mofly roofs adore: thou, better fun!
For ever beameft on the enchanted heart
Love, and harmonious wonder, and delight
Poetic. Brighteft progeny of heaven!   280
How fhall i trace thy features? where felect
The rofeate hues to emulate thy bloom?
Hafte then, my fong, through nature's wide expanfe,
Hafte then, and gather all her comelieft wealth,
Whate'er bright fpoils the florid earth contains,   285
Whate'er the waters, or the liquid air,
To deck thy lovely labour. Wilt thou fly
With laughing Autumn to the Atlantic ifles,
And range with him the Hefperian field, and fee
Where'er his fingers touch the fruitful grove,   290
The branches fhoot with gold; where'er his ftep
Marks the glad foil, the tender clufters grow
With purple ripenefs, and inveft each hill

As

As with the blushes of an evening sky ?
Or wilt thou rather stoop thy vagrant plume,   295
Where gliding through his daughter's honour'd shades,
The smooth Peneus from his glassy flood
Reflects purpureal Tempe's pleasant scene ?
Fair Tempe ! haunt belov'd of sylvan powers,
Of Nymphs and Fauns ; where in the golden age   300
They play'd in secret on the shady brink
With ancient Pan : while round their choral steps
Young Hours and genial Gales with constant hand
Shower'd blossoms, odours, shower'd ambrosial dews,
And spring's Elysian bloom.   Her flowery store   305
To thee nor Tempe shall refuse ; nor watch
Of winged Hydra guard Hesperian fruits
From thy free spoil.   O bear then, unreprov'd,
Thy smiling treasures to the green recess
Where young Dione stays.   With sweetest airs   310
Intice her forth to lend her angel-form
For Beauty's honour'd image.   Hither turn
Thy graceful footsteps ; hither, gentle maid,
Incline thy polish'd forehead : let thy eyes
Effuse the mildness of their azure dawn ;   315
And may the fanning breezes waft aside
Thy radiant locks : disclosing, as it bends
With airy softness from the marble neck,
The cheek fair-blooming, and the rosy lip,

Where

Where winning smiles and pleasures sweet as love,   320
With sanctity and wisdom, tempering blend
Their soft allurement.   Then the pleasing force
Of nature, and her kind parental care
Worthier i'd sing : then all the enamour'd youth,
With each admiring virgin, to my lyre   325
Should throng attentive, while i point on high
Where Beauty's living image, like the morn
That wakes in Zephyr's arms the blushing May,
Moves onward ; or as Venus, when she stood
Effulgent on the pearly car, and smil'd,   330
Fresh from the deep, and conscious of her form,
To see the Tritons tune their vocal shells,
And each cœrulean sister of the flood
With loud acclaim attend her o'er the waves,
To seek the Idalian bower.   Ye smiling band   335
Of youths and virgins, who through all the maze
Of young desire with rival-steps pursue
This charm of beauty ; if the pleasing toil
Can yield a moment's respite, hither turn
Your favourable ear, and trust my words.   340
I do not mean to wake the gloomy form
Of Superstition dress'd in Wisdom's garb,
To damp your tender hopes ; i do not mean
To bid the jealous thunderer fire the heavens,
Or shapes infernal rend the groaning earth   345
                                                    To

To fright you from your joys, my cheerful song
With better omens calls you to the field,
Pleas'd with your generous ardour in the chace,
And warm like you.   Then tell me, for ye know,
Does beauty ever deign to dwell where health   350
And active use are strangers?   Is her charm
Confefs'd in aught, whose moft peculiar ends
Are lame and fruitlefs?· Or did nature mean
This pleasing call the herald of a lye;
To hide the fhame of difcord and difeafe,   355
And catch with fair hypocrify the heart
Of idle faith? O no! with better cares
The indulgent mother, confcious how infirm
Her offspring tread the paths of good and ill,
By this illuftrious image, in each kind   360
Still moft illuftrious where the object holds
Its native powers moft perfect, fhe by this
Illumes the headftrong impulfe of defire,
And fanctifies his choice.   The generous glebe
Whofe bofom fmiles with verdure, the clear tract   365
Of ftreams delicious to the thirfty foul,
The bloom of nectar'd fruitage ripe to fenfe,
And every charm of animated things,
Are only pledges of a ftate fincere,
The integrity and order of their frame,   370
When all is well within, and every end

E   Accomplifh'd.

Accomplish'd.   Thus was beauty sent from heaven,
The lovely ministress of truth and good
In this dark world: for truth and good are one,
And beauty dwells in them, and they in her,   375
With like participation.   Wherefore then,
O sons of earth! would ye dissolve the tye?
O wherefore, with a rash impetuous aim,
Seek ye those flowery joys with which the hand
Of lavish fancy paints each flattering scene   380
Where beauty seems to dwell, nor once inquire
Where is the sanction of eternal truth,
Or where the seal of undeceitful good,
To save your search from folly! Wanting these,
Lo! beauty withers in your void embrace,   385
And with the glittering of an idiot's toy
Did fancy mock your vows.   Nor let the gleam
Of youthful hope that shines upon your hearts,
Be chill'd or clouded at this awful task,
To learn the lore of undeceitful good,   390
And truth eternal.   Though the poisonous charms
Of baleful superstition guide the feet
Of servile numbers, through a dreary way
To their abode, through defarts, thorns and mire;
And leave the wretched pilgrim all forlorn   395
To muse at last, amid the ghostly gloom
Of graves, and hoary vaults, and cloister'd cells;

                                                        To

To walk with spectres through the midnight shade,
And to the screaming owl's accursed song
Attune the dreadful workings of his heart;   400
Yet be not ye dismay'd.   A gentler star
Your lovely search illumines.   From the grove
Where wisdom talk'd with her Athenian sons,
Could my ambitious hand intwine a wreath
Of Plato's olive with the Mantuan bay,   405
Then should my powerful verse at once dispell
Those monkish horrors: then in light divine
Disclose the Elysian prospect, where the steps
Of those whom nature charms, through blooming walks,
Through fragrant mountains and poetic streams,   410
Amid the train of sages, heroes, bards,
Led by their winged Genius and the choir
Of laurell'd science and harmonious art,
Proceed exulting to the eternal shrine,
Where truth conspicuous with her sister-twins,   415
The undivided partners of her sway,
With good and beauty reigns.   O let not us,
Lull'd by luxurious pleasure's languid strain,
Or crouching to the frowns of bigot-rage,
O let us not a moment pause to join   420
That godlike band.   And if the gracious power
Who first awaken'd my untutor'd song,
Will to my invocation breathe anew

The

The tuneful fpirit ; then through all our paths,
Ne'er fhall the found of this devoted lyre   425
Be wanting ; whether on the rofy mead,
When fummer fmiles, to warn the melting heart
Of luxury's allurement ; whether firm
Againft the torrent and the ftubborn hill
To urge bold virtue's unremitted nerve,   430
And wake the ftrong divinity of foul
That conquers chance and fate ; or whether ftruck
For founds of triumph, to proclaim her toils.
Upon the lofty fummit, round her brow
To twine the wreath of incorruptive praife ;   435
To trace her hallow'd light through future worlds,
And blefs heaven's image in the heart of man.

Thus with a faithful aim have we prefum'd,
Adventurous, to delineate nature's form ;
Whether in vaft, majeftic pomp array'd,   440
Or dreft for pleafing wonder, or ferene
In beauty's rofy fmile. It now remains,
Through various being's fair-proportion'd fcale,
To trace the rifing luftre of her charms,
From their firft twilight, fhining forth at length   445
To full meridian fplendour. Of degree
The leaft and lowlieft, in the effufive warmth
Of colours mingling with a random blaze,

Doth

Doth beauty dwell.   Then higher in the line
And variation of determin'd shape,   450
Where truth's eternal measures mark the bound
Of circle, cube, or sphere.   The third ascent
Unites this varied symmetry of parts
With colour's bland allurement; as the pearl
Shines in the concave of its azure bed,   455
And painted shells indent their speckled wreath.
Then more attractive rise the blooming forms
Through which the breath of nature has infus'd
Her genial power to draw with pregnant veins
Nutritious moisture from the bounteous earth,   460
In fruit and seed prolific: thus the flowers
Their purple honours with the spring resume;
And such the stately tree which autumn bends
With blushing treasures.   But more lovely still
Is nature's charm, where to the full consent   465
Of complicated members, to the bloom
Of colour, and the vital change of growth,
Life's holy flame and piercing sense are given,
And active motion speaks the temper'd soul:
So moves the bird of Juno; so the steed   470
With rival ardour beats the dusty plain,
And faithful dogs with eager airs of joy
Salute their fellows.   Thus doth beauty dwell
There most conspicuous, even in outward shape,

Where dawns the high expreſſion of a mind: 475.
By ſteps conducting our inraptur'd ſearch
To that eternal origin, whoſe power,
Through all the unbounded ſymmetry of things,
Like rays effulging from the parent ſun,
This endleſs mixture of her charms diffus'd.   480
Mind, mind alone, (bear witneſs, earth and heaven!)
The living fountains in itſelf contains
Of beauteous and ſublime: here hand in hand,
Sit paramount the Graces; here inthron'd,
Cœleſtial Venus, with divineſt airs,   485
Invites the ſoul to never-fading joy.
Look then abroad through nature, to the range
Of planets, ſuns, and adamantine ſpheres
Wheeling unſhaken through the void immenſe;
And ſpeak, o man! does this capacious ſcene   490
With half that kindling majeſty dilate
Thy ſtrong conception, as when Brutus roſe
Refulgent from the ſtroke of Cæſar's fate,
Amid the croud of patriots; and his arm
Aloft extending, like eternal Jove   495
When guilt brings down the thunder, call'd aloud
On Tully's name, and ſhook his crimſon ſteel,
And bade the father of his country, hail!
For lo! the tyrant proſtrate on the duſt,
And Rome again is free! Is aught ſo fair   500

In

In all the dewy landscapes of the spring,
In the bright eye of Hesper or the morn,
In nature's fairest forms, is aught so fair
As virtuous friendship? as the candid blush
Of him who strives with fortune to be just?   505
The graceful tear that streams for others woes?
Or the mild majesty of private life,
Where peace with ever-blooming olive crowns
The gate; where honour's liberal hands effuse
Unenvied treasures, and the snowy wings   510
Of innocence and love protect the scene?
Once more search, undismay'd, the dark profound
Where nature works in secret; view the beds
Of mineral treasure, and the eternal vault
That bounds the hoary ocean; trace the forms   515
Of atoms moving with incessant change
Their elemental round; behold the seeds
Of being, and the energy of life
Kindling the mass with ever-active flame:
Then to the secrets of the working mind   520
Attentive turn; from dim oblivion call
Her fleet, ideal band; and bid them, go!
Break through time's barrier, and o'ertake the hour
That saw the heavens created: then declare
If aught were found in those external scenes   525
To move thy wonder now.   For what are all

The

The forms which brute, unconfcious matter wears,
Greatnefs of bulk, or fymmetry of parts?
Not reaching to the heart, foon feeble grows
The fuperficial impulfe; dull their charms,   530
And fatiate foon, and pall the languid eye.
Not fo the moral fpecies, nor the powers
Of genius and defign; the ambitious mind
There fees herfelf: by thefe congenial forms
Touch'd and awaken'd, with intenfer act   535
She bends each nerve, and meditates well-pleas'd
Her features in the mirror.   For of all
The inhabitants of earth, to man alone
Creative wifdom gave to lift his eye
To truth's eternal meafures; thence to frame   540
The facred laws of action and of will,
Difcerning juftice from unequal deeds,
And temperance from folly.   But beyond
This energy of truth, whofe dictates bind
Affenting reafon, the benignant fire,   545
To deck the honour'd paths of juft and good,
Has added bright imagination's rays:
Where virtue, rifing from the awful depth
Of truth's myfterious bofom, doth forfake
The unadorn'd condition of her birth;   550
And drefs'd by fancy in ten thoufand hues,
Affumes a various feature, to attract,

With

With charms refponfive to each gazer's eye,
The hearts of men.   Amid his rural walk,
The ingenuous youth, whom folitude infpires   555
With pureft wifhes, from the penfive fhade
Beholds her moving, like a virgin-mufe
That wakes her lyre to fome indulgent theme
Of harmony and wonder : while among
The herd of fervile minds, her ftrenuous form   560
Indignant flafhes on the patriot's eye,
And through the rolls of memory appeals
To ancient honour, or in act ferene,
Yet watchful, raifes the majeftic fword
Of public power, from dark ambition's reach   565
To guard the facred volume of the laws.

    Genius of ancient Greece ! whofe faithful fteps,
Well-pleas'd i follow through the facred paths
Of nature and of fcience ; nurfe divine
Of all heroic deeds and fair defires !   570
O ! let the breath of thy extended praife
Infpire my kindling bofom to the height
Of this untempted theme.   Nor be my thoughts
Prefumptuous counted, if amid the calm
That fooths this vernal evening into fmiles,   575
I fteal impatient from the fordid haunts
Of ftrife and low ambition, to attend
Thy facred prefence in the fylvan fhade,

By their malignant footſteps ne'er profan'd.
Deſcend, propitious! to my favour'd eye;   580
Such in thy mien, thy warm, exalted air,
As when the Perſian tyrant, foil'd and ſtung
With ſhame and deſperation, gnaſh'd his teeth
To ſee thee rend the pageants of his throne;
And at the lightning of thy lifted ſpear   585
Crouch'd like a ſlave.   Bring all thy martial ſpoils,
Thy palms, thy laurels, thy triumphal ſongs,
Thy ſmiling band of arts, thy godlike ſires
Of civil wiſdom, thy heroic youth
Warm from the ſchools of glory.   Guide my way   590
Through fair Lycéum's walk, the green retreats
Of Academus, and the thymy vale,
Where oft inchanted with Socratic ſounds,
Iliſſus pure devolv'd his tuneful ſtream
In gentler murmurs.   From the blooming ſtore   595
Of theſe auſpicious fields, may i unblam'd
Tranſplant ſome living bloſſoms to adorn
My native clime: while far above the flight
Of fancy's plume aſpiring, i unlock
The ſprings of ancient wiſdom; while i join   600
Thy name, thrice honour'd! with the immortal praiſe
Of nature, while to my compatriot youth
I point the high example of thy ſens,
And tune to Attic themes the Britiſh lyre.

E N D   O F   B O O K   I.

THE

PLEASURES

OF

IMAGINATION.

BOOK THE SECOND.

ARGUMENT

OF

THE SECOND BOOK.

*THE separation of the works of imagination from philo-
sophy, the cause of their abuse among the moderns. Prospect
of their re-union under the influence of public liberty. Enu-
meration of accidental pleasures, which increase the effect of
objects delightful to the imagination. The pleasures of sense.
Particular circumstances of the mind. Discovery of truth.
Perception of contrivance and design. Emotion of the paffions. All the natural paffions partake of a pleasing senfa-
tion; with the final cause of this constitution illustrated by an
allegorical vision, and exemplified in sorrow, pity, terror, and
indignation.*

WHEN shall the laurel and the vocal string
Resume their honours?   When shall we behold
The tuneful tongue, the Promethéan hand
Aspire to ancient praise?   Alas! how faint,
How slow the dawn of beauty and of truth   5
Breaks the reluctant shades of Gothic night
Which yet involve the nations!   Long they groan'd
Beneath the furies of rapacious force;
Oft as the gloomy north, with iron-swarms
Tempestuous pouring from her frozen caves,   10
Blasted the Italian shore, and swept the works
Of liberty and wisdom down the gulph
Of all-devouring night.   As long immur'd
In noon-tide darkness by the glimmering lamp,
Each muse and each fair science pin'd away   15

The

The fordid hours : while foul, barbarian hands
Their myfteries profan'd, unftrung the lyre,
And chain'd the foaring pinion down to earth.
At laft the mufes rofe, and fpurn'd their bonds,.
And wildly warbling, fcatter'd, as they flew,   20.
Their blooming wreaths from fair Valclufa's bowers
To Arno's myrtle border and the fhore
Of foft Parthenope.   But ftil' the rage
Of dire ambition and gigantic power,
From public aims and from the bufy walk   25
Of civil commerce, drove the bolder train.
Of penetrating fcience to the cells,
Where ftudious eafe confumes the filent hour
In fhadowy fearches and unfruitful care.
Thus from their guardians torn, the tender arts   30
Of mimic fancy and harmonious joy,.
To prieftly domination and the luft
Of lawlefs courts, their amiable toil
For three inglorious ages have refign'd,
In vain reluctant: and Torquato's tongue   35
Was tun'd for flavifh pæans at the throne
Of tinfel pomp : and Raphael's magic hand
Effus'd its fair creation to enchant
The fond adoring herd in Latian fanes
To blind belief; while on their proftrate necks   40
The fable tyrant plants his heel fecure.

But

But now behold! the radiant æra dawns,
When freedom's ample fabric, fix'd at length
For endlefs years on Albion's happy fhore
In full proportion, once more fhall extend   45
To all the kindred powers of focial blifs
A common manfion, a parental roof.
There fhall the virtues, there fhall wifdom's train,
Their long-loft friends rejoining, as of old,
Embrace the fmiling family of arts,   5?
The mufes and the graces.   Then no more
Shall vice, diftracting their delicious gifts
To aims abhorr'd, with high diftafte and fcorn
Turn from their charms the philofophic eye,
The patriot-bofom; then no more the paths   55
Of public care or intellectual toil,
Alone by footfteps haughty and fevere
In gloomy ftate be trod: the harmonious Mufe
And her perfuafive fifters then fhall plant
Their fheltering laurels o'er the bleak afcent,   60
And fcatter flowers along the rugged way.
Arm'd with the lyre, already have we dar'd
To pierce divine philofophy's retreats,
And teach the Mufe her lore; already ftrove
Their long-divided honours to unite,   65
While tempering this deep argument we fang
Of truth and beauty.   Now the fame glad tafk

Impends;

Impends; now urging our ambitious toil,
We haften to recount the various fprings
Of adventitious pleafure, which adjoin   70
Their grateful influence to the prime effect
Of objects grand or beauteous, and inlarge
The complicated joy.   The fweets of fenfe,
Do they not oft with kind acceffion flow,
To raife harmonious fancy's native charm?   75
So while we tafte the fragrance of the rofe,
Glows not her blufh the fairer?   While we view
Amid the noontide walk a limpid rill
Gufh through the trickling herbage, to the thirft
Of fummer yielding the delicious draught   80.
Of cool refrefhment; o'er the mofly brink
Shines not the furface clearer, and the waves
With fweeter mufic murmur as they flow?

    Nor this alone; the various lot of life
Oft from external circumftance affumes   85
A moment's difpofition to rejoice ·
In thofe delights which at a different hour
Would pafs unheeded.   Fair the face of fpring,
When rural fongs and odours wake the morn,
To every eye; but how much more to his   90
Round whom the bed of ficknefs long diffus'd
Its melancholy gloom!   how doubly fair,

                                                    When

When firſt with freſh-born vigour he inhales
The balmy breeze, and feels the bleſſed ſun
Warm at his boſom, from the ſprings of life   95
Chaſing oppreſſive damps and languid pain !

    Or ſhall i mention, where cœleſtial truth
Her awful light diſcloſes, to beſtow
A more majeſtic pomp on beauty's frame ?
For man loves knowledge, and the beams of truth   100
More welcome touch his underſtanding's eye,
Than all the blandiſhments of ſound his ear,
Than all of taſte his tongue.   Nor ever yet
The melting rainbow's vernal-tinctur'd hues
To me have ſhone ſo pleaſing, as when firſt   105
The hand of ſcience pointed out the path
In which the ſun-beams gleaming from the weſt
Fall on the watry cloud, whoſe darkſome veil
Involves the orient ; and that trickling ſhower
Piercing through every cryſtalline convex   110
Of cluſtering dew-drops to their flight oppos'd,
Recoil at length where concave all behind
The internal ſurface of each glaſſy orb
Repells their forward paſſage into air ;
That thence direct they ſeek the radiant goal   115
From which their courſe began ; and, as they ſtrike
In different lines the gazer's obvious eye,

G

Aſſume

Assume a different lustre, through the brede
Of colours changing from the splendid rose
To the pale violet's dejected hue.   120

Or shall we touch that kind access of joy,
That springs to each fair object, while we trace
Through all its fabric, wisdom's artful aim
Disposing every part, and gaining still
By means proportion'd her benignant end?   125
Speak, ye, the pure delight, whose favour'd steps
The lamp of science through the jealous maze.
Of nature guides,. when haply you reveal:
Her secret honours:. whether in the sky,
The beauteous laws of light, the central powers   130
That wheel the pensile planets round the year;.
Whether in wonders of the rowling deep,.
Or the rich fruits of all-sustaining earth,.
Or fine-adjusted springs of life and sense,.
Ye scan the counsels of their author's hand..   135

What, when to raise the meditated scene;
The flame of passion, through the struggling soul
Deep-kindled, shows across that sudden blaze
The object of its rapture, vast of size,.
With fiercer colours and a night of shade?   140
What? like a storm from their capacious bed

The.

The founding feas o'erwhelming, when the might
Of thefe eruptions, working from the depth
Of man's ftrong apprehenfion, fhakes his frame
Even to the bafe; from every naked fenfe   145
Of pain or pleafure diffipating all
Opinion's feeble coverings, and the veil
Spun from the cobweb fafhion of the times
To hide the feeling heart?   Then nature fpeaks
Her genuine language, and the words of men,   150
Big with the very motion of their fouls,
Declare with what accumulated force,
The impetuous nerve of paffion urges on
The native weight and energy of things.

    Yet more: her honours where nor beauty claims,   155
Nor fhews of good the thirfty fenfe allure,
From paffion's power alone our nature holds
Effential pleafure.   Paffion's fierce illapfe
Rouzes the mind's whole fabric; with fupplies
Of daily impulfe keeps the elaftic powers   160
Intenfely poiz'd, and polifhes anew
By that collifion all the fine machine:
Elfe ruft would rife, and foulnefs, by degrees
Incumbering, choak at laft what heaven defign'd
For ceafelefs motion and a round of toil.   165
—But fay, does every paffion thus to man

G 2   Adminifter

Adminifter delight?   That name indeed
Becomes the rofy breath of love; becomes
The radiant fmiles of joy, the applauding hand
Of admiration: but the bitter fhower   170
That forrow fheds upon a brother's grave,
But the dumb palfy of nocturnal fear,
Or thofe confuming fires that gnaw the heart
Of panting indignation, find we there
To move delight?—Then liften while my tongue   175
The unalter'd will of heaven with faithful awe
Reveals; what old Harmodius wont to teach
My early age; Harmodius, who had weigh'd
Within his learned mind whate'er the fchools
Of wifdom, or thy lonely-whifpering voice,   180
O faithful nature! dictate of the laws
Which govern and fupport this mighty frame
Of univerfal being.   Oft the hours
From morn to eve have ftolen unmark'd away,
While mute attention hung upon his lips,   185
As thus the fage his awful tale began.

  'Twas in the windings of an ancient wood,
When fpotlefs youth with folitude refigns
To fweet philofophy the ftudious day,
What time pale autumn fhades the filent eve,   190
Mufing i rov'd.   Of good and evil much,

                                                        And

And much of mortal man my thought revolv'd;
When starting full on fancy's gushing eye
The mournful image of Parthenia's fate,
That hour, o long belov'd and long deplor'd !   195
When blooming youth, nor gentlest wisdom's arts,
Nor Hymen's honours gather'd for thy brow,
Nor all thy lover's, all thy father's tears
Avail'd to snatch thee from the cruel grave;
Thy agonizing looks, thy last farewel   200
Struck to the inmost feeling of my soul
As with the hand of death.   At once the shade
More horrid nodded o'er me, and the winds
With hoarser murmuring shook the branches.   Dark
As midnight storms, the scene of human things   205
Appear'd before me; defarts, burning sands,
Where the parch'd adder dies; the frozen south,
And defolation blasting all the west
With rapine and with murder: tyrant power
Here sits enthron'd with blood; the baleful charms   210
Of superstition there infect the skies,
And turn the sun to horror.   Gracious heaven !
What is the life of man ? Or cannot these,
Not these portents thy awful will suffice ?
That, propagated thus beyond their scope,   215
They rise to act their cruelties anew
In my afflicted bosom, thus decreed

The univerfal fenfitive of pain,
The wretched heir of evils not its own !

  Thus i impatient ; when, at once effus'd,   220
A flafhing torrent of cœleftial day
Burft through the fhadowy void.   With flow defcent
A purple cloud came floating through the fky,
And pois'd at length within the circling trees,
Hung obvious to my view ; till opening wide   225
Its lucid orb, a more than human form
Emerging lean'd majeftic o'er my head,
And inftant thunder fhook the confcious grove.
Then melted into air the liquid cloud,
And all the fhining vifion ftood reveal'd.   230
A wreath of palm his ample forehead bound,
And o'er his fhoulder, mantling to his knee,
Flow'd the tranfparent robe, around his waift
Collected with a radiant zone of gold
Æthereal : there in myftic figns ingrav'd,   235
I read his office high and facred name,
Genius of human kind.   Appall'd i gaz'd
The godlike prefence ; for athwart his brow
Difpleafure, temper'd with a mild concern,
Look'd down reluctant on me, and his words   240
Like diftant thunders broke the murmuring air.

Vain

Vain are thy thoughts, o child of mortal birth!
And impotent thy tongue.   Is thy fhort fpan
Capacious of this univerfal frame?
Thy wifdom all-fufficient?   Thou, alas!   245
Doft thou afpire to judge between the Lord
Of nature and his works? to lift thy voice
Againft the fovran order he decreed,
All good and lovely? to blafpheme the bands
Of tendernefs innate and focial love,   250
Holieft of things! by which the general orb
Of being, as by adamantine links,
Was drawn to perfect union and fuftain'd
From everlafting?   Haft thou felt the pangs
Of foftening forrow, of indignant zeal   255
So grievous to the foul, as thence to wifh
The ties of nature broken from thy frame;
That fo thy felfifh, unrelenting heart
Might ceafe to mourn its lot, no longer then
The wretched heir of evils not its own?   260
O fair benevolence of generous minds!
O man by nature form'd for all mankind!

He fpoke; abafh'd and filent i remain'd,
As confcious of my tongue's offence, and aw'd
Before his prefence, though my fecret foul   265
                                        Difdain'd

Difdain'd the imputation.   On the ground
I fix'd my eyes; till from his airy couch
He ftoop'd fublime, and touching with his hand
My dazling forehead, Raife thy fight, he cry'd
And let thy fenfe convince thy erring tongue.   270

    I look'd, and lo! the former fcene was chang'd;
For verdant alleys and furrounding trees,
A folitary profpect, wide and wild,
Rufh'd on my fenfes.   'Twas an horrid pile
Of hills with many a fhaggy foreft mix'd,   275
With many a fable cliff and glittering ftream.
Aloft recumbent o'er the hanging ridge,
The brown woods wav'd; while ever-trickling fprings
Wafh'd from the naked roots of oak and pine
The crumbling foil; and ftill at every fall   280
Down the fteep windings of the channel'd rock,
Remurmuring rufh'd the congregated floods
With hoarfer inundation; till at laft
They reach'd a grafly plain, which from the fkirts
Of that high defart fpread her verdant lap,   285
And drank the gufhing moifture, where confin'd
In one fmooth current, o'er the lilied vale
Clearer than glafs it flow'd.   Autumnal fpoils
Luxuriant fpreading to the rays of morn,
Blufh'd o'er the cliffs, whofe half-incircling mound   290

                                                                 As

As in a fylvan theatre inclos'd
That flowery level.   On the river's brink
I fpy'd a fair pavilion, which diffus'd
Its floating umbrage 'mid the filver fhade
Of ofiers.   Now the weftern fun reveal'd   295
Between two parting cliffs his golden orb,
And pour'd acrofs the fhadow of the hills,
On rocks and floods, a yellow ftream of light
That cheer'd the folemn fcene.   My liftening powers
Were aw'd, and every thought in filence hung,   300
And wondering expectation.   Then the voice
Of that cœleftial power, the myftic fhow
Declaring, thus my deep attention call'd.

    Inhabitant of earth, to whom is given
The gracious ways of providence to learn,   305
Receive my fayings with a ftedfaft ear—
Know then, the fovran fpirit of the world,
Though felf-collected from eternal time,
Within his own deep effence he beheld
The bounds of true felicity complete;   310
Yet by immenfe benignity inclin'd
To fpread around him that primæval joy
Which fill'd himfelf, he rais'd his plaftic arm,
And founded through the hollow depth of fpace
The ftrong, creative mandate.   Strait arofe   315
II

Thefe

These heavenly orbs, the glad abodes of life
Effusive kindled by his breath divine
Through endless forms of being.   Each inhal'd
From him its portion of the vital flame,
In measure such, that, from the wide complex   320
Of coexistent orders, one might rise,
One order, all-involving and intire.
He too beholding in the sacred light
Of his essential reason, all the shapes
Of swift contingence, all successive ties   325
Of action propagated through the sum
Of possible existence, he at once,
Down the long series of eventful time,
So fix'd the dates of being, so dispos'd,
To every living soul of every kind   330
The field of motion and the hour of rest,
That all conspir'd to his supreme design,
To universal good: with full accord
Answering the mighty model he had chosen,
The best and fairest of unnumber'd worlds   335
That lay from everlasting in the store
Of his divine conceptions.   Nor content,
By one exertion of creative power
His goodness to reveal; through every age,
Through every moment up the tract of time   340
His parent-hand with ever-new increase

Of

Of happiness and virtue has adorn'd
The vast harmonious frame: his parent-hand,
From the mute shell-fish gasping on the shore,
To men, to angels, to cœlestial minds   345
For ever leads the generations on
To higher scenes of being; while supply'd
From day to day with his enlivening breath,
Inferior orders in succession rise
To fill the void below.   As flame ascends,   350
As bodies to their proper center move,
As the pois'd ocean to the attracting moon
Obedient swells, and every headlong stream
Devolves its winding waters to the main;
So all things which have life aspire to God,   355
The sun of being, boundless, unimpair'd,
Center of souls! Nor does the faithful voice
Of nature cease to prompt their eager steps
Aright; nor is the care of heaven withheld
From granting to the task proportion'd aid;   360
That in their stations all may persevere
To climb the ascent of being, and approach
For ever nearer to the life divine.

That rocky pile thou seest, that verdant lawn
Fresh-water'd from the mountains. Let the scene   365
Paint in thy fancy the primæval seat

Of

Of man, and where the will fupreme ordain'd
His manfion, that pavilion fair-diffus'd
Along the fhady brink; in this recefs
To wear the appointed feafon of his youth,   370
Till riper hours fhould open to his toil
The high communion of fuperior minds,
Of confecrated heroes and of gods.
Nor did the fire omnipotent forget
His tender bloom to cherifh; nor withheld   375
Cœleftial footfteps from his green abode.
Oft from the radiant honours of his throne,.   .
He fent whom moft he lov'd, the fovran fair,
The effluence of his glory, whom he plac'd
Before his eyes for ever to behold;   380.
The goddefs from whofe infpiration flows
The toil of patriots, the delight of friends;
Without whofe work divine, in heaven or earth,
Nought lovely, nought propitious comes to pafs,
Nor hope, nor praife, nor honour.   Her the fire   385.
Gave it in charge to rear the blooming mind,.
The folded powers to open, to direct
The growth luxuriant of his young defires,.
And from the laws of this majeftic world
To teach him what was good.   As thus the nymph   390
Her daily care attended, by her fide
With conftant fteps her gay companion ftay'd,

The

The fair Euphrofyné, the gentle queen
Of fmiles, and graceful gladnefs, and delights
That cheer alike the hearts of mortal men   395
And powers immortal.   See the fhining pair!
Behold, where from his dwelling now difclos'd
They quit their youthful charge and feek the fkies.

I look'd, and on the flowery turf there ftood
Between two radiant forms a fmiling youth   400
Whofe tender cheeks difplay'd the vernal flower
Of beauty; fweeteft innocence illum'd
His bafhful eyes, and on his polifh'd brow.
Sate young fimplicity.   With fond regard
He view'd the affociates, as their fteps they mov'd;   405
The younger chief his ardent eyes detain'd,
With mild regret invoking her return.
Bright as the ftar of evening fhe appear'd.
Amid the dufky feene.   Eternal youth
O'er all her form its glowing honours breath'd;   410
And fmiles eternal from her candid eyes
Flow'd, like the dewy luftre of the morn
Effufive trembling on the placid waves.
The fpring of heaven had fhed its blufhing fpoils
To bind her fable treffes: full diffus'd   415
Her yellow mantle floated in the breeze;
And in her hand fhe wav'd a living branch

Rich

Rich with immortal fruits, of power to calm
The wrathful heart, and from the brightening eyes,
To chafe the cloud of fadnefs.   More fublime   420
The heavenly partner mov'd.   The prime of age
Compos'd her fteps.   The prefence of a god,
High on the circle of her brow inthron'd,
From each majeftic motion darted awe,
Devoted awe! till, cherifh'd by her looks   425
Benevolent and meek, confiding love
To filial rapture foften'd all the foul.
Free in her graceful hand fhe pois'd the fword
Of chafte dominion.   An heroic crown
Difplay'd the old fimplicity of pomp   430
Around her honour'd head.   A matron's robe,
White as the funfhine ftreams through vernal clouds,
Her ftately form invefted.   Hand in hand
The immortal pair forfook the enamel'd green,
Afcending flowly.   Rays of limpid light   435
Gleam'd round their path; cœleftial founds were heard,
And through the fragrant air æthereal dews
Diftill'd around them; till at once the clouds
Difparting wide in midway fky, withdrew
Their airy veil, and left a bright expanfe   340
Of empyrean flame, where fpent and drown'd,
Afflicted vifion plung'd in vain to fcan
What object it involv'd.   My feeble eyes

Indur'd

Indur'd not.   Bending down to earth i ſtood,
With dumb attention.   Soon a female voice,   445
As watry murmurs ſweet, or warbling ſhades,
With ſacred invocation thus began.

      Father of gods and mortals! whoſe right arm·
With reins eternal guides the moving heavens,
Bend thy propitious ear.   Behold well-pleas'd   450
I ſeek to finiſh thy divine decree.
With frequent ſteps I viſit yonder ſeat
Of man, thy offspring; from the tender ſeeds
Of juſtice and of wiſdom, to evolve
The latent honours of his generous frame;   455
Till thy conducting hand ſhall raiſe his lot
From earth's dim ſcene to theſe æthereal walks,
The temple of thy glory.   But not me,
Not my directing voice he oft requires,
Or hears delighted: this inchanting maid,   460
The aſſociate thou haſt given me, her alone
He loves, o Father! abſent, her he craves;
And but for her glad preſence ever join'd,
Rejoices not in mine: that all my hopes
This thy benignant purpoſe to fulfil,   465
I deem uncertain; and my daily cares
Unfruitful all and vain, unleſs by thee
Still farther aided in the work divine.

                                                            She

She ceas'd; a voice more awful thus reply'd.
O thou! in whom for ever i delight,   470
Fairer than all the inhabitants of heaven,
Best image of thy author! far from thee
Be difappointment, or diftafte, or blame;
Who foon or late fhalt every work fulfil,
And no refiftance find.   If man refufe   475
To hearken to thy dictates; or allur'd
By meaner joys, to any other power
Transfer the honours due to thee alone;
That joy which he purfues he ne'er fhall tafte,
That power in whom delighteth ne'er behold.   480
Go then, once more, and happy be thy toil;
Go then! but let not this thy fmiling friend
Partake thy footfteps.   In her ftead, behold!
With thee the fon of Nemefis i fend;
The fiend abhorr'd! whofe vengeance takes account   485
Of facred order's violated laws.
See where he calls thee, burning to be gone,
Fierce to exhauft the tempeft of his wrath
On yon devoted head.   But thou, my child,
Controul his cruel phrenzy, and protect   490
Thy tender charge; that when defpair fhall grafp
His agonizing bofom, he may learn,
Then he may learn to love the gracious hand

Alone

Alone fufficient in the hour of ill,
To fave his feeble fpirit; then confefs   495.
Thy genuine honours, o excelling fair!
When all the plagues that wait the deadly will.
Of this avenging dæmon, all the ftorms
Of night infernal, ferve but to difplay.
The energy of thy fuperior charms   500
With mildeft awe triumphant o'er his rage,
And fhining clearer in the horrid gloom..

Here ceas'd that awful voice, and foon i felt·
The cloudy curtain of refrefhing eve
Was clos'd once more, from that immortal fire   505
Sheltering my eye-lids.   Looking up, i view'd.
A vaft gigantic fpectre ftriding on
Through murmuring thunders and a wafte of clouds,
With dreadful action.   Black as night his brow
Relentlefs frowns involv'd.   His favage limbs   510
With fharp impatience violent he writh'd,
As through convulfive anguifh; and his hand,
Arm'd with a fcorpion-lafh, full oft he rais'd
In madnefs to his bofom; while his eyes
Rain'd bitter tears, and bellowing loud he fhook   515
The void with horror.   Silent by his fide
The virgin came.   No difcompofure ftirr'd

1

Her

Her features.   From the glooms which hung around
No stain of darkness mingled with the beam
Of her divine effulgence.   Now they stoop   520
Upon the river-bank ; and now to hail
His wonted guests, with eager steps advanc'd
The unsuspecting inmate of the shade.

As when a famish'd wolf, that all night long
Had rang'd the Alpine snows, by chance at morn   525
Sees from a cliff incumbent o'er the smoke
Of some lone village, a neglected kid
That strays along the wild for herb or spring ;
Down from the winding ridge he sweeps amain,
And thinks he tears him : so with tenfold rage,   530
The monster sprung remorseless on his prey.
Amaz'd the stripling stood : with panting breast
Feebly he pour'd the lamentable wail
Of helpless consternation, struck at once,
And rooted to the ground.   The queen beheld   535
His terror, and with looks of tenderest care
Advanc'd to save him.   Soon the tyrant felt
Her awful power.   His keen, tempestuous arm
Hung nerveless, nor descended where his rage
Had aim'd the deadly blow : then dumb retir'd   540
With sullen rancour.   Lo ! the sovran maid
Folds with a mother's arms the fainting boy,

Till

Till life rekindles in his rofy cheek;
Then grafps his hands, and cheers him with her tongue.

    O wake thee, rouze thy fpirit!   Shall the fpite   545
Of yon tormentor thus appall thy heart,
While i, thy friend and guardian, am at hand
To refcue and to heal?   O let thy foul
Remember, what the will of heaven ordains
Is ever good for all; and if for all,   550
Then good for thee.   Nor only by the warmth
And foothing funfhine of delightful things,
Do minds grow up and flourifh.   Oft mifled
By that bland light, the young unpractis'd views
Of reafon wander through a fatal road,   555
Far from their native aim: as if to lye
Inglorious in the fragrant fhade, and wait
The foft accefs of ever-circling joys,
Were all the end of being.   Afk thyfelf,
This pleafing error did it never lull   560
Thy wifhes?   Has thy conftant heart refus'd
The filken fetters of delicious eafe?
Or when divine Euphrofyné appear'd
Within this dwelling, did not thy defires
Hang far below the meafure of thy fate,   565
Which i reveal'd before thee? and thy eyes,
Impatient of my counfels, turn away

I 2

To drink the foft effufion of her fmiles?
Know then, for this the everlafting fire
Deprives thee of her prefence, and inftead, 570
O wife and ftill benevolent! ordains
This horrid vifage hither to purfue
My fteps; that fo thy nature may difcern
Its real good, and what alone can fave
Thy feeble fpirit in this hour of ill 575
From folly and defpair. O yet belov'd!
Let not this headlong terror quite o'erwhelm
Thy fcatter'd powers; nor fatal deem the rage
Of this tormentor, nor his proud affault,
While i am here to vindicate thy toil, 580
Above the generous queftion of thy arm.
Brave by thy fears and in thy weaknefs ftrong,
This hour he triumphs: but confront his might,
And dare him to the combat, then with eafe
Difarm'd and quell'd, his fiercenefs he refigns 585
To bondage and to fcorn: while thus inur'd
By watchful danger, by unceafing toil,
The immortal mind, fuperior to his fate,
Amid the outrage of external things,
Firm as the folid bafe of this great world, 590
Refts on his own foundations. Blow, ye winds!
Ye waves! ye thunders! rowl your tempeft on;
Shake, ye old pillars of the marble fky!

Till

Till all its orbs and all its worlds of fire
Be loofen'd from their feats ; yet ftill ferene,   595
The unconquer'd mind looks down upon the wreck ;
And ever ftronger as the ftorms advance,
Firm through the clofing ruin holds his way,
Where nature calls him to the deftin'd goal.

So fpake the goddefs ; while through all her frame   600
Cœleftial raptures flow'd, in every word,
In every motion kindling warmth divine
To feize who liften'd.   Vehement and fwift
As lightening fires the aromatic fhade
In Æthiopian fields, the ftripling felt   605
Her infpiration catch his fervid foul,
And ftarting from his languor thus exclaim'd.

Then let the trial come ! and witnefs thou,
If terror be upon me ; if i fhrink
To meet the ftorm, or faulter in my ftrength   610
When hardeft it befets me.   Do not think
That i am fearful and infirm of foul,
As late thy eyes beheld : for thou haft chang'd
My nature ; thy commanding voice has wak'd
My languid powers to bear me boldly on,   615
Where'er the will divine my path ordains
Through toil or peril : only do not thou

Forfake

Forfake me; o be thou for ever near,
That i may liften to thy facred voice,
And guide by thy decrees my conftant feet.   620
But fay, for ever are my eyes bereft?
Say, fhall the fair Euphrofyné not once
Appear again to charm me?   Thou, in heaven!
O thou eternal arbiter of things!
Be thy great bidding done: for who am i,   625
To queftion thy appointment?   Let the frowns
Of this avenger every morn o'ercaft
The cheerful dawn, and every evening damp
With double night my dwelling; i will learn
To hail them both, and unrepining bear   630
His hateful prefence: but permit my tongue
One glad requeft, and if my deeds may find
Thy awful eye propitious, o reftore
The rofy-featur'd maid; again to cheer
This lonely feat, and blefs me with her fmiles.   635

He fpoke; when inftant through the fable glooms
With which that furious prefence had involv'd
The ambient air, a flood of radiance came
Swift as the lightening flafh; the melting clouds
Flew diverfe, and amid the blue ferene   640
Euphrofyné appear'd.   With fprightly ftep

The

The nymph alighted on the irriguous lawn,
And to her wondering audience thus began.

Lo! i am here to anfwer to your vows,
And be the meeting fortunate! i come   645
With joyful tidings; we fhall part no more—
Hark! how the gentle echo from her cell
Talks through the cliffs, and murmuring o'er the ftream
Repeats the accents; we fhall part no more.
O my delightful friends! well-pleas'd on high   650
The father has beheld you, while the might
Of that ftern foe with bitter trial prov'd
Your equal doings; then for ever fpake
The high decree: that thou, cœleftial maid!
Howe'er that griefly phantom on thy fteps   655
May fometimes dare intrude, yet never more
Shalt thou, defcending to the abode of man,
Alone endure the rancour of his arm,
Or leave thy lov'd Euphrofyné behind.

She ended; and the whole romantic fcene   660
Immediate vanifh'd; rocks, and woods, and rills,
The mantling tent, and each myfterious form
Flew like the pictures of a morning dream,
When fun-fhine fills the bed.   A while i ftood
Perplex'd and giddy; till the radiant power   665

Who

Who bade the vifionary landfcape rife,
As up to him i turn'd, with gentleft looks
Preventing my enquiry, thus began.

There let thy foul acknowledge its complaint
How blind, how impious! There behold the ways   670
Of heaven's eternal deftiny to man,
For ever juft, benevolent and wife:
That virtue's awful fteps, howe'er purfu'd
By vexing fortune and intrufive pain,
Should never be divided from her chafte,   675
Her fair attendant, pleafure.　Need i urge
Thy tardy thought through all the various round
Of this exiftence, that thy foftening foul
At length may learn what energy the hand
Of virtue mingles in the bitter tide   680
Of paffion fwelling with diftrefs and pain,
To mitigate the fharp with gracious drops
Of cordial pleafure?　Afk the faithful youth,
Why the cold urn of her whom long he lov'd
So often fills his arms; fo often draws   685
His lonely footfteps at the filent hour,
To pay the mournful tribute of his tears?
O! he will tell thee, that the wealth of worlds
Should ne'er feduce his bofom to forego
That facred hour, when, ftealing from the noife   690

Of

Of care and envy, fweet remembrance fooths
With virtue's kindeft looks his aking breaft,
And turns his tears to rapture.——Afk the croud
Which flies impatient from the village-walk
To climb the neighbouring clifts, when far below   695
The cruel winds have hurl'd upon the coaft
Some helplefs bark ; while facred pity melts
The general eye, or terror's icy hand
Smites their diftorted limbs and horrent hair ;
While every mother clofer to her breaft   700
Catches her child, and pointing where the waves
Foam through the fhatter'd veffel, fhrieks aloud
As one poor wretch that fpreads his piteous arms
For fuccour, fwallow'd by the roaring furge,
As now another, dafh'd againft the rock,   705
Drops lifelefs down : o! deemeft thou indeed
No kind endearment here by nature given
To mutual terror and compaffion's tears ?
No fweetly-melting foftnefs which attracts,
O'er all that edge of pain, the focial powers   710
To this their proper action and their end ?
——Afk thy own heart ; when at the midnight hour,
Slow through that ftudious gloom thy paufing eye
Led by the glimmering taper moves around
The facred volumes of the dead, the fongs   715
Of Grecian bards, and records writ by fame

K

For

For Grecian heroes, where the prefent power
Of heaven and earth furveys the immortal page,
Even as a father blefling, while he reads
The praifes of his fon.   If then thy foul,
Spurning the yoke of thefe inglorious days,
Mix in their deeds and kindle with their flame;
Say, when the profpect blackens on thy view,
When rooted from the bafe, heroic ftates
Mourn in the duft and tremble at the frown
Of curft ambition; when the pious band
Of youths who fought for freedom and their fires,
Lie fide by fide in gore; when ruffian pride
Ufurps the throne of juftice, turns the pomp
Of public power, the majefty of rule,
The fword, the laurel, and the purple robe,
To flavifh empty pageants, to adorn
A tyrant's walk, and glitter in the eyes
Of fuch as bow the knee; when honour'd urns
Of patriots and of chiefs, the awful buft
And ftoried arch, to glut the coward-rage
Of regal envy, ftrew the public way
With hallow'd ruins; when the Mufe's haunt,
The marble porch where wifdom wont to talk
With Socrates or Tully, hears no more,
Save the hoarfe jargon of contentious monks,
Or female fuperftition's midnight prayer;

When ruthlefs rapine from the hand of time
-Tears the deftroying feythe, with furer blow
To fweep the works of glory from their bafe;   745
'Till defolation o'er the grafs-grown ftreet
Expands his raven-wings, and up the wall,
Where fenates once the price of monarchs doom'd,
Hiffes the gliding fnake through hoary weeds
That clafp the mouldering column; thus defac'd,   750
Thus widely mournful when the profpect thrills
Thy beating bofom, when the patriot's tear
Starts from thine eye, and thy extended arm
In fancy hurls the thunderbolt of Jove
To fire the impious wreath on Philip's brow,   755
Or dafh Octavius from the trophied car;
Say, does thy fecret foul repine to tafte
The big diftrefs?   Or would'ft thou then exchange
Thofe heart-ennobling forrows for the lot
Of him who fits amid the gaudy herd   760
Of mute barbarians bending to his nod,
And bears aloft his gold-invefted front,
And fays within himfelf, " i am a king,
" And wherefore fhould the clamorous voice of woe
" Intrude upon mine ear?—" The baleful dregs   765
Of thefe late ages, this inglorious draught
Of fervitude and folly, have not yet,
Bleft be the eternal ruler of the world!

Defil'd to fuch a depth of fordid fhame
The native honours of the human foul,   770
Nor fo effac'd the image of its fire.

END OF BOOK II.

T H E

P L E A S U R E S

O F

M A G I N A T I O N.

BOOK THE THIRD.

PLEASURE in observing the tempers and manners of men, even where vicious or absurd. The origin of vice, from false representations of the fancy, producing false opinions concerning good and evil. Inquiry into ridicule. The general sources of ridicule in the minds and characters of men, enumerated. Final cause of the sense of ridicule. The resemblance of certain aspects of inanimate things to the sensations and properties of the mind. The operations of the mind in the production of the works of imagination, described. The secondary pleasure from imitation. The benevolent order of the world illustrated in the arbitrary connexion of these pleasures with the objects which excite them. The nature and conduct of taste. Concluding with an account of the natural and moral advantages resulting from a sensible and well-formed imagination.

THE
PLEASURES
OF
IMAGINATION.

BOOK THE THIRD.

WHAT wonder therefore, since the indearing ties
Of passion link the universal kind
Of man so close, what wonder if to search
This common nature through the various change
Of sex, and age, and fortune, and the frame   5
Of each peculiar, draw the busy mind
With unresisted charms ?   The spacious west,
And all the teeming regions of the south
Hold not a quarry, to the curious flight
Of knowledge, half so tempting or so fair,   10
As man to man.   Nor only where the smiles
Of love invite ; nor only where the applause
Of cordial honour turns the attentive eye
On virtue's graceful deeds.   For since the course
Of things external acts in different ways   15

On human apprehensions, as the hand
Of nature temper'd to a different frame
Peculiar minds; so haply where the powers
Of fancy neither lessen nor enlarge
The images of things, but paint in all   20
Their genuine hues, the features which they wore
In nature; there opinion will be true,
And action right.   For action treads the path
In which opinion says he follows good,
Or flies from evil; and opinion gives   25
Report of good or evil, as the scene
Was drawn by fancy, lovely or deform'd:
Thus her report can never there be true
Where fancy cheats the intellectual eye,
With glaring colours and distorted lines.   30
Is there a man, who at the sound of death
Sees ghastly shapes of terror conjur'd up,
And black before him; nought but death-bed groans
And fearful prayers, and plunging from the brink
Of light and being, down the gloomy air,   35
An unknown depth?   Alas! in such a mind,
If no bright forms of excellence attend
The image of his country; nor the pomp
Of sacred senates, nor the guardian voice
Of justice on her throne, nor aught that wakes   40
The conscious bosom with a patriot's flame;

Will

Will not opinion tell him, that to die,
Or stand the hazard, is a greater ill
Than to betray his country?　And in act
Will he not chuse to be a wretch and live?　　　45
Here vice begins then.　From the inchanting cup
Which fancy holds to all, the unwary thirst
Of youth oft swallows a Circæan draught,
That sheds a baleful tincture o'er the eye
Of reason, till no longer he discerns,　　　50
And only guides to err.　Then revel forth
A furious band that spurn him from the throne;
And all is uproar.　Thus ambition grasps
The empire of the soul: thus pale revenge
Unsheaths her murderous dagger; and the hands　　　55
Of lust and rapine, with unholy arts,
Watch to o'erturn the barrier of the laws
That keeps them from their prey: thus all the plagues
The wicked bear, or o'er the trembling scene
The tragic muse discloses, under shapes　　　60
Of honour, safety, pleasure, ease or pomp,
Stole first into the mind.　Yet not by all
Those lying forms which fancy in the brain
Engenders, are the kindling passions driven,
To guilty deeds; nor reason bound in chains,　　　65
That vice alone may lord it: oft adorn'd
With solemn pageants, folly mounts the throne,

L

And

And plays her idiot-anticks, like a queen.
A thoufand garbs fhe wears; a thoufand ways
She wheels her giddy empire.—Lo! thus far   70
With bold adventure, to the Mantuan lyre
I fing of nature's charms, and touch well-pleas'd
A ftricter note: now haply muft my fong
Unbend her ferious meafure, and reveal
In lighter ftrains, how folly's aukward arts   75
Excite impetuous laughter's gay rebuke;
The fportive province of the comic mufe.

See! in what crouds the uncouth forms advance:
Each would outftrip the other, each prevent
Our careful fearch, and offer to your gaze,   80
Unafk'd, his motley features.   Wait awhile,
My curious friends! and let us firft arrange
In proper order your promifcuous throng.

Behold the foremoft band; of flender thought,
And eafy faith; whom flattering fancy fooths   85
With lying fpectres, in themfelves to view
Illuftrious forms of excellence and good,
That fcorn the manfion.   With exulting hearts
They fpread their fpurious treafures to the fun,
And bid the world admire! but chief the glance   90
Of wifhful envy draws their joy-bright eyes,

And

And lifts with felf-applaufe each lordly brow.
In number boundlefs as the blooms of fpring,
Behold their glaring idols, empty fhades
By fancy gilded o'er, and then fet up   95
For adoration.   Some in learning's garb,
With formal band, and fable-cinctur'd gown,
And rags of mouldy volumes.   Some elate
With martial fplendor, fteely pikes and fwords
Of coftly frame, and gay Phœnician robes   100
Inwrought with flowery gold, affume the port
Of ftately valour: liftening by his fide
·There ftands a female form; to her, with looks
Of earneft import, pregnant with amaze,
He talks of deadly deeds, of breaches, ftorms,   105
And fulphurous mines, and ambufh: then at once
Breaks off, and fmiles to fee her look fo pale,
And afks fome wondering queftion of her fears.
Others of graver mien; behold, adorn'd
With holy enfigns, how fublime they move,   110
And bending oft their fanctimonious eyes
Take homage of the fimple-minded throng;
Ambaffadors of heaven ! Nor much unlike
Is he whofe vifage, in the lazy mift
That mantles every feature, hides a brood   115
Of politic conceits; of whifpers, nods,
And hints deep omen'd with unwieldy fchemes,

L 2

And

And dark portents of state.   Ten thousand more,
Prodigious habits and tumultuous tongues,
Pour dauntless in and swell the boastful band.   120

    Then comes the second order; all who seek
The debt of praise, where watchful unbelief
Darts through the thin pretence her squinting eye
On some retir'd appearance which belies
The boasted virtue, or annuls the applause   125
That justice elfe would pay.   Here side by side
I fee two leaders of the folemn train
Approaching: one a female old and grey,
With eyes demure, and wrinkle-furrow'd brow,
Pale as the cheeks of death; yet still she stuns   130
The fickening audience with a naufeous tale;
How many youths her myrtle-chains have worn,
How many virgins at her triumphs pin'd !
Yet how refolv'd she guards her cautious heart;
Such is her terror at the rifques of love,   135
And man's feducing tongue! The other seems
A bearded fage, ungentle in his mien,
And fordid all his habit; peevish want
Grins at his heels, while down the gazing throng
He stalks, refounding in magnific phrafe   140
The vanity of riches, the contempt
Of pomp and power.   Be prudent in your zeal,

                                        Ye

Ye grave affociates! let the filent grace
Of her who blufhes at the fond regard
Her charms infpire, more eloquent unfold   145
The praife of fpotlefs honour: let the man
Whofe eye regards not his illuftrious pomp
And ample ftore, but as indulgent ftreams
To cheer the barren foil and fpread the fruits
Of joy, let him by jufter meafures fix   150
The price of riches and the end of power.

Another tribe fucceeds; deluded long
By fancy's dazling optics, thefe behold
The images of fome peculiar things
With brighter hues refplendent, and portray'd   155
With features nobler far than e'er adorn'd
Their genuine objects.   Hence the fever'd heart
Pants with delirious hope for tinfel charms;
Hence oft obtrufive on the eye of fcorn,
Untimely zeal her witlefs pride betrays!   160
And ferious manhood from the towering aim
Of wifdom, ftoops to emulate the boaft
Of childifh toil.   Behold yon myftic form,
Bedeck'd with feathers, infects, weeds and fhells!
Not with intenfer view the Samian fage   165
Bent his fixt eye on heaven's intenfer fires,
When firft the order of that radiant fcene

Swell'd.

Swell'd his exulting thought, than this furveys
A muckworm's entrails or a fpider's fang.
Next him a youth, with flowers and myrtles crown'd,   170
Attends that virgin form, and blufhing kneels,
With fondeft gefture and a fuppliant's tongue,
To win her coy regard: adieu, for him,
The dull ingagements of the buftling world!
Adieu the fick impertinence of praife!   175
And hope, and action! for with her alone,
By ftreams and fhades, to fteal thefe fighing hours,
Is all he afks, and all that fate can give!
Thee too, facetious Momion, wandering here,
Thee, dreaded cenfor, oft have i beheld   180
Bewilder'd unawares: alas! too long
Flufh'd with thy comic triumphs and the fpoils
Of fly derifion! till on every fide
Hurling thy random bolts, offended truth
Affign'd thee here thy ftation with the flaves   185
Of folly.   Thy once formidable name
Shall grace her humble records, and be heard
In fcoffs and mockery bandied from the lips
Of all the vengeful brotherhood around,
So oft the patient victims of thy fcorn.   190

    But now, ye gay! to whom indulgent fate,
Of all the mufe's empire hath affign'd

                                        The

The fields of folly, hither each advance
Your fickles; here the teeming foil affords
Its richeft growth.   A favourite brood appears;   195
In whom the dæmon, with a mother's joy,
Views all her charms reflected, all her cares
At full repay'd.   Ye moft illuftrious band!
Who, fcorning reafon's tame, pedantic rules,
And order's vulgar bondage, never meant   200
For fouls fublime as yours, with generous zeal
Pay vice the reverence virtue long ufurp'd,
And yield deformity the fond applaufe
Which beauty wont to claim; forgive my fong,
That for the blufhing diffidence of youth,   205
It fhuns the unequal province of your praife.

Thus far triumphant in the pleafing guile
Of bland imagination, folly's train
Have dar'd our fearch : but now a daftard-kind
Advance reluctant, and with faultering feet   210
Shrink from the gazer's eye : infeebled hearts
Whom fancy chills with vifionary fears,
Or bends to fervile tamenefs with conceits
Of fhame, of evil, or of bafe defect,
Fantaftic and delufive.   Here the flave   115
Who droops abafh'd when fullen pomp furveys
His humbler habit; here the trembling wretch

Unnerv'd and ſtruck with terror's icy bolts,
Spent in weak wailings, drown'd in ſhameful tears,
At every dream of danger: here ſubdued   220
By frontleſs laughter and the hardy ſcorn
Of old, unfeeling vice, the abjeĉt ſoul,
Who bluſhing half reſigns the candid praiſe
Of temperance and honour; half diſowns
A freeman's hatred of tyrannic pride;   225
And hears with ſickly ſmiles the venal mouth
With fouleſt licence mock the patriot's name.

Laſt of the motley bands on whom the power
Of gay deriſion bends her hoſtile aim,
Is that where ſhameful ignorance preſides.   230
Beneath her ſordid banners, lo! they march,
Like blind and lame. Whate'er their doubtful hands
Attempt, confuſion ſtraight appears behind,
And troubles all the work. Through many a maze,
Perplex'd they ſtruggle, changing every path,   235
O'erturning every purpoſe; then at laſt
Sit down diſmay'd, and leave the entangled ſcene
For ſcorn to ſport with. Such then is the abode
Of folly in the mind; and ſuch the ſhapes
In which ſhe governs her obſequious train.   240

                                        Through

Through every fcene of ridicule in things
To lead the tenour of my devious lay;
Through every fwift occafion, which the hand
Of laughter points at, when the mirthful fling
Diftends her fallying nerves and choaks her tongue;   245
What were it but to count each cryftal drop
Which morning's dewy fingers on the blooms
Of May diftill?   Suffice it to have faid,
Where'er the power of ridicule difplays
Her quaint-ey'd vifage, fome incongruous form,   250
Some ftubborn diflonance of things combin'd,
Strikes on the quick obferver: whether pomp,
Or praife, or beauty, mix their partial claim
Where fordid fafhions, where ignoble deeds,
Where foul deformity are wont to dwell;   255
Or whether thefe with violation loath'd,
Invade refplendent pomp's imperious mien,
The charms of beauty, or the boaft of praife.

Afk we for what fair end, the almighty fire
In mortal bofoms wakes this gay contempt,   260
Thefe grateful flings of laughter, from difguft
Educing pleafure?   Wherefore, but to aid
The tardy fteps of reafon, and at once
By this prompt impulfe urge us to deprefs

M

The

The giddy aims of folly?   Though the light   265
Of truth flow-dawning on the inquiring mind,
At length unfolds, through many a fubtile tie,
How thefe uncouth diforders end at laft
In public evil! yet benignant heaven,
Confcious how dim the dawn of truth appears   270
To thoufands; confcious what a fcanty paufe
From labours and from care, the wider lot
Of humble life affords for ftudious thought
To fcan the maze of nature; therefore ftamp'd.
The glaring fcenes with characters of fcorn,   275
As broad, as obvious, to the paffing clown,
As to the letter'd fage's curious eye.

Such are the various afpects of the mind—
Some heavenly genius, whofe unclouded thoughts
Attain that fecret harmony which blends   280
The æthereal fpirit with its mold of clay;
O! teach me to reveal the grateful charm
That fearchlefs nature o'er the fenfe of man
Diffufes, to behold, in lifelefs things,
The inexpreffive femblance of himfelf,   285
Of thought and paffion.   Mark the fable woods
That fhade fublime yon mountain's nodding brow;
With what religious awe the folemn fcene
Commands your fteps! as if the reverend form

Of

Of Minos or of Numa fhould forfake   290
The Elyfian feats, and down the embowering glade
Move to your paufing eye!   Behold the expanfe
Of yon gay landfcape, where the filver clouds
Flit o'er the heavens before the fprightly breeze:
Now their grey cincture fkirts the doubtful fun;   295
Now ftreams of fplendor, through their opening veil
Effulgent, fweep from off the gilded lawn
The aërial fhadows; on the curling brook,
And on the fhady margin's quivering leaves
With quickeft luftre glancing; while you view   300
The profpect, fay, within your cheerful breaft
Plays not the lively fenfe of winning mirth
With clouds and fun-fhine chequer'd, while the round
Of focial converfe, to the infpiring tongue
Of fome gay nymph amid her fubject train,   305
Moves all obfequious?   Whence is this effect,
This kindred power of fuch difcordant things?
Or flows their femblance from that myftic tone
To which the new-born mind's harmonious powers
At firft were ftrung?   Or rather from the links   310
Which artful cuftom twines around her frame?

For when the different images of things
By chance combin'd, have ftruck the attentive foul
With deeper impulfe, or connected long,

M 2

Have

Have drawn her frequent eye; howe'er diſtinct   315
The external ſcenes, yet oft the ideas gain
From that conjunction an eternal tie,
And ſympathy unbroken.   Let the mind
Recall one partner of the various league,
Immediate, lo! the firm confederates riſe,   320
And each his former ſtation ſtrait reſumes:
One movement governs the conſenting throng,
And all at once with roſy pleaſure ſhine,
Or all are ſadden'd with the glooms of care.
'Twas thus, if ancient fame the truth unfold,   325
Two faithful needles, from the informing touch
Of the ſame parent-ſtone, together drew
Its myſtic virtue, and at firſt conſpir'd
With fatal impulſe quivering to the pole:
Then, though disjoin'd by kingdoms, though the main   330
Rowl'd its broad ſurge betwixt, and different ſtars.
Beheld their wakeful motions, yet preſerv'd
The former friendſhip, and remember'd ſtill
The alliance of their birth: whate'er the line
Which one poſſeſs'd, nor pauſe, nor quiet knew   335
The ſure aſſociate, ere with trembling ſpeed
He found its path and fix'd unnerring there.
Such is the ſecret union, when we feel
A ſong, a flower, a name, at once reſtore
Thoſe long-connected ſcenes where firſt they mov'd.   340

The

The attention : backward through her mazy walks
Guiding the wanton fancy to her fcope,
To temples, courts or fields ; with all the band
Of painted forms, of paflions and defigns
Attendant : whence, if pleafing in itfelf,   345
The profpect from that fweet acceflion gains
Redoubled influence o'er the liftening mind.

By thefe myfterious ties the bufy power
Of memory her ideal train preferves
Intire ; or when they would elude her watch,   350
Reclaims their fleeting footfteps from the wafte
Of dark oblivion ; thus collecting all
The various forms of being to prefent,
Before the curious aim of mimic art,
Their largeft choice : like fpring's unfolded blooms   355
Exhaling fweetnefs, that the fkillful bee
May tafte at will, from their felected fpoils
To work her dulcet food.   For not the expanfe
Of living lakes in fummer's noontide calm,
Reflects the bordering fhade, and fun-bright heavens   360
With fairer femblance ; not the fculptur'd gold
More faithful keeps the graver's lively trace,
Than he whofe birth the fifter powers of art
Propitious view'd, and from his genial ftar
Shed influence to the feeds of fancy kind ;   365

Than

Than his attemper'd bofom muft preferve
The feal of nature.   There alone unchang'd,
Her form remains.   The balmy walks of May
There breathe perennial fweets: the trembling chord
Refounds for ever in the abftracted ear,   370
Melodious: and the virgin's radiant eye,
Superior to difeafe, to grief, and time,
Shines with unbating luftre.   Thus at length
Indow'd with all that nature can beftow,
The child of fancy oft in filence bends   375
O'er thefe mixt treafures of his pregnant breaft,
With confcious pride.   From them he oft refolves
To frame he knows not what excelling things ;
And win he knows not what fublime reward
Of praife and wonder.   By degrees, the mind   380
Feels her young nerves dilate: the plaftic powers
Labour for action: blind emotions heave
His bofom ; and with lovelieft frenzy caught,
From earth to heaven he rowls his daring eye,
From heaven to earth.   Anon ten thoufand fhapes,   385
Like fpectres trooping to the wifard's call,
Flit fwift before him.   From the womb of earth,
From ocean's bed they come: the eternal heavens
Difclofe their fplendors, and the dark abyfs
Pours out her births unknown.   With fixed gaze   390
He marks the rifing phantoms.   Now compares

Their

Their different forms; now blends them, now divides,
Inlarges and extenuates by turns;
Oppofes, ranges in fantaftic bands,
And infinitely varies.   Hither now,   395
Now thither fluctuates his inconftant aim,
With endlefs choice perplex'd.   At length his plan
Begins to open.   Lucid order dawns;
And as from Chaos old the jarring feeds
Of nature at the voice divine repair'd   400
Each to its place, till rofy earth unveil'd
Her fragrant bofom, and the joyful fun
Sprung up the blue ferene; by fwift degrees
Thus difentangled, his entire defign
Emerges.   Colours mingle, features join,   405
And lines converge: the fainter parts retire;
The fairer eminent in light advance;
And every image on its neighbour fmiles.
A while he ftands, and with a father's joy
Contemplates.   Then with Promethéan art,   410
Into its proper vehicle he breathes
The fair conception; which, imbodied thus,
And permanent, becomes to eyes or ears
An object afcertain'd: while thus inform'd,
The various organs of his mimic fkill,   415
The confonance of founds, the featur'd rock,
The fhadowy picture and impaffion'd verfe,

Beyond

Beyond their proper powers attract the soul
By that expreſſive ſemblance, while in ſight
Of nature's great original we ſcan   420
The lively child of art; while line by line,
And feature after feature we refer
To that ſublime exemplar whence it ſtole
Thoſe animating charms.   Thus beauty's palm
Betwixt them wavering hangs: applauding love   425
Doubts where to chuſe; and mortal man aſpires
To tempt creative praiſe.   As when a cloud
Of gathering hail with limpid cruſts of ice
Incloſ'd and obvious to the beaming ſun,
Collects his large effulgence; ſtrait the heavens   430
With equal flames preſent on either hand
The radiant viſage: Perſia ſtands at gaze,
Appall'd; and on the brink of Ganges doubts
The ſnowy-veſted ſeer, in Mithra's name,
To which the fragrance of the ſouth ſhall burn,   435
To which his warbled oriſons aſcend.

Such various bliſs the well-tun'd heart enjoys,
Favour'd of heaven! while plung'd in ſordid cares,
The unfeeling vulgar mocks the boon divine:
And harſh auſterity, from whoſe rebuke   440
Young love and ſmiling wonder ſhrink away
Abaſh'd and chill of heart, with ſager frowns

Condemns

Condemns the fair inchantment.   On my brain,
Perhaps even now, some cold, fastidious judge
Casts a disdainful eye ; and calls my toil,   445
And calls the love and beauty which i sing,
The dream of folly.   Thou, grave censor! say,
Is beauty then a dream, because the glooms
Of dulness hang too heavy on thy sense,
To let her shine upon thee ?   So the man   450
Whose eye ne'er open'd on the light of heaven,
Might smile with scorn while raptur'd vision tells
Of the gay-colour'd radiance flushing bright
O'er all creation.   From the wise be far
Such gross unhallow'd pride ; nor needs my song   455
Descend so low ; but rather now unfold,
If human thought could reach, or words unfold,
By what mysterious fabric of the mind,
The deep-felt joys and harmony of sound
Result from airy motion ; and from shape   460
The lovely phantoms of sublime and fair.
By what fine ties hath God connected things
When present in the mind, which in themselves
Have no connection ?   Sure the rising sun
O'er the cærulean convex of the sea,   465
With equal brightness and with equal warmth
Might rowl his fiery orb ; nor yet the soul
Thus feel her frame expanded, and her powers

N

Exulting

Exulting in the fplendor fhe beholds;
Like a young conqueror moving through the pomp   470
Of fome triumphal day.   When join'd at eve,
Soft-murmuring ftreams and gales of gentleft breath
Melodious Philomela's wakeful ftrain
Attemper, could not man's difcerning ear
Through all its tones the fympathy purfue;   475
Nor yet this breath divine of namelefs joy
Steal through his veins and fan the awaken'd heart,
Mild as the breeze, yet rapturous as the fong.

But were not nature ftill endow'd at large
With all which life requires, though unadorn'd   480
With fuch inchantment?   Wherefore then her form
So exquifitely fair?   her breath perfum'd
With fuch æthereal fweetnefs?   whence her voice
Inform'd at will to raife or to deprefs
The impaffion'd foul?   and whence the robes of light   485
Which thus inveft her with more lovely pomp
Than fancy can defcribe?   Whence but from thee,
O fource divine of ever-flowing love,
And thy unmeafur'd goodnefs?   Not content
With every food of life to nourifh man,   490.
By kind illufions of the wondering fenfe·
Thou mak'ft all nature beauty to his eye,
Or mufic to his ear: well-pleas'd he fcans.

The.

The goodly profpect; and with inward fmiles
Treads the gay verdure of the painted plain :   495
Beholds the azure canopy of heaven,
And living lamps that over-arch his head
With more than regal fplendor; bends his ears
To the full choir of water, air, and earth ;
Nor heeds the pleafing error of his thought,   500
Nor doubts the painted green or azure arch,
Nor queftions more the mufic's mingling founds
Than fpace, or motion, or eternal time ;
So fweet he feels their influence to attract
The fixed foul; to brighten the dull glooms   505
Of care, and make the deftin'd road of life
Delightful to his feet.   So fables tell,
The adventurous heroe, bound on hard exploits,
Beholds with glad furprife, by fecret fpells
Of fome kind fage, the patron of his toils,   510
A vifionary paradife difclos'd
Amid the dubious wild : with ftreams, and fhades,
And airy fongs, the enchanted landfcape fmiles,
Cheers his long labours and renews his frame.

What then is tafte, but thefe internal powers   515
Active, and ftrong, and feelingly alive
To each fine impulfe ? a difcerning fenfe
Of decent and fublime, with quick difguft

N 2

From things deform'd, or difarrang'd, or grofs
In fpecies?   This, nor gems, nor ftores of gold,   520
Nor purple ftate, nor culture can beftow;
But God alone, when firft his active hand
Imprints the fecret byafs of the foul.
He, mighty parent! wife and juft in all,
Free as the vital breeze or light of heaven,   525
Reveals the charms of nature.   Afk the fwain
Who journeys homeward from a fummer day's
Long labour, why, forgetful of his toils
And due repofe, he loiters to behold
The funfhine gleaming as through amber clouds,   530
O'er all the weftern fky; full foon, I ween,
His rude expreffion and untutor'd airs,
Beyond the power of language, will unfold
The form of beauty fmiling at his heart,
How lovely! how commanding!   But though heaven   535.
In every breaft hath fown thefe early feeds
Of love and admiration, yet in vain,
Without fair culture's kind parental aid;
Without inlivening funs, and genial fhowers,
And fhelter from the blaft, in vain we hope   540
The tender plant fhould rear its blooming head,
Or yield the harveft promis'd in its fpring.
Nor yet will every foil with equal ftores
Repay the tiller's labour; or attend

His

His will, obfequious, whether to produce   545
The olive or the laurel.   Different minds
Incline to different objects : one purfues
The vaft alone, the wonderful, the wild;
Another fighs for harmony, and grace,
And gentleft beauty.   Hence when lightening fires   550
The arch of heaven, and thunders rock the ground,
When furious whirlwinds rend the howling air,
And ocean, groaning from his loweft bed,
Heaves his tempeftuous billows to the fky;
Amid the mighty uproar, while below   555
The nations tremble, Shakefpeare looks abroad
From fome high cliff, fuperior, and enjoys
The elemental war.   But Waller longs,
All on the margin of fome flowery ftream
To fpread his carelefs limbs amid the cool   560
Of plantane fhades, and to the liftening deer
The tale of flighted vows and love's difdain
Refound foft-warbling all the live-long day :
Confenting Zephyr fighs; the weeping rill
Joins in his plaint, melodious; mute the groves ;   565
And hill and dale with all their echoes mourn.
Such and fo various are the taftes of men.

   Oh ! bleft of heaven, whom not the languid fongs
Of luxury, the Siren ! not the bribes

Of sordid wealth, nor all the gaudy spoils
Of pageant honour can seduce to leave
Those ever-blooming sweets, which from the store
Of nature fair imagination culls
To charm the inliven'd soul!   What though not all
Of mortal offspring can attain the heights
Of envied life; though only few possess
Patrician treasures or imperial state;
Yet nature's care, to all her children just,
With richer treasures and an ampler state,
Indows at large whatever happy man
Will deign to use them.   His the city's pomp,
The rural honors his.   Whate'er adorns
The princely dome, the column and the arch,
The breathing marbles and the sculptur'd gold,
Beyond the proud possessor's narrow claim,
His tuneful breast injoys.   For him, the spring
Distills her dews, and from the silken gem
Its lucid leaves unfolds: for him, the hand
Of autumn tinges every fertile branch
With blooming gold and blushes like the morn.
Each passing hour sheds tribute from her wings;
And still new beauties meet his lonely walk,
And loves unfelt attract him.   Not a breeze
Flies o'er the meadow, not a cloud imbibes
The setting sun's effulgence, not a strain

From all the tenants of the warbling fhade
Afcends, but whence his bofom can partake
Frefh pleafure, unreprov'd.   Nor thence partakes
Frefh pleafure only: for the attentive mind,
By this harmonious action on her powers   600
Becomes herfelf harmonious: wont fo oft
In outward things to meditate the charm
Of facred order, foon fhe feeks at home
To find a kindred order, to exert
Within herfelf this elegance of love,   605
This fair-infpir'd delight: her temper'd powers
Refine at length, and every paffion wears
A chafter, milder, more attractive mien.
But if to ampler profpects, if to gaze
On nature's form, where, negligent of all   610
Thefe leffer graces, fhe affumes the port
Of that eternal majefty that weigh'd
The world's foundations, if to thefe the mind
Exalts her daring eye; then mightier far
Will be the change, and nobler.   Would the forms   615
Of fervile cuftom cramp her generous powers?
Would fordid policies, the barbarous growth
Of ignorance and rapine, bow her down
To tame purfuits, to indolence and fear?
Lo! fhe appeals to nature, to the winds   620
And rowling waves, the fun's unwearied courfe,

The

The elements and feafons: all declare
For what the eternal maker has ordain'd
The powers of man: we feel within ourfelves
His energy divine: he tells the heart,   625
He meant, he made us to behold and love
What he beholds and loves, the general orb
Of life and being; to be great like him,
Beneficent and active.   Thus the men
Whom nature's works can charm, with God himfelf   630
Hold converfe; grow familiar, day by day,
With his conceptions, act upon his plan;
And form to his, the relifh of their fouls.

END OF BOOK III.

NOTES

N O T E S

ON THE

THREE BOOKS

OF THE

PLEASURES

OF

MAGINATION.

()

N O T E S

O N T H E

F I R S T B O O K.

VER. 151. *Say, why was man, &c.*] In apologizing for the frequent negligences of the sublimeſt authors of *Greece*, *Thoſe god-like geniuſes*, ſays *Longinus*, *were well aſſured, that Nature had not intended man for a low-ſpirited or ignoble being : but bringing us into life and the midſt of this wide univerſe, as before a multitude aſſembled at ſome heroic ſolemnity, that we might be ſpectators of all her magnificence, and candidates high in emulation for the prize of glory; ſhe has therefore implanted in our ſouls an inextinguiſhable love of every thing great and exalted, of every thing which appears divine beyond our comprehenſion. Whence it comes to paſs, that even the whole world is not an object ſufficient for the depth and rapidity of human imagination, which often ſallies forth beyond the limits of all that ſurrounds us. Let any man caſt his eye through the whole circle of our exiſtence, and conſider how eſpecially it abounds in excellent and grand objects, he will ſoon acknowledge for what irjoyments and purſuits we were deſtined. Thus by the very propenſity of nature we are led to admire, not little ſprings or ſhallow rivulets, however clear and delicious, but the Nile, the Rhine, the Danube, and, much more than all, the Ocean, &c.* Dionyſ. Longin. de Sublim. § xxiv.

Ver. 202. *The empyreal waſte.*] *Ne ſe peut-il point qu'il y a un grand eſpace au de'a de la region des etoiles? Que ce ſeit le ciel empyrée, ou non, toujours cet eſpace immenſe qui environne toute cette region, pourra etre rempli de bonheur & de gloire. Il pourra etre conçu comme l'ocean, où ſe rendent les fleuves de toutes les creatures bienheureuſes, quand elles ſeront venues à leur perfection dans le ſyſteme des etoiles.* Leibnitz dans la Theodicee, part. i. § 19.

Ver. 204. *Whoſe unfading light, &c.*] It was a notion of the great Mr. *Huygens*, that there may be fixed ſtars at ſuch a diſtance from our ſolar ſyſtem, as that their light ſhould not have had time to reach us, even from the creation of the world to this day.

Ver. 234. ———— *the neglect*
Of all familiar proſpects, &c.] It is here ſaid, that in conſequence of the love of novelty, objects which at firſt were highly delightful to the mind, loſe

that

that effect by repeated attention to them. But the instance of *habit* is opposed to this observation; for *there*, objects at first distasteful are in time rendered intirely agreeable by repeated attention.

The difficulty in this case will be removed, if we consider, that, when objects at first agreeable, lose that influence by frequently recurring, the mind is wholly *passive*, and the perception *involuntary*; but habit, on the other hand, generally supposes *choice* and *activity* accompanying it: so that the pleasure arises here not from the object, but from the mind's *conscious* determination of its own activity; and consequently increases in proportion to the frequency of that determination.

It will still be urged perhaps, that a familiarity with disagreeable objects renders them at length acceptable, even when there is no room for the mind to *resolve* or *act* at all. In this case, the appearance must be accounted for, one of these ways.

The pleasure from habit may be merely negative. The object at first gave uneasiness: this uneasiness gradually wears off as the object grows familiar: and the mind, finding it at last intirely removed, reckons its situation really pleasurable, compared with what it had experienced before.

The dislike conceived of the object at first, might be owing to prejudice or want of attention. Consequently the mind being necessitated to review it often, may at length perceive its own mistake, and be reconciled to what it had looked on with aversion. In which case, a sort of instinctive justice naturally leads it to make amends for the injury, by running toward the other extreme of fondness and attachment.

Or lastly, though the object itself should always continue disagreeable, yet circumstances of pleasure or good fortune may occur along with it. Thus an association may arise in the mind, and the object never be remembered without those pleasing circumstances attending it; by which means the disagreeable impression which it at first occasioned will in time be quite obliterated.

Ver. 240.   ——— *this desire*

         Of objects new *and* strange ———] These two ideas are oft confounded; though it is evident the mere *novelty* of an object makes it agreeable, even where the mind is not affected with the least degree of *wonder*: whereas *wonder* indeed always implies *novelty*, being never excited by common or well-known appearances. But the pleasure in both cases is explicable from the same final cause, the acquisition of knowledge and inlargement of our views of nature: on this account, it is natural to treat of them together.

Ver. 374.   ——— *Truth and good are one,*

         And beauty dwells in them, &c.] *Do you imagine,* says *Socrates* to *Aristippus, that what is good is not beautiful? Have you not observed that those appearances always coincide? Virtue, for instance, in the same respect as to which we*

               call

call it good, is ever acknowledged to be beautiful also. In the characters of men we always * *join the two denominations together. The beauty of human bodies corresponds, in like manner, with that œconomy of parts which constitutes them good; and in every circumstance of life, the same object is constantly accounted both beautiful and good, inasmuch as it answers the purposes for which it was designed.* Xenophont. Memorab. Socrat. l. iii. c. 8.

This excellent observation has been illustrated and extended by the noble reformer of ancient philosophy; *see the Characteristicks,* vol. ii. p. 339 and 422. and vol. iii. p. 181. And another ingenious author has particularly shewn, that it holds in the general laws of nature, in the works of art, and the conduct of the sciences. *Inquiry into the original of our ideas of beauty and virtue,* Treat. i. § 8. As to the connection between *beauty* and *truth,* there are two opinions concerning it. Some philosophers assert an independent and invariable law in nature, in consequence of which *all rational beings must alike perceive beauty in some certain proportions, and deformity in the contrary.* And this necessity being supposed the same with that which commands the assent or dissent of the understanding, it follows of course that *beauty* is founded on the universal and unchangeable law of *truth.*

But others there are, who believe *beauty* to be merely a relative and arbitrary thing; that indeed it was a benevolent provision in nature to annex so delightful a sensation to those objects which are *best and most perfect in themselves,* that so we might be ingaged to the choice of them at once and without staying to infer their *usefulness* from their structure and effects; but that it is not impossible, in a physical sense, that two beings, of equal capacities for *truth,* should perceive, one of them *beauty,* and the other *deformity,* in the same proportions. And upon this supposition, by that *truth* which is always connected with *beauty,* nothing more can be meant than the conformity of any object to those proportions upon which, after careful examination, the beauty of that species is found to depend. *Polycletus,* for instance, a famous ancient sculptor, from an accurate mensuration of the several parts of the most perfect human bodies, deduced a canon or system of proportions, which was the rule of all succeeding artists. Suppose a statue modelled according to this: a man of mere natural taste, upon looking at it, without entering into its proportions, confesses and admires its *beauty;* whereas a professor of the art applies his measures to the head, the neck, or the hand, and, without attending to its beauty, pronounces the workmanship to be *just* and *true.*

Ver. 492. *As when Brutus rose,* &c.] *Cicero* himself describes this fact—*Cæsare interjecto——statim cruentum alte extollens M. Brutus pugionem, Ciceronem neminatim exclamavit, atque ei recuperatam libertatem est gratulatus.* Cic. Philipp. ii. 12.

---

* This the *Athenians* did in a peculiar manner, by the word καλοκαγαθὸς, καλοκαγαθία.

Ver. 548.   *Where virtue rifing from the awful depth*

           Of truth's myfterious bofom, &c.]   According to the opinion of thofe who affert *moral obligation* to be founded on an immutable and univerfal law, and that which is ufually called the *moral fenfe*, to be determined by the peculiar temper of the imagination and the earlieft affociations of ideas.

Ver. 591.   *Lycéum.*]   The fchool of *Ariftotle*.

Ver. 592.   *Academus.*]   The fchool of *Plato*.

Ver. 594.   *Iliffus.*]   One of the rivers on which *Athens* was fituated. *Plato*, in fome of his fineft dialogues, lays the fcene of the converfation with *Socrates* on its banks.

VER. 19. *At laſt the muſes roſe, &c.*] About the age of *Hugh Capet,* founder of the third race of *French* kings, the poets of *Provence* were in high reputation ; a ſort of ſtrolling bards or rhapſodiſts, who went about the courts of princes and noblemen, entertaining them at feſtivals with muſic and poetry. They attempted both the epic, ode, and ſatire ; and abounded in a wild and fantaſtic vein of fable, partly allegorical, and partly founded on traditionary legends of the *Saracen* wars. Theſe were the rudiments of *Italian* poetry. But their taſte and compoſition muſt have been extremely barbarous, as we may judge by thoſe who followed the turn of their fable in much politer times ; ſuch as *Boiardo, Bernardo Taſſo, Arioſto,* &c.

Ver. 21. *Valchuſa.*] The famous retreat of *Franciſo Petrarcha,* the father of *Italian* poetry, and his miſtreſs *Laura,* a lady of *Avignon.*

Ver. 22. *Arno.*] The river which runs by *Florence,* the birth-place of *Dante* and *Boccacio.*

Ver. 23. *Parthenope.*] Or *Naples,* the birth-place of *Sannazaro.* The great *Torquato Taſſo* was born at *Sorrento* in the kingdom of *Naples.*

Ibid. —— *the rage*

Of dire ambition, &c.] This relates to the cruel wars among the republics of *Italy,* and abominable politics of its little princes, about the fifteenth century. Theſe at laſt, in conjunction with the papal power, intirely extinguiſhed the ſpirit of liberty in that country, and eſtabliſhed that abuſe of the fine arts which has been ſince propagated over all *Europe.*

Ver. 30. *Thus from their guardians torn, the tender arts,* &c.] Nor were they only loſers by the ſeparation. For philoſophy itſelf, to uſe the words of a noble philoſopher, *being thus ſevered by the ſprightly arts and ſciences, muſt conſequently grow droniſh, inſipid, pedantic, uſeleſs, and directly oppoſite to the real knowledge and practice of the world.* Inſomuch that *a gentleman,* ſays another excellent writer, *cannot eaſily bring himſelf to like ſo auſtere and ungainly a form : ſo greatly is it changed from what was once the delight of the fineſt gentlemen of antiquity, and their recreation after the hurry of public affairs !* From this condition it cannot be

recovered

recovered but by uniting it once more with the works of imagination; and we have had the pleasure of obferving a very great progrefs made towards their union in *England* within thefe few years.   It is hardly poffible to conceive them at a greater diftance from each other than at the Revolution, when *Locke* flood at the head of one party, and *Dryden* of the other.   But the general fpirit of liberty, which has ever fince been growing, naturally invited our men of wit and genius to improve that influence which the arts of perfuafion gave them with the people, by applying them to fubjects of importance to fociety.   Thus poetry and eloquence became confiderable; and philofophy is now of courfe obliged to borrow of their embellifhments, in order even to gain audience with the public.

Ver. 157. *From paffion's power alone,* &c.]   This very myfterious kind of pleafure, which is often found in the exercife of paffions generally counted painful, has been taken notice of by feveral authors.   *Lucretius* refolves it into felf-love :

Suave mari magno, &c. lib. ii. 1.

As if a man was never pleafed in being moved at the diftrefs of a tragedy, without a cool reflection that though thefe fictitious perfonages were fo unhappy, yet he himfelf was perfectly at eafe and in fafety.   The ingenious author of the *Reflections critiques fur la poefie & fur la peinture,* accounts for it by the general delight which the mind takes in its own activity, and the abhorrence it feels of an indolent and inattentive ftate : and this, joined with the moral approbation of its own temper, which attends thefe emotions when natural and juft, is certainly the true foundation of the pleafure, which, as it is the origin and bafis of tragedy and epic, deferved a very particular confideration in this poem.

Ver. 304. *Inhabitant of earth,* &c.]   The account of the œconomy of providence here introduced, as the moft proper to calm and fatisfy the mind when under the compunction of private evils, feems to have come originally from the *Pythagorean* fchool : but of the ancient philofophers, *Plato* has moft largely infifted upon it, has eftablifhed it with all the ftrength of his capacious underftanding, and ennobled it with all the magnificence of his divine imagination.   He has one paffage fo full and clear on this head, that I am perfuaded the reader will be pleafed to fee it here, though fomewhat long.   Addreffing himfelf to fuch as are not fatisfied concerning divine providence : *The Being who prefides over the whole,* fays he, *has difpofed and complicated all things for the happinefs and virtue of the whole, every part of which, according to the extent of its influence, does and fuffers what is fit and proper. One of thefe parts is yours, O unhappy man, which though in itfelf moft inconfiderable and minute, yet being connected with the univerfe, ever feeks to co-operate with that fupreme order. You in the mean time are ignorant of the very end for which all particular natures are brought into exiftence, that the all-comprehending nature of the whole may be perfect and happy ; exifting, as it does, not for your fake, but the caufe and reafon of your exiftence, which, as in the fymmetry of every artificial work, muft*

of

of neceſſity concur with the general deſign of the artiſt, and be ſubſervient to the whole of which it is a part. Your complaint therefore is ignorant and groundleſs; ſince, according to the various energy of creation, and the common laws of nature, there is a conſtant proviſion of that which is beſt at the ſame time for you and for the whole. --- For the governing intelligence clearly beholding all the actions of animated and ſelf-moving creatures, and that mixture of good and evil which diverſifies them, conſidered firſt of all by what diſpoſition of things, and by what ſituation of each individual in the general ſyſtem, vice might be depreſſed and ſubdued, and virtue made ſecure of victory and happineſs with the greateſt facility and in the higheſt degree poſſible: In this manner he ordered through the entire circle of being, the internal conſtitution of every mind, where ſhould be its ſtation in the univerſal fabric, and through what variety of circumſtances it ſhould proceed in the whole tenour of its exiſtence. He goes on in his ſublime manner to aſſert a future ſtate of retribution, *as well for thoſe who, by the exerciſe of good diſpoſitions being harmonized and aſſimilated into the divine virtue, are conſequently removed to a place of unblemiſhed ſanctity and happineſs; as of thoſe who by the moſt flagitious arts have riſen from contemptible beginnings to the greateſt affluence and power, and whom you therefore look upon as unanſwerable inſtances of negligence in the gods, becauſe you are ignorant of the purpoſes to which they are ſubſervient, and in what manner they contribute to that ſupreme intention of good to the whole.* Plato de Leg. x. 16.

This theory has been delivered of late, eſpecially abroad, in a manner which ſubverts the freedom of human actions; whereas *Plato* appears very careful to preſerve it, and has been in that reſpect imitated by the beſt of his followers.

Ver. 321.   ——*one might riſe,*

                One order, &c.]   See the Meditations of *Antoninus* and the Characteriſticks, paſſim.

Ver. 355. *The beſt and faireſt, &c.*]   This opinion is ſo old, that *Timæus Locrus* calls the ſupreme being δαμιεργὸς τῶ βελτίϛϖ, *the artificer of that which is beſt*; and repreſents him as reſolving in the beginning to produce the moſt excellent work, and as copying the world moſt exactly from his own intelligible and eſſential idea; *ſo that it yet remains, as it was at firſt, perfect in beauty, and will never ſtand in need of any correction or improvement.* There can be no room for a caution here, to underſtand the expreſſions, not of any particular circumſtances of human life ſeparately conſidered, but of the ſum or univerſal ſyſtem of life and being.   See alſo the viſion at the end of the *Theodicée* of *Leibnitz.*

Ver. 350. *As flame aſcends, &c.*]   This opinion, though not held by *Plato* nor any of the ancients, is yet a very natural conſequence of his principles.   But the diſquiſition is too complex and extenſive to be entered upon here.

Ver. 755. *Philip.*]   The *Macedonian.*

P

N O T E S

N O T E S

ON THE

T H I R D B O O K.

Of fancy, &c.] The influence of the imagination on the conduct of life, is one of the moſt important points in moral philoſophy. It were eaſy by an inducſtion of facſts to prove that the imagination direcſts almoſt all the paſſions, and mixes with almoſt every circumſtance of acſtion or pleaſure. Let any man, even of the coldeſt head and ſobereſt induſtry, analyſe the idea of what he calls his intereſt; he will find that it conſiſts chiefly of certain degrees of decency, beauty, and order, variouſly combined into one ſyſtem, the idol which he ſeeks to enjoy by labour, hazard, and ſelf-denial. It is on this account of the laſt conſequence to regulate theſe images by the ſtandard of nature and the general good; otherwiſe the imagination, by heightening ſome objecſts beyond their real excellence and beauty, or by repreſenting others in a more odious or terrible ſhape than they deſerve, may of courſe engage us in purſuits utterly inconſiſtent with the moral order of things.

If it be objecſted that this account of things ſuppoſes the paſſions to be merely accidental, whereas there appears in ſome a natural and hereditary diſpoſition to certain paſſions prior to all circumſtances of education or fortune; it may be anſwered, that though no man is born *ambitious* or a *miſer,* yet he may inherit from his parents a peculiar temper or complexion of mind, which ſhall render his imagination more liable to be ſtruck with ſome particular objecſts, conſequently diſpoſe him to form opinions of good and ill, and entertain paſſions of a particular turn. Some men, for inſtance, by the original frame of their minds, are more delighted with the vaſt and magnificent, others on the contrary with the elegant and gentle aſpecſts of nature. And it is very remarkable, that the diſpoſition of the moral powers is always ſimilar to this of the imagination; that thoſe who are moſt inclined to admire prodigious and ſublime objecſts in the phyſical world, are alſo moſt inclined to applaud examples of fortitude and heroic virtue in the moral. While thoſe who are charmed rather with the *delicacy* and *ſweetneſs* of colours, and forms, and ſounds, never fail in like manner to yield the preference to the ſofter ſcenes of

virtue

virtue and the fympathies of a domeſtic life. And this is ſufficient to account for the objection.

Among the ancient philoſophers, though we have ſeveral hints concerning this influence of the imagination upon morals among the remains of the *Socratic* ſchool, yet the *Stoics* were the firſt who paid it a due attention. *Zeno*, their founder, thought it impoſſible to preſerve any tolerable regularity in life, without frequently inſpecting thoſe pictures or appearances of things, which the imagination offers to the mind (*Diog. Laert.* l. vii.) The Meditations of *M. Aurelius*, and the diſcourſes of *Epictetus*, are full of the ſame ſentiment; inſomuch that the latter makes the Χρῆσις οἵα δῆ φαντασιῶν, or *right management of the fancies*, the only thing for which we are accountable to providence, and without which a man is no other than ſtupid or frantic. *Arrian.* l. i. c. 12. & l. ii. c. 22. See alſo the *Characteriſtics*, vol. i. from p. 313. to 321. where this *Stoical* doctrine is embelliſhed with all the elegance and graces of *Plato*.

Ver. 75. —— *how folly's awkward arts*, &c.] Notwithſtanding the general influence of *ridicule* on private and civil life, as well as on learning and the ſciences, it has been almoſt conſtantly neglected or miſrepreſented, by divines eſpecially. The manner of treating theſe ſubjects in the ſcience of human nature, ſhould be preciſely the ſame as in natural philoſophy; from particular facts to inveſtigate the ſtated order in which they appear, and then apply the general law, thus diſcovered, to the explication of other appearances and the improvement of uſeful arts.

Ver. 84. *Behold the foremoſt band*, &c.] The firſt and moſt general ſource of ridicule in the characters of men, is vanity, or ſelf-applauſe for ſome deſirable quality or poſſeſſion which evidently does not belong to thoſe who aſſume it.

Ver. 121. *Then comes the ſecond order*, &c.] Ridicule from the ſame vanity, where, though the poſſeſſion be real, yet no merit can ariſe from it, becauſe of ſome particular circumſtances, which, though obvious to the ſpectator, are yet overlooked by the ridiculous character.

Ver. 152. *Another tribe ſucceeds*, &c.] Ridicule from a notion of excellence in particular objects diſproportioned to their intrinſic value, and inconſiſtent with the order of nature.

Ver. 191. *But now ye gay*, &c.] Ridicule from a notion of excellence, when the object is abſolutely odious or contemptible. This is the higheſt degree of the ridiculous; as in the affectation of diſeaſes or vices.

Ver. 207. *Thus far triumphant*, &c.] Ridicule from falſe ſhame or groundleſs fear.

Ver. 228. *Laſt of the*, &c.] Ridicule from the ignorance of ſuch things as our circumſtances require us to know.

Ver. 248. —— *Suffice it to have ſaid*, &c.] By comparing theſe general ſources of ridicule with each other, and examining the ridiculous in other objects, we may

obtain

obtain a general definition of it, equally applicable to every species. The most important circumstance of this definition is laid down in the lines referred to; but others more minute we shall subjoin here. *Aristotle's* account of the matter seems both imperfect and false; τὸ γὰρ γελοῖον, says he, ἐστὶν ἁμάρτημά τι καὶ αἶσχος, ἀνώδυνον καὶ οὐ φθαρτικόν: *the ridiculous is some certain fault or turpitude without pain, and not destructive to its subject.* (*Poët.* c. 5.) For allowing it to be true, as it is not, that the ridiculous is never accompanied with pain, yet we might produce many instances of such a fault or turpitude which cannot with any tolerable propriety be called ridiculous. So that the definition does not distinguish the thing designed. Nay farther; even when we perceive the turpitude tending to the destruction of its subject, we may still be sensible of a ridiculous appearance, till the ruin become imminent, and the keener sensations of pity or terror banish the ludicrous apprehension from our minds. For the sensation of ridicule is not a bare perception of the agreement or disagreement of ideas; but a passion or emotion of the mind consequential to that perception. So that the mind may perceive the agreement or disagreement, and yet not feel the ridiculous, because it is engrossed by a more violent emotion. Thus it happens that some men think those objects ridiculous, to which others cannot endure to apply the name; because in them they excite a much intenser and more important feeling. And this difference, among other causes, has brought a good deal of confusion into this question.

That which makes objects ridiculous, is some ground of admiration or esteem connected with other more general circumstances comparatively worthless or deformed; or it is some circumstance of turpitude or deformity connected with what is in general excellent or beautiful: the inconsistent properties existing either in the objects themselves, or in the apprehension of the person to whom they relate; belonging always to the same order or class of being; implying sentiment or design; and exciting no acute or vehement emotion of the heart.

To prove the several parts of this definition: *The appearance of excellence or beauty connected with a general condition comparatively sordid or deformed,* is ridiculous: for instance, pompous pretensions of wisdom joined with ignorance or folly in the *Socrates* of *Aristophanes;* and the ostentations of military glory with cowardice and stupidity in the *Thraso* of *Terence.*

The appearance of deformity or turpitude in conjunction with what is in general excellent or venerable, is also ridiculous: for instance, the personal weaknesses of a magistrate appearing in the solemn and public functions of his station.

The incongruous properties may either exist in the objects themselves, or in apprehension of the person to whom they relate: in the last-mentioned instance, they both exist in the objects; in the instances from *Aristophanes* and *Terence,* one of them is objective and real, the other only founded in the apprehension of the ridiculous character.

The.

The inconfiftent properties muft belong to the fame order or clafs of being. A coxcomb in fine cloaths, bedaubed by accident in foul weather, is a ridiculous object; becaufe his general apprehenfion of excellence and efteem is referred to the fplendour and expence of his drefs. A man of fenfe and merit, in the fame circumftances, is not counted ridiculous; becaufe the general ground of excellence and efteem in him is, both in fact and in his own apprehenfion, of a very different fpecies.

Every ridiculous object implies fentiment or defign. A column placed by an architect without a capital or bafe, is laughed at: the fame column in a ruin caufes a very different fenfation.

And laftly, *the occurrence muft excite no acute or vehement emotion of the heart,* fuch as terror, pity, or indignation; for in that cafe, as was obferved above, the mind is not at leifure to contemplate the ridiculous.

Whether any appearance not ridiculous be involved in this defcription, and whether it comprehend every fpecies and form of the ridiculous, muft be determined by repeated applications of it to particular inftances.

Ver. 259. *Afk we for what fair end,* &c.] Since it is beyond all contradiction evi lent that we have a *natural* fenfe or feeling of the ridiculous, and fince fo good a reafon may be affigned to juftify the fupreme being for beftowing it; one cannot without aftonifhment reflect on the conduct of thofe men who imagine it is for the fervice of true religion to vilify and blacken it without diftinction, and endeavour to perfuade us that it is never applied but in a bad caufe. Ridicule is not concerned with mere fpeculative truth or falfehood. It is not in abftract propofitions or theorems, but in actions and paffions, good and evil, beauty and deformity, that we find materials for it; and all thefe terms are *relative,* implying approbation or blame. To afk them whether *ridicule be a teft of truth,* is, in other words, to afk whether that which is ridiculous can be *morally true,* can be juft and becoming; or whether that which is juft and becoming, can be ridiculous. A queftion that does not deferve a ferious anfwer. For it is moft evident, that, as in a metaphyfical propofition offered to the underftanding for its affent, the faculty of reafon examines the terms of the propofition, and finding one idea, which was fuppofed equal to another, to be in fact unequal, of confequence rejects the propofition as a falfehood; fo, in objects offered to the mind for its efteem or applaufe, the faculty of ridicule, finding an incongruity in the claim, urges the mind to reject it with laughter and contempt. When therefore we obferve fuch a claim obtruded upon mankind, and the inconfiftent circumftances carefully concealed from the eye of the public, it is our bufinefs, if the matter be of importance to fociety, to drag out thofe latent circumftances, and, by fetting them in full view, to convince the world how ridiculous the claim is: and thus a double advantage is gained; for we both detect the *moral falfehood* fooner than in the way of fpeculative inquiry, and imprefs the minds of

men

men with a stronger sense of the vanity and error of its authors. And this and no more is meant by the application of ridicule.

But it is said, the practice is dangerous, and may be inconsistent with the regard we owe to objects of real dignity and excellence. I answer, the practice fairly managed can never be dangerous; men may be dishonest in obtruding circumstances foreign to the object, and we may be inadvertent in allowing those circumstances to impose upon us: but the sense of ridicule always judges right. The *Socrates* of *Aristophanes* is as *truly* ridiculous a character as ever was drawn: — True; but it is not the character of *Socrates*, the divine moralist and father of ancient wisdom. What then? did the ridicule of the poet hinder the philosopher from detecting and disclaiming those foreign circumstances which he had falsely introduced into his character, and thus rendered the satirist doubly ridiculous in his turn? No; but it nevertheless had an ill influence on the minds of the people. And so has the reasoning of *Spinoza* made many atheists: he has founded it indeed on suppositions utterly false; but allow him these, and his conclusions are unavoidably true. And if we must reject the use of ridicule, because, by the imposition of false circumstances, things may be made to seem ridiculous, which are not so in themselves; why we ought not in the same manner to reject the use of reason, because, by proceeding on false principles, conclusions will appear true which are impossible in nature, let the vehement and obstinate declaimers against ridicule determine.

Ver. 285. *The inexpressive semblance*, &c.] This similitude is the foundation of almost all the ornaments of poetic diction.

Ver. 326. *Two faithful needles*, &c.] See the elegant poem recited by Cardinal *Bembo* in the character of *Lucretius; Strada Proluf.* vi. *Academ.* 2. c. v.

Ver. 348. *By these mysterious ties*, &c.] The act of remembering seems almost wholly to depend on the association of ideas.

Ver. 411. *Into its proper vehicle*, &c.] This relates to the different sorts of corporeal mediums, by which the ideas of the artists are rendered palpable to the senses; as by sounds, in music; by lines and shadows, in painting; by diction, in poetry, *&c.*

Ver. 547.   —— *One pursues*
        The vast alone, &c.] See the note to ver. 18. of this book.

Ver. 558.   *Waller longs*, &c.]
        O! how I long my careless limbs to lay
        Under the plantane shade; and all the day
        With amorous airs my fancy entertain, &c.
                WALLER, Battle of the Summer-Islands, Canto I.

And again,
        While in the park I sing, the list'ning deer
        Attend my passion, and forget to fear, &c.
                At *Pens-hurst.*
                        Ver.

Ver. 593. ——- *Not a breeze,* &c.] That this account may not appear rather poetically extravagant than juſt in philoſophy, it may be proper to produce the ſentiment of one of the greateſt, wiſeſt, and beſt of men on this head; one ſo little to be ſuſpected of partiality in the caſe, that he reckons it among thoſe favours for which he was eſpecially thankful to the gods, that they had not ſuffered him to make any great proficiency in the arts of eloquence and poetry, leſt by that means he ſhould have been diverted from purſuits of more importance to his high ſtation. Speaking of the beauty of univerſal nature, he obſerves, that there *is a pleaſing and graceful aſpect in every object we perceive,* when once we conſider its connection with that general order. He inſtances in many things which at firſt ſight would be thought rather deformities; and then adds, *that a man who enjoys a ſenſibility of temper with a juſt comprehenſion of the univerſal order — will diſcern many amiable things, not credible to every mind, but to thoſe alone who have entered into an honourable familiarity with nature and her works.* M. Antoniu. iii. 2.

THE

THE

PLEASURES

OF THE

IMAGINATION:

A

POEM.

The pleasures of the imagination proceed either from natural objects, as from a flourishing grove, a clear and murmuring fountain, a calm sea by moon-light; or from works of art, such as a noble edifice, a musical tune, a statue, a picture, a poem. In treating of these pleasures, we must begin with the former class; they being original to the other; and nothing more being necessary, in order to explain them, than a view of our natural inclination toward greatness and beauty, and of those appearances, in the world around us, to which that inclination is adapted. This is the subject of the first book of the following poem.

But the pleasures which we receive from the elegant arts, from music, sculpture, painting, and poetry, are much more various and complicated. In them (besides greatness and beauty, or forms proper to the imagination) we find interwoven frequent representations of truth, of virtue and vice, of circumstances proper to move us with laughter, or to excite in us pity, fear, and the other passions. These moral and intellectual objects are described in the second book; to which the third properly belongs as an episode, though too large to have been included in it.

Q 2

With

*With the above-mentioned caufes of pleafure, which are univer-
fal in the courfe of human life and appertain to our higher
faculties, many others do generally concur, more limited in
their operation, or of an inferior origin: fuch are the novelty
of objects, the affociation of ideas, affections of the bodily
fenfes, influences of education, national habits, and the like.
To illuftrate thefe, and from the whole to determine the character of a perfect tafte, is the argument of the fourth book.*

*Hitherto the pleafures of the imagination belong to the human fpe-
cies in general. But there are certain particular men whofe
imagination is indowed with powers, and fufceptible of pleafures, which the generality of mankind never participate.
thefe are the men of genius, deftined by nature to excell in
one or other of the arts already mentioned. It is propofed
therefore, in the laft place, to delineate that genius which in
fome degree appears common to them all; yet with a more
peculiar confideration of poetry: inafmuch as poetry is the
moft extenfive of thofe arts, the moft philofophical, and the
moft ufeful.*

THE

T H E

P L E A S U R E S

.

O F   T H E

M A G I N A T I O N:

B O O K   T H E   F I R S T.

MDCCLVII.

* Truth is here taken, not in a logical, but in a mixed and popular sense, or for what has been called the truth of things; denoting as well their natural and regular condition, as a proper estimate or judgment concerning them.

T H E.

THE PLEASURES OF THE IMAGINATION:

BOOK THE FIRST.

WITH what inchantment nature's goodly scene
Attracts the sense of mortals; how the mind
For its own eye doth objects nobler still
Prepare; how men by various lessons learn
To judge of beauty's praise; what raptures fill   5
The breast with fancy's native arts indow'd
And what true culture guides it to renown;
My verse unfolds. Ye gods, or godlike powers,
Ye guardians of the sacred task, attend
Propitious. Hand in hand around your bard   10
Move in majestic measures, leading on
His doubtful step through many a solemn path
Conscious of secrets which to human sight
Ye only can reveal. Be great in him:
And let your favor make him wise to speak   15

Of

Of all your wonderous empire; with a voice
So temper'd to his theme, that those, who hear,
May yield perpetual homage to yourselves.
Thou chief, o daughter of eternal Love,
Whate'er thy name; or Muse, or Grace, ador'd   20
By Grecian prophets; to the sons of heaven
Known, while with deep amazement thou dost there
The perfect counsels read, the ideas old,
Of thine omniscient father; known on earth
By the still horror and the blissful tear   25
With which thou seizest on the soul of man;
Thou chief, Poetic Spirit, from the banks
Of Avon, whence thy holy fingers cull
Fresh flowers and dews to sprinkle on the turf
Where Shakespear lies, be present. and with thee   30
Let Fiction come; on her aërial wings
Wafting ten thousand colors; which in sport,
By the light glances of her magic eye,
She blends and shifts at will through countless forms,
Her wild creation. Goddess of the lyre   35
Whose awful tones controul the moving sphere,
Wilt thou, eternal Harmony, descend,
And join this happy train? for with thee comes
The guide, the guardian of their mystic rites,
Wise Order: and, where Order deigns to come,   40
Her sister, Liberty, will not be far.

Be

Be prefent all ye Genii, who conduct
Of youthful bards the lonely-wandering ftep
New to your fprings and fhades; who touch their ear
With finer founds, and heighten to their eye   45
The pomp of nature, and before them place
The faireft, loftieft countenance of things.

    Nor thou, my Dyfon, to the lay refufe
Thy wonted partial audience.   What, though firft
In years unfeafon'd, haply ere the fports   50
Of childhood yet were o'er, the adventurous lay
With many fplendid profpects, many charms,
Allur'd my heart, nor confcious whence they fprung,
Nor heedful of their end? yet ferious truth
Her empire o'er the calm, fequefter'd theme   55
Afferted foon; while falfehood's evil brood,
Vice and deceitful pleafure, fhe at once
Excluded, and my fancy's carelefs toil
Drew to the better caufe.   Maturer aid
Thy friendfhip added, in the paths of life,   60
The bufy paths, my unaccuftom'd feet
Preferving: nor to truth's recefs divine,
Through this wide argument's unbeaten fpace,
Witholding furer guidance; while by turns
We trac'd the fages old, or while the queen   65
Of fciences (whom manners and the mind

R

Acknowledge)

Acknowledge) to my true companion's voice
Not unattentive, o'er the wintry lamp
Inclin'd her fcepter, favoring.   Now the fates
Have other tafks impos'd.   to thee, my friend,   70
The miniftry of freedom and the faith
Of popular decrees, in early youth,
Not vainly they committed.   me they fent
To wait on pain ; and filent arts to urge,
Inglorious : not ignoble ; if my cares,   75
To fuch as languifh on a grievous bed,
Eafe and the fweet forgetfulnefs of ill
Conciliate : nor delightlefs ; if the Mufe,
Her fhades to vifit and to tafte her fprings,
If fome diftinguifh'd hours the bounteous Mufe   80
Impart, and grant (what fhe and fhe alone
Can grant to mortals) that my hand thofe wreaths
Of fame and honeft favor, which the blefs'd
Wear in Elyfium, and which never felt
The breath of envy or malignant tongues,   85
That thefe my hand for thee and for myfelf
May gather.   Meanwhile, o my faithful friend,
O early chofen, ever found the fame,
And trufted and belov'd ; once more the verfe
Long deftin'd, always obvious to thine ear,   90
Attend, indulgent.   fo in lateft years,
When time thy head with honors fhall have cloth'd

                                        Sacred

Sacred to even virtue, may thy mind,
Amid the calm review of feafons paft,
Fair offices of friendfhip or kind peace   95
Or public zeal, may then thy mind well pleas'd
Recall thefe happy ftudies of our prime.

From heaven my ftrains begin.   from heaven defcends
The flame of genius to the chofen breaft,
And beauty with poetic wonder join'd,   100
And infpiration.   Ere the rifing fun
Shone o'er the deep, or 'mid the vault of night
The moon her filver lamp fufpended : ere
The vales with fprings were water'd, or with groves
Of oak or pine the ancient hills were crown'd ;   105
Then the great fpirit, whom his works adore,
Within his own deep effence view'd the forms,
The forms eternal of created things :
The radiant fun ; the moon's nocturnal lamp ;
The mountains and the ftreams ; the ample ftores   110
Of earth, of heaven, of nature.   From the firft,
On that full fcene his love divine he fix'd,
His admiration.   till, in time compleat,
What he admir'd and lov'd his vital power
Unfolded into being.   Hence the breath   115
Of life informing each organic frame :
Hence the green earth, and wild-refounding waves :
R 2   Hence

Hence light and fhade, alternate ; warmth and cold ;
And bright autumnal fkies, and vernal fhowers,
And all the fair variety of things.   120

    But not alike to every mortal eye
Is this great fcene unveil'd.   For while the claims
Of focial life to different labours urge
The active powers of man, with wifeft care
Hath nature on the multitude of minds   125
Imprefs'd a various bias ; and to each
Decreed its province in the common toil.
To fome fhe taught the fabric of the fphere,
The changeful moon, the circuit of the ftars,
The golden zones of heaven.   to fome fhe gave   130
To fearch the ftory of eternal thought ;
Of fpace, and time ; of fate's unbroken chain,
And will's quick movement.   others by the hand
She led o'er vales and mountains, to explore
What healing virtue dwells in every vein   135
Of herbs or trees.   But fome to nobler hopes
Were deftin'd : fome within a finer mould
She wrought, and temper'd with a purer flame.
To thefe the fire omnipotent unfolds,
In fuller afpects and with fairer lights,   140
This picture of the world.   Through every part
They trace the lofty fketches of his hand :

                                                            In

In earth, or air, the meadow's flowery store,
The moon's mild radiance, or the virgin's mien
Drefs'd in attractive fmiles, they fee portray'd   145
(As far as mortal eyes the portrait fcan)
Thofe lineaments of beauty which delight
The mind fupreme.   They alfo feel their force,
Inamor'd: they partake the eternal joy.

For as old Memnon's image long renown'd   150
Through fabling Egypt, at the genial touch
Of morning, from its inmoft frame fent forth
Spontaneous mufic; fo doth nature's hand,
To certain attributes which matter claims,
Adapt the finer organs of the mind: 155
So the glad impulfe of thofe kindred powers
(Of form, of colour's cheerful pomp, of found
Melodious, or of motion aptly fped)
Detains the inliven'd fenfe; till foon the foul
Feels the deep concord and affents through all   160
Her functions.   Then the charm by fate prepar'd
Diffufeth its inchantment. Fancy dreams,
Rapt into high difcourfe with prophets old,
And wandering through Elyfium, fancy dreams
Of facred fountains, of o'erfhadowing groves,   165
Whofe walks with godlike harmony refound:
Fountains, which Homer vifits; happy groves,

Where Milton dwells. the intellectual power,
On the mind's throne, suspends his graver cares,
And smiles. the passions, to divine repose,   170
Persuaded yield: and love and joy alone
Are waking: love and joy, such as await
An angel's meditation.   O! attend,
Whoe'er thou art whom these delights can touch;
Whom nature's aspect, nature's simple garb   175
Can thus command; o! listen to my song;
And i will guide thee to her blissful walks,
And teach thy solitude her voice to hear,
And point her gracious features to thy view.

Know then, whate'er of the world's ancient store,   180
Whate'er of mimic art's reflected scenes,
With love and admiration thus inspire
Attentive fancy, her delighted sons
In two illustrious orders comprehend,
Self-taught.   from him whose rustic toil the lark   185
Cheers warbling, to the bard whose daring thoughts
Range the full orb of being, still the form,
Which fancy worships, or sublime or fair
Her votaries proclaim.   I see them dawn:
I see the radiant visions where they rise,   190
More lovely than when Lucifer displays

His

His glittering forehead through the gates of morn,
To lead the train of Phœbus and the spring.

Say, why was man so eminently rais'd
Amid the vast creation; why impower'd   195
Through life and death to dart his watchful eye,
With thoughts beyond the limit of his frame;
But that the omnipotent might send him forth,
In sight of angels and immortal minds,
As on an ample theatre to join   200
In contest with his equals, who shall best
The task atchieve, the course of noble toils,
By wisdom and by mercy preordain'd?
Might send him forth the sovran good to learn;
To chace each meaner purpose from his breast;   205
And through the mists of passion and of sense,
And through the pelting storms of chance and pain,
To hold strait on with constant heart and eye
Still fix'd upon his everlasting palm,
The approving smile of heaven? Else wherefore burns   210
In mortal bosoms this unquenched hope,
That seeks from day to day sublimer ends;
Happy, though restlefs? Why departs the soul
Wide from the track and journey of her times,
To grasp the good she knows not? in the field   215
Of things which may be, in the spacious field

Of

Of fcience, potent arts, or dreadful arms,
To raife up fcenes in which her own defires
Contented may repofe; when things, which are,
Pall on her temper, like a twice-told tale: 220
Her temper, ftill demanding to be free;
Spurning the rude controul of willful might;
Proud of her dangers brav'd, her griefs indur'd
Her ftrength feverely prov'd?   To thefe high aims,
Which reafon and affection prompt in man,   225
Not adverfe nor unapt hath nature fram'd
His bold imagination.   For, amid
The various forms which this full world prefents
Like rivals to his choice, what human breaft
E'er doubts, before the tranfient and minute,   230
To prize the vaft, the ftable, the fublime?
Who, that from heights aërial fends his eye
Around a wild horizon, and furveys
Indus or Ganges rolling his broad wave
Through mountains, plains, through fpacious cities old,   235
And regions dark with woods; will turn away
To mark the path of fome penurious rill
Which murmureth at his feet?   Where does the foul
Confent her foaring fancy to reftrain,
Which bears her up, as on an eagle's wings,   240
Deftin'd for higheft heaven; or which of fate's
Tremendous barriers fhall confine her flight

To

To any humbler quarry? The rich earth
Cannot detain her; nor the ambient air
With all its changes.   For a while with joy   245
She hovers o'er the fun, and views the fmall
Attendant orbs, beneath his facred beam,
Emerging from the deep, like clufter'd ifles
Whofe rocky fhores to the glad failor's eye
Reflect the gleams of morning: for a while   250
With pride fhe fees his firm, paternal fway
Bend the reluctant planets to move each
Round its perpetual year.   But foon fhe quits
That profpect: meditating loftier views,
She darts adventurous up the long career   255
Of comets; through the conftellations holds
Her courfe, and now looks back on all the ftars
Whofe blended flames as with a milky ftream
Part the blue region.   Empyrean tracts,
Where happy fouls beyond this concave heaven   260
Abide, fhe then explores, whence purer light
For countlefs ages travels through the abyfs
Nor hath in fight of mortals yet arriv'd.
Upon the wide creation's utmoft fhore
At length fhe ftands, and the dread fpace beyond   265
Contemplates, half-recoiling: nathlefs down
The gloomy void, aftonifh'd, yet unquell'd,
She plungeth; down the unfathomable gulph

S

Where

Where God alone hath being.   There her hopes
Reſt at the fated goal.   For, from the birth   270
Of human kind, the ſovran maker ſaid
That not in humble, nor in brief delight,
Not in the fleeting echos of renown,
Power's purple robes, nor pleaſure's flowery lap,
The ſoul ſhould find contentment; but, from theſe   275
Turning diſdainful to an equal good,
Through nature's opening walks inlarge her aim,
Till every bound at length ſhould diſappear,
And infinite perfection fill the ſcene.

But lo, where beauty, dreſs'd in gentler pomp,   280.
With comely ſteps advancing, claims the verſe
Her charms inſpire.   O beauty, ſource of praiſe,
Of honour, even to mute and lifeleſs things;
O thou that kindleſt in each human heart
Love, and the wiſh of poets, when their tongue   285
Would teach to other boſoms what ſo charms
Their own; o child of nature and the ſoul,
In happieſt hour brought forth; the doubtful garb
Of words, of earthly language, all too mean,
Too lowly i account, in which to clothe   290
Thy form divine.   for thee the mind alone
Beholds; nor half thy brightneſs can reveal
Through thoſe dim organs, whoſe corporeal touch

O'er-

O'erfhadoweth thy pure effence.   Yet, my Mufe,
If fortune call thee to the tafk, wait thou   295
Thy favorable feafons: then, while fear
And doubt are abfent, through wide nature's bounds
Expatiate with glad ftep, and choofe at will
Whate'er bright fpoils the florid earth contains,
Whate'er the waters, or the liquid air,   300
To manifeft unblemifh'd beauty's praife,
And o'er the breafts of mortals to extend
Her gracious empire.   Wilt thou to the ifles
Atlantic, to the rich Hefperian clime,
Fly in the train of Autumn; and look on,   305
And learn from him; while, as he roves around,
Where'er his fingers touch the fruitful grove,
The branches bloom with gold; where'er his foot
Imprints the foil, the ripening clufters fwell,
Turning afide their foliage, and come forth   310
In purple lights, till every hilloc glows
As with the blufhes of an evening fky?
Or wilt thou that Theffalian landfcape trace,
Where flow Penéus his clear glaffy tide
Draws fmooth along, between the winding cliffs   315
Of Offa and the pathlefs woods unfhorn
That wave o'er huge Olympus?   Down the ftream,
Look how the mountains with their double range
Imbrace the vale of Tempe; from each fide

S 2

Afcending

Afcending fteep to heaven, a rocky mound   320
Cover'd with ivy and the laurel boughs
That crown'd young Phœbus for the Python flain.
Fair Tempe! on whofe primrofe banks the morn
Awoke moft fragrant, and the noon repos'd
In pomp of lights and fhadows moft fublime: 325
Whofe lawns, whofe glades, ere human footfteps yet
Had trac'd an entrance, were the hallow'd haunt
Of fylvan powers immortal: where they fate
Oft in the golden age, the Nymphs and Fauns,
Beneath fome arbor branching o'er the flood,   330
And leaning round hung on the inftructive lips
Of hoary Pan, or o'er fome open dale
Danc'd in light meafures to his fevenfold pipe,
While Zephyr's wanton hand along their path
Flung fhowers of painted bloffoms, fertile dews,   335
And one perpetual fpring.   But if our tafk
More lofty rites demand, with all good vows
Then let us haften to the rural haunt
Where young Meliffa dwells.   Nor thou refufe
The voice which calls thee from thy lov'd retreat,   340
But hither, gentle maid, thy footfteps turn:
Here, to thy own unqueftionable theme,
O fair, o graceful, bend thy polifh'd brow,
Affenting; and the gladnefs of thy eyes
Impart to me, like morning's wifhed light   345
Seen

Seen through the vernal air.   By yonder ftream,
Where beech and elm along the bordering mead
Send forth wild melody from every bough,
Together let us wander; where the hills
Cover'd with fleeces to the lowing vale   350
Reply; where tidings of content and peace
Each echo brings.   Lo, how the weftern fun
O'er fields and floods, o'er every living foul,
Diffufeth glad repofe! There while i fpeak
Of beauty's honors, thou, Meliffa, thou   355
Shalt hearken, not unconfcious.   while i tell
How firft from heaven fhe came: how after all
The works of life, the elemental fcenes,
The hours, the feafons, fhe had oft explor'd,
At length her favorite manfion and her throne   360
She fix'd in woman's form: what pleafing ties
To virtue bind her; what effectual aid
They lend each other's power; and how divine
Their union, fhould fome unambitious maid,
To all the inchantment of the Idalian queen,   365
Add fanctity and wifdom: while my tongue
Prolongs the tale, Meliffa, thou may'ft feign
To wonder whence my rapture is infpir'd;
But foon the fmile which dawns upon thy lip
Shall tell it, and the tenderer bloom o'er all   370
That foft cheek fpringing to the marble neck.

                                    Which

Which bends aside in vain, revealing more
What it would thus keep silent, and in vain
The sense of praise diffembling.   Then my song
Great nature's winning arts, which thus inform   375
With joy and love the rugged breast of man,
Should found in numbers worthy of such a theme:
While all whose souls have ever felt the force
Of those inchanting paffions, to my lyre
Should throng attentive, and receive once more   380
Their influence, unobscur'd by any cloud
Of vulgar care, and purer than the hand
Of fortune can bestow : nor, to confirm
Their sway, should awful contemplation scorn
To join his dictates to the genuine strain   385
Of pleasure's tongue ; nor yet should pleafure's ear
Be much averse.   Ye chiefly, gentle band
Of youths and virgins, who through many a wish
And many a fond pursuit, as in some scene
Of magic bright and fleeting, are allur'd   390
By various beauty ; if the pleasing toil
Can yield a moment's refpite, hither turn
Your favorable ear, and trust my words.
I do not mean, on blefs'd religion's feat
Presenting superstition's gloomy form,   395
To dash your foothing hopes : i do not mean
To bid the jealous thunderer fire the heavens,

Or

Or shapes infernal rend the groaning earth,
And scare you from your joys.   my cheerful song
With happier omens calls you to the field,   400
Pleas'd with your generous ardor in the chace,
And warm like you.   Then tell me (for ye know)
Doth beauty ever deign to dwell where use
And aptitude are strangers? is her praise
Confefs'd in aught whose moft peculiar ends   405
Are lame and fruitlefs? or did nature mean
This pleafing call the herald of a lye,
To hide the fhame of difcord and difeafe,
And win each fond admirer into fnares,
Foil'd, baffled?   No.   with better providence   410
The general mother, confcious how infirm
Her offspring tread the paths of good and ill,
Thus, to the choice of credulous defire,
Doth objects the completeft of their tribe
Diftinguifh and commend.   Yon flowery bank   415
Cloth'd in the foft magnificence of fpring,
Will not the flocks approve it? will they afk
The reedy fen for pafture?   That clear rill
Which trickleth murmuring from the mofly rock,
Yields it lefs wholefome beverage to the worn   420
And thirfty traveler, than the ftanding pool
With muddy weeds o'ergrown?   Yon ragged vine
Whofe lean and fullen clufters mourn the rage

Of Eurus, will the wine-press or the bowl
Report of her, as of the swelling grape   425
Which glitters through the tendrils, like a gem
When first it meets the sun?   Or what are all
The various charms to life and sense adjoin'd?
Are they not pledges of a state intire,
Where native order reigns, with every part   430
In health, and every function well perform'd?

Thus then at first was beauty sent from heaven,
The lovely ministress of truth and good
In this dark world.   for truth and good are one;
And beauty dwells in them, and they in her,   435
With like participation.   Wherefore then,
O sons of earth, would ye diffolve the tie?
O! wherefore with a rash and greedy aim
Seek ye to rove through every flattering scene
Which beauty seems to deck, nor once inquire   440
Where is the suffrage of eternal truth,
Or where the seal of undeceitful good,
To save your search from folly?   Wanting these,
Lo, beauty withers in your void embrace;
And with the glittering of an idiot's toy   445
Did fancy mock your vows.   Nor yet let hope,
That kindlieft inmate of the youthful breaft,
Be hence appall'd; be turn'd to coward floth

Sitting

Sitting in silence, with dejected eyes
Incurious and with folded hands.   far lefs   450
Let fcorn of wild fantaftic folly's dreams
Or hatred of the bigot's favage pride
Perfuade you e'er that beauty, or the love
Which waits on beauty, may not brook to hear
The facred lore of undeceitful good   455
And truth eternal.   From the vulgar croud
Though fuperftition, tyrannefs abhorr'd,
The reverence due to this majeftic pair
With threats and execration ftill demands;
Though the tame wretch, who afks of her the way   460
To their celeftial dwelling, fhe conftrains
To quench or fet at nought the lamp of God
Within his frame; through many a cheerlefs wild
Though forth fhe leads him credulous and dark
And aw'd with dubious notion; though at length   465
Haply fhe plunge him into cloifter'd cells
And manfions unrelenting as the grave,
But void of quiet, there to watch the hours
Of midnight; there, amid the fcreaming owl's
Dire fong, with fpectres or with guilty fhades   470
To talk of pangs and everlafting woe;
Yet be not ye difmay'd.   a gentler ftar
Prefides o'er your adventure.   From the bower
Where wifdom fate with her Athenian fons,

T

Could

Could but my happy hand intwine a wreath   475
Of Plato's olive with the Mantuan bay,
Then (for what need of cruel fear to you,
To you whom godlike love can well command ?)
Then fhould my powerful voice at once difpell
Thofe monkifh horrors; fhould in words divine   480
Relate how favor'd minds like you infpir'd,
And taught their infpiration to conduct
By ruling heaven's decree, through various walks
And profpects various, but delightful all,
Move onward; while now myrtle groves appear,   485
Now arms and radiant trophies, now the rods
Of empire with the curule throne, or now
The domes of contemplation and the Mufe.
Led by that hope fublime, whofe cloudlefs eye
Through the fair toils and ornaments of earth   490
Difcerns the nobler life referv'd for heaven,
Favor'd alike they worfhip round the fhrine
Where truth confpicuous with her fifter-twins,
The undivided partners of her fway,
With good and beauty reigns.   O! let not us   495
By pleafure's lying blandifhments detain'd,
Or crouching to the frowns of bigot rage,
O! let not us one moment paufe to join
That chofen band.   And if the gracious power,
Who firft awaken'd my untutor'd fong,   500

Will

Will to my invocation grant anew
The tuneful fpirit, then through all our paths
Ne'er fhall the found of this devoted lyre
Be wanting; whether on the rofy mead
When fummer fmiles, to warn the melting heart   505
Of luxury's allurement; whether firm
Againft the torrent and the ftubborn hill
To urge free virtue's fteps, and to her fide
Summon that ftrong divinity of foul
Which conquers chance and fate; or on the height,   510
The goal affign'd her, haply to proclaim
Her triumph; on her brow to place the crown
Of uncorrupted praife; through future worlds
To follow her interminated way,
And blefs heaven's image in the heart of man.   515

   Such is the worth of beauty: fuch her power,
So blamelefs, fo rever'd.   It now remains,
In juft gradation through the various ranks
Of being, to contemplate how her gifts
Rife in due meafure, watchful to attend   520
The fteps of rifing nature.   Laft and leaft,
In colors mingling with a random blaze,
Doth beauty dwell.   Then higher in the forms
Of fimpleft, eafieft meafure; in the bounds
Of circle, cube, or fphere.   The third afcent   525

T 2

To fymmetry adds color: thus the pearl
Shines in the concave of its purple bed,
And painted fhells along fome winding fhore
Catch with indented folds the glancing fun.
Next, as we rife, appear the blooming tribes　　530
Which clothe the fragrant earth; which draw from her
Their own nutrition; which are born and die;
Yet, in their feed, immortal: fuch the flowers
With which young Maia pays the village-maids
That hail her natal morn; and fuch the groves　　535
Which blithe Pomona rears on Vaga's bank,
To feed the bowl of Ariconian fwains
Who quaff beneath her branches.　Nobler ftill
Is beauty's name where, to the full confent
Of members and of features, to the pride　　540
Of color, and the vital change of growth,
Life's holy flame with piercing fenfe is given,
While active motion fpeaks the temper'd foul:
So moves the bird of Juno: fo the fteed
With rival fwiftnefs beats the dufty plain,　　545
And faithful dogs with eager airs of joy
Salute their fellows.　What fublimer pomp
Adorns the feat where virtue dwells on earth,
And truth's eternal day-light fhines around;
What palm belongs to man's imperial front,　　550
And woman powerful with becoming fmiles,

Chief

Chief of terreſtrial natures ; need we now
Strive to inculcate ?   Thus hath beauty there
Her moſt conſpicuous praiſe to matter lent,
Where moſt conſpicuous through that ſhadowy veil   555
Breaks forth the bright expreſſion of a mind :
By ſteps directing our inraptur'd ſearch
To him, the firſt of minds ; the chief ; the ſole ;
From whom, through this wide, complicated world,
Did all her various lineaments begin ;   560
To whom alone, conſenting and intire,
At once their mutual influence all diſplay.
He, God moſt high (bear witneſs, earth and heaven)
The living fountains in himſelf contains
Of beauteous and ſublime.   with him inthron'd   565
Ere days or years trod their ethereal way,
In his ſupreme intelligence inthron'd,
The queen of love holds her unclouded ſtate,.
Urania.   Thee, o father, this extent
Of matter ; thee the ſluggiſh earth and tract   570
Of ſeas, the heavens and heavenly ſplendors feel
Pervading, quickening, moving.   From the depth
Of thy great eſſence, forth did'ſt thou conduct
Eternal Form ; and there, where Chaos reign'd,
Gav'ſt her dominion to erect her ſeat,   575
And ſanctify the manſion.   All her works
Well-pleas'd thou did'ſt behold.   the gloomy fires

Of

Of ſtorm or earthquake, and the pureſt light
Of ſummer; ſoft Campania's new-born roſe
And the ſlow weed, which pines on Ruſſian hills,   580
Comely alike to thy full viſion ſtand:
To thy ſurrounding viſion, which unites
All eſſences and powers of the great world
In one ſole order, fair alike they ſtand,
As features well conſenting, and alike   585
Requir'd by nature ere ſhe could attain
Her juſt reſemblance to the perfect ſhape
Of univerſal beauty, which with thee
Dwelt from the firſt.   Thou alſo, ancient mind,
Whom love and free beneficence await   590
In all thy doings; to inferior minds,
Thy offspring, and to man, thy youngeſt ſon,
Refuſing no convenient gift nor good;
Their eyes did'ſt open, in this earth, yon heaven,
Thoſe ſtarry worlds, the countenance divine   595
Of beauty to behold.   But not to them
Didſt thou her awful magnitude reveal
Such as before thine own unbounded ſight
She ſtands, (for never ſhall created ſoul
Conceive that object) nor, to all their kinds,   600
The ſame in ſhape or features didſt thou frame
Her image.   Meaſuring well their different ſpheres
Of ſenſe and action, thy paternal hand

                                                  Hath

Hath for each race prepar'd a different teſt
Of beauty, own'd and reverenc'd as their guide   605
Moſt apt, moſt faithful.   Thence inform'd, they ſcan
The objects that ſurround them ; and ſelect,
Since the great whole diſclaims their ſcanty view,
Each for himſelf ſelects peculiar parts
Of nature ; what the ſtandard fix'd by heaven   610
Within his breaſt approves : acquiring thus
A partial beauty, which becomes his lot ;
A beauty which his eye may comprehend,
His hand may copy : leaving, o ſupreme,
O thou whom none hath utter'd, leaving all   615
To thee that infinite, conſummate form,
Which the great powers, the gods around thy throne
And neareſt to thy counſels, know with thee
For ever to have been ; but who ſhe is,
Or what her likeneſs, know not.   Man ſurveys   620
A narrower ſcene, where, by the mix'd effect
Of things corporeal on his paſſive mind,
He judgeth what is fair.   Corporeal things
The mind of man impell with various powers,
And various features to his eye diſcloſe.   625
The powers which move his ſenſe with inſtant joy,
The features which attract his heart to love,
He marks, combines, repoſits.   other powers
And features of the ſelf-ſame thing (unleſs

The

The beauteous form, the creature of his mind,   630
Requeſt their cloſe alliance) he o'erlooks
Forgotten ; or with ſelf-beguiling zeal,
Whene'er his paſſions mingle in the work,
Half alters, half diſowns.   The tribes of men
Thus from their different funƈtions and the ſhapes   635
Familiar to their eye, with art obtain,
Unconſcious of their purpoſe, yet with art
Obtain the beauty fitting man to love :
Whoſe proud deſires from nature's homely toil
Oft turn away, faſtidious : aſking ſtill   640
His mind's high aid, to purify the form
From matter's groſs communion ; to ſecure
For ever, from the meddling hand of change
Or rude decay, her features ; and to add
Whatever ornaments may ſuit her mien,   645
Where'er he finds them ſcatter'd through the paths
Of nature or of fortune.   Then he ſeats
The accompliſh'd image deep within his breaſt,
Reviews it, and accounts it good and fair.

Thus the one beauty of the world intire,   650
The univerſal Venus, far beyond
The keeneſt effort of created eyes,
And their moſt wide horizon, dwells inthron'd
In ancient ſilence.   At her footſtool ſtands

An

An altar burning with eternal fire   655
Unfullied, unconfum'd.   Here every hour,
Here every moment, in their turns arrive
Her offspring; an innumerable band
Of fifters, comely all; but differing far
In age, in ftature, and expreffive mien,   660
More than bright Helen from her new-born babe.
To this maternal fhrine in turns they come,
Each with her facred lamp; that from the fource
Of living flame, which here immortal flows,
Their portions of its luftre they may draw   665
For days, or months, or years; for ages, fome;
As their great parent's difcipline requires.
Then to their feveral manfions they depart,
In ftars, in planets, through the unknown fhores
Of yon ethereal ocean.   Who can tell,   670
Even on the furface of this rowling earth,
How many make abode?   The fields, the groves,
The winding rivers and the azure main,
Are render'd folemn by their frequent feet,
Their rites fublime.   There each her deftin'd home   675
Informs with that pure radiance from the fkies
Brought down, and fhines throughout her little fphere,
Exulting.   Strait, as travellers by night
Turn toward a diftant flame, fo fome fit eye,
Among the various tenants of the fcene,   680
U

Difcerns

Difcerns the heaven-born phantom feated there,
And owns her charms.   Hence the wide univerfe,
Through all the feafons of revolving worlds,
Bears witnefs with its people, gods and men,
To beauty's blifsful power, and with the voice   685
Of grateful admiration ftill refounds:
That voice, to which is beauty's frame divine
As is the cunning of the mafter's hand
To the fweet accent of the well-tun'd lyre.

Genius of ancient Greece, whofe faithful fteps   690
Have led us to thefe awful folitudes
Of nature and of fcience; nurfe rever'd
Of generous counfels and heroic deeds;
O! let fome portion of thy matchlefs praife
Dwell in my breaft, and teach me to adorn   695
This unattempted theme.   Nor be my thoughts
Prefumptuous counted, if amid the calm
Which Hefper fheds along the vernal heaven,
If i, from vulgar fuperftition's walk,
Impatient fteal, and from the unfeemly rites   700
Of fplendid adulation, to attend
With hymns thy prefence in the fylvan fhade,
By their malignant footfteps unprofan'd.
Come, o renowned power; thy glowing mien.
Such, and fo elevated all thy form,   705

As

As when the great barbaric lord, again
And yet again diminish'd, hid his face
Among the herd of fatraps and of kings;
And, at the lightning of thy lifted fpear,
Crouch'd like a flave.   Bring all thy martial fpoils,   710
Thy palms, thy laurels, thy triumphal fongs,
Thy fmiling band of arts, thy godlike fires
Of civil wifdom, thy unconquer'd youth
After fome glorious day rejoicing round
Their new-erected trophy.   Guide my feet   715
Through fair Lycéum's walk, the olive fhades
Of Academus, and the facred vale
Haunted by fteps divine, where once beneath
That ever-living platane's ample boughs
Iliffus, by Socratic founds detain'd,   720
On his neglected urn attentive lay;
While Boreas, lingering on the neighboring fteep
With beauteous Orithyía, his love-tale
In filent awe fufpended.   There let me
With blamelefs hand, from thy unenvious fields,   725
Tranfplant fome living bloffoms, to adorn
My native clime: while, far beyond the meed
Of fancy's toil afpiring, i unlock
The fprings of antient wifdom: while i add
(What cannot be disjoin'd from beauty's praife)   730
Thy name and native drefs, thy works belov'd

U 2

And

And honor'd : while to my compatriot youth
I point the great example of thy fons,
And tune to Attic themes the Britifh lyre.

THE END OF BOOK THE FIRST.

T H E

THE

PLEASURES

OF THE

IMAGINATION:

BOOK THE SECOND.

MDCCLXV.

THE ARGUMENT.

Introduction to this more difficult part of the subject. Of truth and its three classes, matter of fact, experimental or scientifical truth, (contradistinguished from opinion) and universal truth: which last is either metaphysical or geometrical, either purely intellectual or perfectly abstracted. On the power of discerning truth depends that of acting with the view of an end; a circumstance essential to virtue. Of virtue, considered in the divine mind as a perpetual and universal beneficence. Of human virtue, considered as a system of particular sentiments and actions, suitable to the design of providence and the condition of man; to whom it constitutes the chief good and the first beauty. Of vice and its origin. Of ridicule: its general nature and final cause. Of the passions; particularly of those which relate to evil natural or moral, and which are generally accounted painful, though not always unattended with pleasure.

T H E

P L E A S U R E S

O F   T H E

I M A G I N A T I O N:

B O O K   T H E   S E C O N D.

THUS far of beauty and the pleafing forms
Which man's untutor'd fancy, from the fcenes
Imperfect of this ever-changing world,
Creates; and views, inamor'd.   Now my fong
Severer themes demand: myfterious truth;
And virtue, fovran good: the fpells, the trains,
The progeny of error: the dread fway
Of paffion; and whatever hidden ftores
From her own lofty deeds and from herfelf
The mind acquires.   Severer argument:.   10
Not lefs attractive; nor deferving lefs
A conftant ear.   For what are all the forms
Educ'd by fancy from corporeal things,
Greatnefs, or pomp, or fymmetry of parts?
Not tending to the heart, foon feeble grows,   15

A 3

As the blunt arrow 'gainſt the knotty trunk,
Their impulſe on the ſenſe: while the pall'd eye
Expects in vain its tribute; aſks in vain,
Where are the ornaments it once admir'd?
Not ſo the moral ſpecies, nor the powers   20
Of paſſion and of thought.   the ambitious mind
With objects boundleſs as her own deſires
Can there converſe: by theſe unfading forms
Touch'd and awaken'd ſtill, with eager act
She bends each nerve, and meditates well-pleas'd   25
Her gifts, her godlike fortune.   Such the ſcenes
Now opening round us.   May the deſtin'd verſe
Maintain its equal tenor, though in tracts
Obſcure and arduous.   may the ſource of light
All-preſent, all ſufficient, guide our ſteps   30
Through every maze: and whom in childiſh years
From the loud throng, the beaten paths of wealth
And power, thou did'ſt apart ſend forth to ſpeak
In tuneful words concerning higheſt things,
Him ſtill do thou, o father, at thoſe hours   35
Of penſive freedom, when the human ſoul
Shuts out the rumour of the world, him ſtill
Touch thou with ſecret leſſons: call thou back
Each erring thought; and let the yielding ſtrains
From his full boſom, like a welcome rill   40
Spontaneous from its healthy fountain, flow.

But

But from what name, what favorable fign,
What heavenly aufpice, rather fhall i date
My perilous excurfion, than from truth,
That neareft inmate of the human foul ;   45
Eftrang'd from whom, the countenance divine
Of man disfigur'd and difhonor'd finks
Among inferior things ?   For to the brutes
Perception and the tranfient boons of fenfe
Hath fate imparted : but to man alone   50
Of fublunary beings was it given
Each fleeting impulfe on the fenfual powers
At leifure to review ; with equal eye
To fcan the paffion of the ftricken nerve
Or the vague object ftriking : to conduct   55
From fenfe, the portal turbulent and loud,
Into the mind's wide palace one by one
The frequent, preffing, fluctuating forms,
And queftion and compare them.   Thus he learns
Their birth and fortunes ; how allied they haunt   60
The avenues of fenfe ; what laws direct
Their union ; and what various difcords rife,
Or fix'd or cafual : which when his clear thought
Retains and when his faithful words exprefs,
That living image of the external fcene,   65
As in a polifh'd mirror held to view,

X

Is truth: where'er it varies from the shape
And hue of its exemplar, in that part
Dim error lurks.   Moreover, from without
When oft the same society of forms   70
In the same order have approach'd his mind,
He deigns no more their steps with curious heed
To trace; no more their features or their garb
He now examines; but of them and their
Condition, as with some diviner's tongue,   75
Affirms what heaven in every distant place,
Through every future season, will decree.
This too is truth: where'er his prudent lips
Wait till experience diligent and slow
Has authoriz'd their sentence, this is truth;   80
A second, higher kind: the parent this
Of science; or the lofty power herself,
Science herself: on whom the wants and cares
Of social life depend; the substitute
Of God's own wisdom in this toilsome world;   85
The providence of man.   Yet oft in vain,
To earn her aid, with fix'd and anxious eye
He looks on nature's and on fortune's course:
Too much in vain.   His duller visual ray
The stillness and the persevering acts   ·   90
Of nature oft elude; and fortune oft
With step fantastic from her wonted walk

                                                  Turns

Turns into mazes dim. his fight is foil'd;
And the crude fentence of his faltering tongue
Is but opinion's verdict, half believ'd   95
And prone to change. Here thou, who feel'ft thine ear
Congenial to my lyre's profounder tone,
Paufe, and be watchful. Hitherto the ftores,
Which feed thy mind and exercife her powers,
Partake the relifh of their native foil,   100
Their parent earth. But know, a nobler dower
Her fire at birth decreed her; purer gifts
From his own treafure; forms which never deign'd
In eyes or ears to dwell, within the fenfe
Of earthly organs; but fublime were plac'd   105
In his efiential reafon, leading there
That vaft ideal hoft which all his works
Through endlefs ages never will reveal.
Thus then indow'd, the feeble creature man,
The flave of hunger and the prey of death,   110
Even now, even here, in earth's dim prifon bound,
The language of intelligence divine
Attains; repeating oft concerning one
And many, pafs'd and prefent, parts and whole,
Thofe fovran dictates which in fartheft heaven,   115
Where no orb rowls, eternity's fix'd ear
Hears from coeval truth, when chance nor change,
Nature's loud progeny, nor nature's felf

X 2

Dares

Dares intermeddle or approach her throne.
Ere long, o'er this corporeal world he learns　　120
To extend her fway; while calling from the deep,
From earth and air, their multitudes untold
Of figures and of motions round his walk,
For each wide family fome fingle birth
He fets in view, the impartial type of all　　125
Its brethren; fuffering it to claim, beyond
Their common heritage, no private gift,
No proper fortune.　Then whate'er his eye
In this difcerns, his bold unerring tongue
Pronounceth of the kindred, without bound,　　130
Without condition.　Such the rife of forms
Sequefter'd far from fenfe and every fpot
Peculiar in the realms of fpace or time:
Such is the throne which man for truth amid
The paths of mutability hath built　　135
Secure, unfhaken, ftill; and whence he views,
In matter's mouldering ftructures, the pure forms
Of triangle or circle, cube or cone,
Impaffive all; whofe attributes nor force
Nor fate can alter.　There he firft conceives　　140
True being, and an intellectual world
The fame this hour and ever.　Thence he deems
Of his own lot; above the painted fhapes
That fleeting move o'er this terreftrial fcene

Looks

Looks up; beyond the adamantine gates 145
Of death expatiates; as his birthright claims
Inheritance in all the works of God;
Prepares for endlefs time his plan of life,
And counts the univerfe itfelf his home.

Whence alfo but from truth, the light of minds, 150
Is human fortune gladden'd with the rays
Of virtue? with the moral colors thrown
On every walk of this our focial fcene,
Adorning for the eye of gods and men
The paffions, actions, habitudes of life, 155
And rendering earth like heaven, a facred place·
Where love and praife may take delight to dwell?
Let none with heedlefs tongue from truth disjoin
The reign of virtue. Ere the dayfpring flow'd,
Like fifters link'd in concord's golden chain, 160
They ftood before the great eternal mind,
Their common parent; and by him were both
Sent forth among his creatures, hand in hand,
Infeparably join'd: nor e'er did truth
Find an apt ear to liften to her lore, 165
Which knew not virtue's voice; nor, fave where truth's
Majeftic words are heard and underftood,
Doth virtue deign to inhabit. Go, inquire
Of nature: not among Tartarian rocks,

Whither

Whither the hungry vulture with its prey
Returns: not where the lion's sullen roar
At noon refounds along the lonely banks
Of ancient Tigris: but her gentler fcenes,
The dove-cote and the fhepherd's fold at morn,
Confult; or by the meadow's fragrant hedge,
In fpring-time when the woodlands firft are green,
Attend the linnet finging to his mate
Couch'd o'er their tender young.   To this fond care
Thou doft not virtue's honorable name
Attribute: wherefore, fave that not one gleam
Of truth did e'er difcover to themfelves
Their little hearts, or teach them, by the effects
Of that parental love, the love itfelf
To judge, and meafure its officious deeds?
But man, whofe eyelids truth has fill'd with day,
Difcerns how fkilfully to bounteous ends
His wife affections move; with free accord
Adopts their guidance; yields himfelf fecure
To nature's prudent impulfe; and converts
Inftinct to duty and to facred law.
Hence right and fit on earth: while thus to man
The almighty legiflator hath explain'd
The fprings of action fix'd within his breaft;
Hath given him power to flacken or reftrain
Their effort; and hath fhewn him how they join

Their partial movements with the mafter wheel
Of the great world, and ferve that facred end
Which he, the unerring reafon, keeps in view.

    For (if a mortal tongue may fpeak of him
And his dread ways) even as his boundlefs eye,   200
Connecting every form and every change,
Beholds the perfect beauty ; fo his will,
Through every hour producing good to all
The family of creatures, is itfelf
The perfect virtue.   Let the grateful fwain   205
Remember this, as oft with joy and praife
He looks upon the falling dews which clothe
His lawns with verdure, and the tender feed
Nourifh within his furrows : when between
Dead feas and burning fkies, where long unmov'd   210
The bark had languifh'd, now a ruftling gale
Lifts o'er the fickle waves her dancing prow,
Let the glad pilot, burfting out in thanks,
Remember this : left blind o'erweening pride
Pollute their offerings : left their felfifh heart   215
Say to the heavenly ruler, " At our call
" Relents thy power : by us thy arm is mov'd."
Fools ! who of God as of each other deem :
Who his invariable acts deduce
From fudden counfels tranfient as their own ;   220

                                        Nor

Nor farther of his bounty, than the event
Which haply meets their loud and eager prayer,
Acknowledge; nor, beyond the drop minute
Which haply they have tafted, heed the fource
That flows for all; the fountain of his love   225
Which, from the fummit where he fits inthron'd,
Pours health and joy, unfailing ftreams, throughout
The fpacious region flourifhing in view,
The goodly work of his eternal day,
His own fair univerfe; on which alone   230
His counfels fix, and whence alone his will
Affumes her ftrong direction.   Such is now
His fovran purpofe: fuch it was before
All multitude of years.   For his right arm
Was never idle: his beftowing love   235
Knew no beginning; was not as a change
Of mood that woke at laft and ftarted up
After a deep and folitary floth
Of boundlefs ages.   No: he now is good,
He ever was.   The feet of hoary time   240
Through their eternal courfe have travell'd o'er
No fpeechlefs, lifelefs defart; but through fcenes
Cheerful with bounty ftill; among a pomp
Of worlds, for gladnefs round the maker's throne
Loud-fhouting, or, in many dialects   245
Of hope and filial truft, imploring thence

The

The fortunes of their people: where fo fix'd
Were all the dates of being, fo difpos'd
To every living foul of every kind
The field of motion and the hour of reft,   250
That each the general happinefs might ferve;
And, by the difcipline of laws divine
Convinc'd of folly or chaftiz'd from guilt,
Each might at length be happy.   What remains
Shall be like what is pafs'd; but fairer ftill,   255
And ftill increafing in the godlike gifts
Of life and truth.   The fame paternal hand,
From the mute fhell-fifh gafping on the fhore,
To men, to angels, to celeftial minds,
Will ever lead the generations on   260
Through higher fcenes of being: while, fupply'd
From day to day by his inlivening breath,
Inferior orders in fucceffion rife
To fill the void below.   As flame afcends,
As vapors to the earth in fhowers return,   265
As the pois'd ocean toward the attracting moon
Swells, and the ever-liftening planets charm'd
By the fun's call their onward pace incline,
So all things which have life afpire to God,
Exhauftlefs fount of intellectual day,   270
Center of fouls.   Nor doth the maftering voice
Of nature ceafe within to prompt aright

Y

Their

Their steps ; nor is the care of heaven witheld
From sending to the toil external aid ;
That in their stations all may persevere   275
To climb the ascent of being, and approach
For ever nearer to the life divine.

    But this eternal fabric was not rais'd
For man's inspection.   Though to some be given
To catch a transient visionary glimpse   280
Of that majestic scene which boundless power
Prepares for perfect goodness, yet in vain
Would human life her faculties expand
To imbosom such an object.   Nor could e'er
Virtue or praise have touch'd the hearts of men,   285
Had not the sovran guide, through every stage
Of this their various journey, pointed out
New hopes, new toils, which to their humble sphere
Of sight and strength might such importance hold
As doth the wide creation to his own.   290
Hence all the little charities of life,
With all their duties : hence that favorite palm
Of human will, when duty is suffic'd,
And still the liberal soul in ampler deeds
Would manifest herself ; that sacred sign   295
Of her rever'd affinity to him
Whose bounties are his own ; to whom none said

                                          " Create

" Create the wifeft, fulleft, faireft world,
" And make its offspring happy ;" who, intent
Some likenefs of himfelf among his works   300
To view, hath pour'd into the human breaft
A ray of knowledge and of love, which guides
Earth's feeble race to act their maker's part,
Self-judging, felf-oblig'd : while, from before
That godlike function, the gigantic power   305
Neceffity, though wont to curb the force
Of Chaos and the favage elements,
Retires abafh'd, as from a fcene too high
For her brute tyranny, and with her bears
Her fcorned followers, terror, and bafe awe   310
Who blinds herfelf, and that ill-fuited pair,
Obedience link'd with hatred.   Then the foul
Arifes in her ftrength ; and, looking round
Her bufy fphere, whatever work fhe views,
Whatever counfel bearing any trace   315
Of her creator's likenefs, whether apt
To aid her fellows or preferve herfelf
In her fuperior functions unimpair'd,
Thither fhe turns exulting : that fhe claims
As her peculiar good : on that, through all   320
The fickle feafons of the day, fhe looks
With reverence ftill : to that, as to a fence
Againft affliction and the darts of pain,

Y 2

Her

Her drooping hopes repair: and, once oppos'd
To that, all other pleafure, other wealth   325
Vile, as the drofs upon the molten gold,
Appears, and loathfome as the briny fea
To him who languifhes with thirft and fighs
For fome known fountain pure.   For what can ftrive
With virtue?   Which of nature's regions vaft   330
Can in fo many forms produce to fight
Such powerful beauty? beauty, which the eye
Of hatred cannot look upon fecure:
Which envy's felf contemplates, and is turn'd
Ere long to tendernefs, to infant fmiles,   335
Or tears of humbleft love.   Is aught fo fair
In all the dewy landfcapes of the fpring,
The fummer's noontide groves, the purple eve
At harveft-home, or in the frofty moon
Glittering on fome fmooth fea, is aught fo fair   340
As virtuous friendfhip? as the honor'd roof
Whither from higheft heaven immortal Love
His torch ethereal and his golden bow
Propitious brings, and there a temple holds
To whofe unfpotted fervice gladly vow'd   345
The focial band of parent, brother, child,
With fmiles and fweet difcourfe and gentle deeds
Adore his power? What gift of richeft clime
E'er drew fuch eager eyes, or prompted fuch

Deep

Deep wishes, as the zeal that snatcheth back   350
From slander's poisonous tooth a foe's renown ;
Or crosseth danger in his lion walk,
A rival's life to rescue ? as the young
Athenian warrior sitting down in bonds,
That his great father's body might not want   355
A peaceful, humble tomb ? the Roman wife
Teaching her lord how harmless was the wound
Of death, how impotent the tyrant's rage,.
Who nothing more could threaten to afflict
Their faithful love ?   Or is there in the abyss,   360
Is there, among the adamantine spheres
Wheeling unshaken through the boundless void,
Aught that with half such majesty can fill
The human bosom, as when Brutus rose
Refulgent from the stroke of Cæsar's fate   365
Amid the croud of patriots ; and, his arm.
Aloft extending like eternal Jove.
When guilt brings down the thunder, call'd aloud
On Tully's name, and shook the crimson sword.
Of justice in his rapt astonish'd eye,.   370
And bade the father of his country hail ;.
For lo the tyrant prostrate on the dust,
And Rome again is free ?   Thus, through the paths
Of human life, in various pomp array'd
Walks the wise daughter of the judge of heaven,   375

Fair

Fair virtue; from her father's throne supreme
Sent down to utter laws, such as on earth
Most apt he knew, most powerful to promote
The weal of all his works, the gracious end
Of his dread empire. And though haply man's 380
Obscurer fight, so far beyond himself
And the brief labors of his little home,
Extends not; yet, by the bright presence won
Of this divine instructress, to her sway
Pleas'd he assents, nor heeds the distant goal 385
To which her voice conducts him. Thus hath God,
Still looking toward his own high purpose, fix'd
The virtues of his creatures; thus he rules
The parent's fondness and the patriot's zeal;
Thus the warm sense of honor and of shame; 390
The vows of gratitude, the faith of love;
And all the comely intercourse of praise,
The joy of human life, the earthly heaven.

How far unlike them must the lot of guilt
Be found! Or what terrestrial woe can match 395
The self-convicted bosom, which hath wrought
The bane of others or inflav'd itself
With shackles vile? Not poison, nor sharp fire,
Nor the worst pangs that ever monkish hate
Suggested, or despotic rage impos'd, 400

Were

Were at that feafon an unwifh'd exchange:
When the foul loaths herfelf: when, flying thence
To crouds, on every brow fhe fees portray'd
Fell demons, hate or fcorn, which drive her back
To folitude, her judge's voice divine   405
To hear in fecret, haply founding through
The troubled dreams of midnight, and ftill, ftill
Demanding for his violated laws
Fit recompence, or charging her own tongue
To fpeak the award of juftice on herfelf.   410
For well fhe knows what faithful hints within
Were whifper'd, to beware the lying forms
Which turn'd her footfteps from the fafer way:
What cautions to fufpect their painted drefs,
And look with fteady eyelid on their fmiles,   415
Their frowns, their tears.   In vain.   the dazzling hues
Of fancy, and opinion's eager voice,
Too much prevail'd.   For mortals tread the path
In which opinion fays they follow good
Or fly from evil: and opinion gives   420
Report of good or evil, as the fcene
Was drawn by fancy, pleafing or deform'd:
Thus her report can never there be true
Where fancy cheats the intellectual eye
With glaring colors and diftorted lines.   425
Is there a man to whom the name of death

Brings

Brings terror's ghaſtly pageants conjur'd up
Before him, death-bed groans, and diſmal vows,
And the frail ſoul plung'd headlong from the brink
Of life and daylight down the gloomy air,   430
An unknown depth, to gulphs of torturing fire
Unviſited by mercy?   Then what hand
Can ſnatch this dreamer from the fatal toils
Which fancy and opinion thus conſpire
To twine around his heart?   or who ſhall huſh   435
Their clamor, when they tell him that to die,
To riſk thoſe horrors, is a direr curſe
Than baſeſt life can bring?   Though love with prayers
Moſt tender, with affliction's ſacred tears,
Beſeech his aid; though gratitude and faith   440
Condemn each ſtep which loiters; yet let none
Make anſwer for him that, if any frown
Of danger thwart his path, he will not ſtay,
Content, and be a wretch to be ſecure.
Here vice begins then: at the gate of life,   445
Ere the young multitude to diverſe roads
Part, like fond pilgrims on a journey unknown,
Sits fancy, deep inchantreſs; and to each
With kind maternal looks preſents her bowl,
A potent beverage.   Heedleſs they comply: 450
Till the whole ſoul from that myſterious draught
Is ting'd, and every tranſient thought imbibes

Of

Of gladnefs or difguft, defire or fear,
One homebred color: which not all the lights
Of fcience e'er fhall change; not all the ftorms   455
Of adverfe fortune wafh away, nor yet
The robe of pureft virtue quite conceal.
Thence on they pafs, where meeting frequent fhapes
Of good and evil, cunning phantoms apt
To fire or freeze the breaft, with them they join   460
In dangerous parley; liftening oft, and oft
Gazing with recklefs paffion, while its garb
The fpectre heightens, and its pompous tale
Repeats with fome new circumftance to fuit
That early tincture of the hearer's foul.   465
And fhould the guardian, reafon, but for one
Short moment yield to this illufive fcene
His ear and eye, the intoxicating charm
Involves him, till no longer he difcerns,
Or only guides to err.   Then revel forth   470
A furious band that fpurn him from the throne,
And all is uproar.   Hence ambition climbs
With fliding feet and hands impure, to grafp
Thofe folemn toys which glitter in his view
On fortune's rugged fteep: hence pale revenge   475
Unfheaths her murderous dagger: rapine hence
And envious luft, by venal fraud upborne,
Surmount the reverend barrier of the laws

Z

Which kept them from their prey: hence all the crimes
That e'er defil'd the earth, and all the plagues   480
That follow them for vengeance, in the guife
Of honor, fafety, pleafure, eafe, or pomp,
Stole firft into the fond believing mind.

    Yet not by fancy's witchcraft on the brain
Are always the tumultuous paffions driven   485
To guilty deeds, nor reafon bound in chains
That vice alone may lord it. Oft, adorn'd
With motley pageants, folly mounts his throne,
And plays her ideot antics, like a queen.
A thoufand garbs fhe wears: a thoufand ways   490
She whirls her giddy empire. Lo, thus far
With bold adventure to the Mantuan lyre
I fing for contemplation link'd with love
A penfive theme. Now haply fhould my fong
Unbend that ferious countenance, and learn   495
Thalia's tripping gait, her fhrill-ton'd voice,
Her wiles familiar: whether fcorn fhe darts
In wanton ambufh from her lip or eye,
Or whether with a fad difguife of care
O'ermantling her gay brow, fhe acts in fport   500
The deeds of folly, and from all fides round
Calls forth impetuous laughter's gay rebuke;
Her province. But through every comic fcene

                                        To

To lead my Mufe with her light pencil arm'd;
Through every fwift occafion which the hand   505
Of laughter points at, when the mirthful fting
Diftends her laboring fides and chokes her tongue;
Were endlefs as to found each grating note
With which the rooks, and chattering daws, and grave
Unwieldy inmates of the village pond,   510
The changing feafons of the fky proclaim;
Sun, cloud, or fhower.   Suffice it to have faid,
Where'er the power of ridicule difplays
Her quaint-ey'd vifage, fome incongruous form,
Some ftubborn diffonance of things combin'd,   515
Strikes on her quick perception : whether pomp,
Or praife, or beauty be dragg'd in and fhown
Where fordid fafhions, where ignoble deeds,
Where foul deformity is wont to dwell;
Or whether thefe with fhrewd and wayward fpite   520
Invade refplendent pomp's imperious mien,
The charms of beauty, or the boaft of praife.

Afk we for what fair end the almighty fire
In mortal bofoms ftirs this gay contempt,
Thefe grateful pangs of laughter; from difguft   525
Educing pleafure?   Wherefore, but to aid
The tardy fteps of reafon, and at once
By this prompt impulfe urge us to deprefs

Z 2

Wild

Wild folly's aims ?   For though the fober light
Of truth flow-dawning on the watchful mind   530
At length unfolds, through many a fubtile tie,
How thefe uncouth diforders end at laft
In public evil ; yet benignant heaven,
Confcious how dim the dawn of truth appears
To thoufands, confcious what a fcanty paufe   535
From labor and from care the wider lot
Of humble life affords for ftudious thought
To fcan the maze of nature, therefore ftamp'd
Thefe glaring fcenes with characters of fcorn,
As broad, as obvious to the pafling clown.   540
As to the letter'd fage's curious eye.

But other evils o'er the fteps of man.
Through all his walks impend ; againft whofe might
The flender darts of laughter nought avail :
A trivial warfare.   Some, like cruel guards,   545
On nature's ever-moving throne attend ;
With mifchief arm'd for him whoe'er fhall thwart
The path of her inexorable wheels,
While fhe purfues the work that muft be done
Through ocean, earth, and air.   Hence frequent forms   550
Of woe ; the merchant, with his wealthy bark,
Bury'd by dafhing waves ; the traveller.
Pierc'd by the pointed lightening in his hafte ;

                                                   And

And the poor hufbandman, with folded arms,
Surveying his loft labors, and a heap   555
Of blafted chaff the product of the field
Whence he expected bread.   But worfe than thefe
I deem, far worfe, that other race of ills
Which human kind rear up among themfelves;
That horrid offspring which mifgovern'd will   560
Bears to fantaftic error; vices, crimes,
Furies that curfe the earth, and make the blows,
The heavieft blows, of nature's innocent hand
Seem fport: which are indeed but as the care
Of a wife parent, who follicits good   565
To all her houfe, though haply at the price
Of tears and froward wailing and reproach
From fome unthinking child, whom not the lefs
Its mother deftines to be happy ftill.

Thefe fources then of pain, this double lot   570
Of evil in the inheritance of man,
Requir'd for his protection no flight force,
No carelefs watch.   and therefore was his breaft
Fenc'd round with paffions quick to be alarm'd,
Or ftubborn to oppofe; with fear, more fwift   5
Than beacons catching flame from hill to hill,
Where armies land; with anger, uncontroul'd
As the young lion bounding on his prey;

With forrow, that locks up the ftruggling heart,
And fhame, that overcafts the drooping eye 580
As with a cloud of lightening. Thefe the part
Perform of eager monitors, and goad
The foul more fharply than with points of fteel,
Her enemies to fhun or to refift.

And as thofe paffions, that converfe with good, 585
Are good themfelves; as hope and love and joy,
Among the faireft and the fweeteft boons
Of life, we rightly count; fo thefe, which guard
Againft invading evil, ftill excite
Some pain, fome tumult: thefe, within the mind 590
Too oft admitted or too long retain'd,
Shock their frail feat, and by their uncurb'd rage
To favages more fell than Libya breeds
Transform themfelves: till human thought becomes
A gloomy ruin, haunt of fhapes unblefs'd, 595
Of felf-tormenting fiends; horror, defpair,
Hatred, and wicked envy: foes to all
The works of nature and the gifts of heaven.

But when through blamelefs paths to righteous ends
Thofe keener paffions urge the awaken'd foul, 600
I would not, as ungracious violence,
Their fway defcribe, nor from their free career
The fellowfhip of pleafure quite exclude.

For

For what can render, to the self-approv'd,
Their temper void of comfort, though in pain?   605
Who knows not with what majesty divine
The forms of truth and justice to the mind
Appear, ennobling oft the sharpest woe
With triumph and rejoicing?   Who, that bears
A human bosom, hath not often felt   610
How dear are all those ties which bind our race
In gentleness together, and how sweet
Their force, let fortune's wayward hand the while
Be kind or cruel?   Ask the faithful youth
Why the cold urn, of her whom long he lov'd,   615
So often fills his arms; so often draws
His lonely footsteps, silent and unseen,
To pay the mournful tribute of his tears?
O! he will tell thee that the wealth of worlds,
Should ne'er seduce his bosom to forego   620
Those sacred hours when, stealing from the noise
Of care and envy, sweet remembrance sooths
With virtue's kindest looks his aking breast,
And turns his tears to rapture?   Ask the croud,
Which flies impatient from the village walk   625
To climb the neighbouring cliffs, when far below
The savage winds have hurl'd upon the coast
Some helpless bark; while holy pity melts
The general eye, or terror's icy hand

Smites

Smites their diftorted limbs and horrent hair;   630
While every mother clofer to her breaft
Catcheth her child, and, pointing where the waves
Foam through the fhatter'd veffel, fhrieks aloud
As one poor wretch, who fpreads his piteous arms
For fuccour, fwallow'd by the roaring furge,   635
As now another, dafh'd againft the rock,
Drops lifelefs down.   o! deemeft thou indeed
No pleafing influence here by nature given
To mutual terror and compaffion's tears?
No tender charm myfterious, which attracts   640
O'er all that edge of pain the focial powers
To this their proper action and their end?
Afk thy own heart; when, at the midnight hour,
Slow through that penfive gloom thy paufing eye,
Led by the glimmering taper, moves around   645
The reverend volumes of the dead, the fongs
Of Grecian bards, and records writ by fame
For Grecian heroes, where the fovran power
Of heaven and earth furveys the immortal page
Even as a father meditating all   650
The praifes of his fon, and bids the reft
Of mankind there the faireft model learn
Of their own nature, and the nobleft deeds
Which yet the world hath feen.   If then thy foul
Join in the lot of thofe diviner men;   655

Say,

Say, when the profpect darkens on thy view;
When, funk by many a wound, heroic ftates
Mourn in the duft and tremble at the frown
Of hard ambition; when the generous band
Of youths who fought for freedom and their fires 660
Lie fide by fide in death; when brutal force
Ufurps the throne of juftice, turns the pomp
Of guardian power, the majefty of rule,
The fword, the laurel, and the purple robe,
To poor difhoneft pageants, to adorn 665
A robber's walk, and glitter in the eyes
Of fuch as bow the knee; when beauteous works,
Rewards of virtue, fculptur'd forms which deck'd
With more than human grace the warrior's arch
Or patriot's tomb, now victims to appeafe 670
Tyrannic envy, ftrew the common path
With awful ruins; when the Mufe's haunt,
The marble porch where wifdom wont to talk
With Socrates or Tully, hears no more
Save the hoarfe jargon of contentious monks, 675
Or female fuperftition's midnight prayer;
When ruthlefs havoc from the hand of time
Tears the deftroying fcythe, with furer ftroke
To mow the monuments of glory down;
Till defolation o'er the grafs-grown ftreet 680
Expands her raven wings, and, from the gate

A a

Where

Where senates once the weal of nations plann'd,
Hisseth the gliding snake through hoary weeds
That clasp the mouldering column: thus when all
The widely-mournful scene is fix'd within   685
Thy throbbing bosom; when the patriot's tear
Starts from thine eye, and thy extended arm
In fancy hurls the thunderbolt of Jove
To fire the impious wreath on Philip's brow,
Or dash Octavius from the trophied car;   690
Say, doth thy secret soul repine to taste
The big distress? or wouldst thou then exchange
Those heart-ennobling sorrows for the lot
Of him who sits amid the gaudy herd
Of silent flatterers bending to his nod,   695
And o'er them, like a giant, casts his eye,
And says within himself, "I am a king,
" And wherefore should the clamorous voice of woe
" Intrude upon mine ear?" The dregs corrupt
Of barbarous ages, that Circæan draught   700
Of servitude and folly, have not yet,
Bless'd be the eternal ruler of the world!
Yet have not so dishonor'd, so deform'd
The native judgement of the human soul,
Nor so effac'd the image of her sire.   705

THE END OF BOOK THE SECOND.

                                        THE

THE PLEASURES OF THE IMAGINATION:

BOOK THE THIRD.

MDCCLXX.

THE

WHAT tongue then may explain the various fate
Which reigns o'er earth? or who to mortal eyes
Illuſtrate this perplexing labyrinth
Of joy and woe through which the feet of man
Are doom'd to wander?   That eternal mind   5
From paſſions, wants and envy far eſtrang'd,
Who built the ſpacious univerſe, and deck'd
Each part ſo richly with whate'er pertains
To life, to health, to pleaſure; why bade he
The viper Evil, creeping in, pollute   10
The goodly ſcene, and with inſidious rage,
While the poor inmate looks around and ſmiles,
Dart her fell ſting with poiſon to his ſoul?
Hard is the queſtion, and from ancient days
Hath ſtill oppreſs'd with care the ſage's thought; 15

Hath

Hath drawn forth accents from the poet's lyre
Too fad, too deeply plaintive : nor did e'er
Thofe chiefs of human kind, from whom the light
Of heavenly truth firft gleam'd on barbarous lands,
Forget this dreadful fecret when they told   20
What wonderous things had to their favor'd eyes
And ears on cloudy mountain been reveal'd,
Or in deep cave by nymph or power divine,
Portentous oft and wild.   Yet one i know,
Could i the fpeech of lawgivers afiume,   25
One old and fplendid tale i would record
With which the Mufe of Solon in fweet ftrains
Adorn'd this theme profound, and render'd all
Its darknefs, all its terrors, bright as noon,
Or gentle as the golden ftar of eve.   30
Who knows not Solon ? laft, and wifeft far,
Of thofe whom Greece triumphant in the height
Of glory, ftyl'd her fathers ? him whofe voice
Through Athens hufh'd the ftorm of civil wrath ;
Taught envious want and cruel wealth to join   35
In friendfhip ; and, with fweet compulfion, tam'd
Minerva's eager people to his laws,
Which their own goddefs in his breaft infpir'd ?

'Twas now the time when his heroic tafk
Seem'd but perform'd in vain : when footh'd by years   40

Of

Of flattering fervice, the fond multitude
Hung with their fudden counfels on the breath
Of great Pififtratus: that chief renown'd,
Whom Hermes and the Idalian queen had train'd
Even from his birth to every powerful art   45
Of pleafing and perfuading: from whofe lips
Flow'd eloquence which like the vows of love
Could fteal away fufpicion from the hearts
Of all who liften'd.   Thus from day to day
He won the general fuffrage, and beheld   50
Each rival overfhadow'd and deprefs'd
Beneath his ampler ftate: yet oft complain'd,
As one lefs kindly treated, who had hop'd
To merit favor, but fubmits perforce
To find another's fervices preferr'd,   55
Nor yet relaxeth aught of faith or zeal.
Then tales were fcatter'd of his envious foes,
Of fnares that watch'd his fame, of daggers aim'd
Againft his life.   At laft with trembling limbs,
His hair diffus'd and wild, his garments loofe,   60
And ftain'd with blood from felf-inflicted wounds,
He burft into the public place, as there,
There only, were his refuge; and declar'd
In broken words, with fighs of deep regret,
The mortal danger he had fcarce repell'd.   65
Fir'd with his tragic tale, the indignant croud,

To

To guard his fteps, forthwith a menial band,
Array'd beneath his eye for deeds of war,
Decree.   O ftill too liberal of their truft,
And oft betray'd by over-grateful love,   70
The generous people !   Now behold him fenc'd
By mercenary weapons, like a king,
Forth iffuing from the city gate at eve
To feek his rural manfion, and with pomp
Crouding the public road.   the fwain ftops fhort,   75
And fighs: the officious townsmen ftand at gaze
And fhrinking give the fullen pageant room.
Yet not the lefs obfequious was his brow ;
Nor lefs profufe of courteous words his tongue,
Of gracious gifts his hand: the while by ftealth,   80
Like a fmall torrent fed with evening fhowers,
His train increas'd.   till, at that fatal time
Juft as the public eye, with doubt and fhame
Startled, began to queftion what it faw,
Swift as the found of earthquakes rufh'd a voice   85
Through Athens, that Pififtratus had fill'd
The rocky citadel with hoftile arms,
Had barr'd the fteep afcent, and fate within
Amid his hirelings, meditating death
To all whofe ftubborn necks his yoke refus'd.   90
Where then was Solon ?   After ten long years
Of abfence, full of hafte from foreign fhores

The

The fage, the lawgiver had now arriv'd :
Arriv'd, alafs, to fee that Athens, that
Fair temple rais'd by him and facred call'd   95
To liberty and concord, now profan'd
By favage hate, or funk into a den
Of flaves who crouch beneath the mafter's fcourge,
And deprecate his wrath and court his chains.
Yet did not the wife patriot's grief impede   100
His virtuous will, nor was his heart inclin'd
One moment with fuch woman-like diftrefs
To view the tranfient ftorms of civil war,
As thence to yield his country and her hopes
To all-devouring bondage.   His bright helm,   105
Even while the traitor's impious act is told,
He buckles on his hoary head : he girds
With mail his ftooping breaft : the fhield, the fpear
He fnatcheth ; and with fwift indignant ftrides
The affembled people feeks : proclaims aloud   110
It was no time for counfel : in their fpears
Lay all their prudence now : the tyrant yet
Was not fo firmly feated on his throne,
But that one fhock of their united force
Would dafh him from the fummit of his pride   115
Headlong and groveling in the duft.   What elfe
Can re-aftert the loft Athenian name
So cheaply to the laughter of the world

B b

Betray'd ;

Betray'd; by guile beneath an infant's faith
So mock'd and fcorn'd?   Away then: freedom now   120
And fafety dwell not but with fame in arms:
Myfelf will fhew you where their manfion lies,
And through the walks of danger or of death
Conduct you to them.   While he fpake, through all
Their crouded ranks his quick fagacious eye   125
He darted; where no cheerful voice was heard
Of focial daring; no ftretch'd arm was feen
Haftening their common tafk: but pale miftruft
Wrinkled each brow: they fhook their heads, and down
Their flack hands hung: cold fighs and whifper'd doubts 130
From breath to breath ftole round.   The fage mean time
Look'd fpeechlefs on, while his big bofom heav'd
Struggling with fhame and forrow: till at laft
A tear broke forth; and, O immortal fhades,
O Thefeus, he exclaim'd, o Codrus, where,   135
Where are ye now?   behold for what ye toil'd
Through life?   behold for whom ye chofe to die.
No more he added; but with lonely fteps
Weary and flow, his filver beard deprefs'd,
And his ftern eyes bent heedlefs on the ground,   140
Back to his filent dwelling he repair'd.
There o'er the gate, his armor, as a man
Whom from the fervice of the war his chief
Difmiffeth after no inglorious toil,

He

He fix'd in general view.   One wishful look   145
He sent, unconscious, toward the public place
At parting: then beneath his quiet roof
Without a word, without a sigh, retir'd.

     Scarce had the morrow's sun his golden rays
From sweet Hymettus darted o'er the fanes   150
Of Cecrops to the Salaminian shores,
When, lo, on Solon's threshold met the feet
Of four Athenians by the same sad care
Conducted all: than whom the state beheld
None nobler.   First came Megacles, the son   155
Of great Alcmæon, whom the Lydian king
The mild, unhappy Crœsus, in his days
Of glory had with costly gifts adorn'd,
Fair vessels, splendid garments, tinctur'd webs
And heaps of treasur'd gold beyond the lot   160
Of many sovrans; thus requiting well
That hospitable favor which erewhile
Alcmæon to his messengers had shewn,
Whom he with offerings worthy of the God
Sent from his throne in Sardis to revere   165
Apollo's Delphic shrine.   With Megacles
Approach'd his son, whom Agarista bore,
The virtuous child of Clisthenes whose hand
Of Grecian scepters the most ancient far

B b 2

In Sicyon fway'd : but greater fame he drew   170
From arms controul'd by juftice, from the love
Of the wife Mufes, and the unenvied wreath
Which glad Olympia gave.   For thither once
His warlike fteeds the heroe led, and there
Contended through the tumult of the courfe   175
With fkillful wheels.   Then victor at the goal,
Amid the applaufes of affembled Greece,
High on his car he ftood and wav'd his arm..
Silence infu'd : when ftrait the herald's voice
Was heard, inviting every Grecian youth,   180
Whom Clifthenes content might call his fon,.
To vifit, ere twice thirty days were pafs'd,
The towers of Sicyon.. there the chief decreed,.
Within the circuit of the following year,
To join at Hymen's altar, hand in hand   185
With his fair daughter, him among the guefts.
Whom worthieft he fhould deem.   Forthwith from all
The bounds of Greece the ambitious wooers came :.
From rich Hefperia; from the Illyrian. fhore
Where Epidamnus over Adria's furge   190
Looks on the fetting fun.; from thofe brave tribes
Chaonian or Moloffian whom the race
Of great Achilles governs, glorying ftill
In Troy o'erthrown; from rough Ætolia, nurfe
Of men who firft among the Greeks threw off   195
The

The yoke of kings, to commerce and to arms
Devoted ; from Theſſalia's fertile meads,
Where flows Penéus near the lofty walls
Of Cranon old ; from ſtrong Eretria, queen
Of all Eubœan cities, who, ſublime   200
On the ſteep margin of Euripus, views
Acroſs the tide the Marathonian plain,
Not yet the haunt of glory.   Athens too,
Minerva's care, among her graceful ſons,
Found equal lovers for the princely maid :   205
Nor was proud Argos wanting ; nor the domes
Of ſacred Elis ; nor the Arcadian groves
That overſhade Alphéus, echoing oft
Some ſhepherd's ſong.   But through the illuſtrious band
Was none who might with Megacles compare   210
In all the honors of unblemiſh'd youth.
Ilis was the beauteous bride : and now their ſon
Young Cliſthenes, betimes, at Solon's gate
Stood anxious ; leaning forward on the arm
Of his great ſire, with earneſt eyes that aſk'd   215
When the ſlow hinge would turn, with reſtleſs feet,
And cheeks now pale, now glowing : for his heart
Throbb'd, full of burſting paſſions, anger, grief.
With ſcorn imbitter'd, by the generous boy.
Scarce underſtood, but which, like noble ſeeds,   220
Are deſtin'd for his country and himſelf.

In

In riper years to bring forth fruits divine
Of liberty and glory.   Next appear'd
Two brave companions whom one mother bore
To different lords; but whom the better ties   225
Of firm esteem and friendship render'd more
Than brothers: first Miltiades, who drew
From godlike Æacus his ancient line;
That Æacus whose unimpeach'd renown
For sanctity and justice won the lyre   230
Of elder bards to celebrate him thron'd
In Hades o'er the dead, where his decrees
The guilty foul within the burning gates
Of Tartarus compel, or fend the good
To inhabit with eternal health and peace   235
The vallies of Elysium.   From a stem
So facred, ne'er could worthier fcyon fpring
Than this Miltiades; whose aid erelong
The chiefs of Thrace, already on their ways
Sent by the infpir'd foreknowing maid who fits   240
Upon the Delphic tripod, fhall implore
To wield their fceptre, and the rural wealth
Of fruitful Cherfonefus to protect
With arms and laws.   But, nothing careful now
Save for his injur'd country, here he ftands   245
In deep follicitude with Cymon join'd:
Unconfcious both what widely-different lots

                                              Await

Await them, taught by nature as they are
To know one common good, one common ill.
For Cimon not his valor, not his birth   250
Deriv'd from Codrus, not a thousand gifts
Dealt round him with a wise, benignant hand,
No, not the Olympic olive by himself
From his own brow transferr'd to sooth the mind
Of this Pisistratus, can long preserve   255
From the fell envy of the tyrant's sons,
And their assassin dagger.   But if death.
Obscure upon his gentle steps attend,
Yet fate an ample recompense prepares
In his victorious son, that other great   260
Miltiades, who o'er the very throne
Of glory shall with Time's assiduous hand
In adamantine characters ingrave
The name of Athens; and, by freedom arm'd
'Gainst the gigantic pride of Asia's king,   265
Shall all the achievements of the heroes old:
Surmount, of Hercules, of all who sail'd,
From Thessaly with Jason, all who fought:
For empire or for fame at Thebes or Troy.

   Such were the patriots who within the porch   270
Of Solon had assembled.   But the gate
Now opens, and across the ample floor

                                        Strait

Strait they proceed into an open fpace
Bright with the beams of morn: a verdant fpot,
Where ftands a rural altar, pil'd with fods   275
Cut from the graffy turf and girt with wreaths
Of branching palm.   Here Solon's felf they found
Clad in a robe of purple pure, and deck'd
With leaves of olive on his reverend brow.
He bow'd before the altar, and o'er cakes   280
Of barley from two earthen veffels pour'd
Of honey and of milk a plenteous ftream;
Calling meantime the Mufes to accept
His fimple offering, by no victim ting'd
With blood, nor fullied by deftroying fire,   285
But fuch as for himfelf Apollo claims
In his own Delos, where his favorite haunt
Is thence the Altar of the Pious nam'd.
Unfeen the guefts drew near, and filent view'd
That worfhip; till the heroe prieft his eye   290
Turn'd toward a feat on which prepar'd there lay
A branch of laurel.   Then his friends confefs'd
Before him ftood.   Backward his ftep he drew,
As loth that care or tumult fhould approach
Thofe early rites divine: but foon their looks,   295
So anxious, and their hands, held forth with fuch
Defponding gefture, bring him on perforce
To fpeak to their affliction.   Are ye come,

He

He cried, to mourn with me this common fhame?
Or afk ye fome new effort which may break   300
Our fetters?   Know then, of the public caufe
Not for yon traitor's cunning or his might
Do i defpair: nor could i wifh from Jove
Aught dearer, than at this late hour of life,
As once by laws, fo now by ftrenuous arms,   305
From impious violation to affert
The rights our fathers left us.   But, alas!
What arms? or who fhall wield them?   Ye beheld
The Athenian people.   Many bitter days
Muft pafs, and many wounds from cruel pride   310
Be felt, ere yet their partial hearts find room
For juft refentment, or their hands indure
To fmite this tyrant brood, fo near to all
Their hopes, fo oft admir'd, fo long belov'd.
That time will come, however.   Be it yours   315
To watch its fair approach, and urge it on
With honeft prudence: me it ill befeems
Again to fupplicate the unwilling croud
To refcue from a vile deceiver's hold
That envied power which once with eager zeal   320
They offer'd to myfelf; nor can i plunge
In counfels deep and various, nor prepare
For diftant wars, thus faultering as i tread
On life's laft verge, erelong to join the fhades

C c

Of

Of Minos and Lycurgus.   But behold   325
What care imploys me now.   My vows i pay
To the fweet Mufes, teachers of my youth
And folace of my age.   If right i deem
Of the ftill voice that whifpers at my heart,
The immortal fifters have not quite withdrawn   330
Their old harmonious influence.   Let your tongues
With facred filence favor what i fpeak,
And haply fhall my faithful lips be taught
To unfold celeftial counfels, which may arm
As with impenetrable fteel your brealts   335
For the long ftrife before you, and repel
The darts of adverfe fate.   He faid, and fnatch'd
The laurel bough, and fate in filence down,
Fix'd, wrapp'd in folemn mufing, full before
The fun, who now from all his radiant orb   340
Drove the gray clouds, and pour'd his genial light
Upon the breaft of Solon.   Solon rais'd
Aloft the leafy rod, and thus began.

Ye beauteous offspring of Olympian Jove
And Memory divine, Picrian maids,   345
Hear me, propitious.   In the morn of life,
When hope fhone bright and all the profpect fmil'd,
To your fequefter'd manfion oft my fteps

                                                      Were

Were turn'd, o Muses, and within your gate
My offerings paid.   Ye taught me then with strains   350
Of flowing harmony to soften war's
Dire voice, or in fair colors, that might charm
The public eye, to clothe the form austere
Of civil counsel.   Now my feeble age
Neglected, and supplanted of the hope   355
On which it lean'd, yet sinks not, but to you,
To your mild wisdom flies, refuge belov'd
Of solitude and silence.   Ye can teach
The visions of my bed whate'er the gods
In the rude ages of the world inspir'd,   360
Or the first heroes acted : ye can make
The morning light more gladsome to my sense
Than ever it appear'd to active youth
Pursuing careless pleasure : ye can give
To this long leisure, these unheeded hours,   365
A labor as sublime, as when the sons
Of Athens throng'd and speechless round me stood
To hear pronounc'd for all their future deeds
The bounds of right and wrong.   Celestial powers,
I feel that ye are near me : and behold,   370
To meet your energy divine, i bring
A high and sacred theme ; not less than those
Which to the eternal custody of fame
Your lips intrusted, when of old ye deign'd

C c 2

With Orpheus or with Homer to frequent   375
The groves of Hæmus or the Chian shore.

    Ye know, harmonious maids, (for what of all
My various life was e'er from you estrang'd?)
Oft hath my solitary song to you
Reveal'd that duteous pride which turn'd my steps   380
To willing exile; earnest to withdraw
From envy and the disappointed thirst
Of lucre, left the bold familiar strife,
Which in the eye of Athens they upheld
Against her legislator, should impair   385
With trivial doubt the reverence of his laws.
To Egypt therefore through the Ægean isles
My course i steer'd, and by the banks of Nile
Dwelt in Canopus.   Thence the hallow'd domes
Of Saïs, and the rites to Isis paid,   390
I sought, and in her temple's silent courts,
Through many changing moons, attentive heard
The venerable Sonchis, while his tongue
At morn or midnight the deep story told
Of her who represents whate'er has been,   395
Or is, or shall be; whose mysterious veil
No mortal hand hath ever yet remov'd.
By him exhorted, southward to the walls
Of On i pass'd, the city of the sun,

The

The ever-youthful god.   'Twas there amid   400
His priests and sages, who the live-long night
Watch the dread movements of the starry sphere,
Or who in wonderous fables half disclose
The secrets of the elements, 'twas there
That great Psenophis taught my raptur'd ears   405
The fame of old Atlantis, of her chiefs,
And her pure laws, the first which earth obey'd.
Deep in my bosom sunk the noble tale;
And often, while i listen'd, did my mind
Foretell with what delight her own free lyre   410
Should sometime for an Attic audience raise
Anew that lofty scene, and from their tombs
Call forth those ancient demigods to speak.
Of justice and the hidden providence
That walks among mankind.   But yet meantime   415
The mystic pomp of Ammon's gloomy sons
Became less pleasing.   With contempt i gaz'd
On that tame garb and those unvarying paths
To which the double yoke of king and priest
Had cramp'd the sullen race.   At last with hymns   420
Invoking our own Pallas and the gods
Of cheerful Greece, a glad farewell i gave
To Egypt, and before the southern wind
Spread my full sails.   What climes i then survey'd,
What fortunes i incounter'd in the realm   425

Of

Of Crœsus or upon the Cyprian shore,
The Muse, who prompts my bosom, doth not now
Consent that i reveal.　But when at length
Ten times the sun returning from the south
Had strow'd with flowers the verdant earth and fill'd   430
The groves with music, pleas'd i then beheld
The term of those long errors drawing nigh.
Nor yet, i said, will i sit down within
The walls of Athens, till my feet have trod
The Cretan soil, have pierc'd those reverend haunts   435
Whence law and civil concord issued forth
As from their ancient home, and still to Greece
Their wisest, loftiest discipline proclaim.
Strait where Amnisus, mart of wealthy ships,
Appears beneath fam'd Cnossus and her towers   440
Like the fair handmaid of a stately queen,
I check'd my prow, and thence with eager steps
The city of Minos enter'd.　O ye gods,
Who taught the leaders of the simpler time
By written words to curb the untoward will   445
Of mortals, how within that generous isle
Have ye the triumphs of your power display'd
Munificent!　Those splendid merchants, lords
Of traffic and the sea, with what delight
I saw them at their public meal, like sons   450
Of the same houshold, join the plainer sort

Whose

Whose wealth was only freedom! whence to these
Vile envy, and to those fantastic pride,
Alike was strange; but noble concord still
Cherish'd the strength untam'd, the rustic faith,   455
Of their first fathers.   Then the growing race,
How pleasing to behold them in their schools,
Their sports, their labors, ever plac'd within,
O shade of Minos, thy controuling eye!
Here was a docile band in tuneful tones   460
Thy laws pronouncing, or with lofty hymns
Praising the bounteous gods, or, to preserve
Their country's heroes from oblivious night,
Resounding what the Muse inspir'd of old;
There, on the verge of manhood, others met,   465
In heavy armor through the heats of noon
To march, the rugged mountains height to climb
With measur'd swiftness, from the hard-bent bow
To send resistless arrows to their mark,
Or for the fame of prowess to contend,   470
Now wrestling, now with fists and staves oppos'd,
Now with the biting falchion, and the fence
Of brazen shields; while still the warbling flute
Presided o'er the combat, breathing strains
Grave, solemn, soft; and changing headlong spite   475
To thoughtful resolution cool and clear.
Such i beheld those islanders renown'd,

So

So tutor'd from their birth to meet in war
Each bold invader, and in peace to guard
That living flame of reverence for their laws   480
Which nor the storms of fortune, nor the flood
Of foreign wealth diffus'd o'er all the land,
Could quench or flacken. First of human names
In every Cretan's heart was Minos still;   485
And holieft far, of what the fun furveys
Through his whole courfe, were thofe primeval feats
Which with religious footfteps he had taught
Their fires to approach ; the wild Dictæan cave
Where Jove was born ; the ever-verdant meads   490
Of Ida, and the fpacious grotto, where
His active youth he pafs'd, and where his throne
Yet ftands myfterious ; whither Minos came
Each ninth returning year, the king of gods
And mortals there in fecret to confult   495
On juftice, and the tables of his law
To infcribe anew. Oft alfo with like zeal
Great Rhea's manfion from the Cnoflian gates
Men vifit ; nor lefs oft the antique fane
Built on that facred fpot, along the banks   500
Of fhady Theron, where benignant Jove
And his majeftic confort join'd their hands
And fpoke their nuptial vows. Alafs, 'twas there
That the dire fame of Athens funk in bonds

I firft

I firſt receiv'd; what time an annual feaſt   505
Had ſummon'd all the genial country round,
By ſacrifice and pomp to bring to mind
That firſt great ſpouſal; while the inamor'd youths
And virgins, with the prieſt before the ſhrine,
Obſerve the ſame pure ritual and invoke   510
The ſame glad omens.   There, among the croud
Of ſtrangers from thoſe naval cities drawn
Which deck, like gems, the iſland's northern ſhore,
A merchant of Ægina i deſcried,
My ancient hoſt.   but, forward as i ſprung   515
To meet him, he, with dark dejected brow,
Stopp'd half-averſe; and, O Athenian gueſt,
He ſaid, art thou in Crete; theſe joyful rites
Partaking?   Know thy laws are blotted out:
Thy country kneels before a tyrant's throne.   520
He added names of men, with hoſtile deeds
Diſaſtrous; which obſcure and indiſtinct
I heard: for, while he ſpake, my heart grew cold
And my eyes dim: the altars and their train
No more were preſent to me: how i far'd,   525
Or whither turn'd, i know not; nor recall
Aught of thoſe moments other than the ſenſe
Of one who ſtruggles in oppreſſive ſleep
And, from the toils of ſome diſtreſsful dream
To break away, with palpitating heart,   530

D d

Weak.

Weak limbs, and temples bath'd in death-like dew,
Makes many a painful effort.   When at laſt
The ſun and nature's face again appear'd,
Not far I found me; where the public path,
Winding through cypreſs groves and ſwelling meads,
From Cnoſſus to the cave of Jove aſcends.
Heedleſs i follow'd on; till ſoon the ſkirts
Of Ida roſe before me, and the vault
Wide-opening pierc'd the mountain's rocky ſide.
Entering within the threſhold, on the ground
I flung me, ſad, faint, overworn with toil,

*   *   *   *   *   *   *   *

HE BEGINNING

OF THE

FOURTH BOOK

OF THE

PLEASURES

OF THE

MAGINATION:

MDCCLXX.

THE

THE

PLEASURES

OF THE

IMAGINATION:

BOOK THE FOURTH.

ONE effort more, one cheerful fally more,
Our deftin'd courfe will finifh.   and in peace
Then, for an offering facred to the powers
Who lent us gracious guidance, we will then
Infcribe a monument of deathlefs praife,   5
O my adventurous fong.   With fteady fpeed
Long haft thou, on an untried voyage bound,
Sail'd between earth and heaven : haft now furvey'd,
Stretch'd out beneath thee, all the mazy tracts
Of paffion and opinion ; like a wafte   10
Of fands and flowery lawns and tangling woods,
Where mortals roam bewilder'd : and haft now
Exulting foar'd among the worlds above,
Or hover'd near the eternal gates of heaven,
If haply the difcourfes of the Gods,   15

A curious

A curious, but an unpresuming gueft,
Thou might'ft partake, and carry back some ftrain
Of divine wifdom, lawful to repeat,
And apt to be conceiv'd ofi man below.
A different tafk remains; the fecret paths   20
Of early genius to explore: to trace
Thofe haunts where Fancy her predeftin'd fons,
Like to the Demigods of old, doth nurfe
Remote from eyes profane.   Ye happy fouls
Who now her tender difcipline obey,   25
Where dwell ye?   What wild river's brink at eve
Imprint your fteps?   What folemn groves at noon
Ufe ye to vifit, often breaking forth
In rapture 'mid your dilatory walk, .
Or mufing, as in flumber, on the green?   30
—Would i again were with you!—O ye dales
Of Tyne, and ye moft ancient woodlands; where
Oft as the giant flood obliquely ftrides,
And his banks open, and his lawns extend,
Stops fhort the pleafed traveller to view   35
Prefiding o'er the fcene fome ruftic tower
Founded by Norman or by Saxon hands:
O ye Northumbrian fhades, which overlook
The rocky pavement and the moffy falls
Of folitary Wenfbeck's limpid ftream;   40
How gladly i recall your well-known feats

Belov'd

Belov'd of old, and that delightful time
When all alone, for many a fummer's day,
I wander'd through your calm receffes, led
In filence by fome powerful hand unfeen.   45

    Nor will i e'er forget you.   nor fhall e'er
The graver tafks of manhood, or the advice
Of vulgar wifdom, move me to difclaim
Thofe ftudies which poffefs'd me in the dawn
Of life, and fix'd the color of my mind   50
For every future year: whence even now
From fleep i refcue the clear hours of morn,
And, while the world around lies overwhelm'd
In idle darknefs, am alive to thoughts
Of honourable fame, of truth divine   55
Or moral, and of minds to virtue won
By the fweet magic of harmonious verfe;
The themes which now expect us.   For thus far
On general habits, and on arts which grow
Spontaneous in the minds of all mankind,   60
Hath dwelt our argument; and how felf-taught,
Though feldom confcious of their own imploy,
In nature's or in fortune's changeful fcene
Men learn to judge of beauty, and acquire
Thofe forms fet up, as idols in the foul   65
For love and zealous praife.   Yet indiftinct,

                                                           In

In vulgar bofoms, and unnotic'd lie
Thefe pleafing ftores, unlefs the cafual force
Of things external prompt the heedlefs mind
To recognize her wealth.   But fome there are
Confcious of nature, and the rule which man
O'er nature holds: fome who, within themfelves
Retiring from the trivial fcenes of chance
And momentary paffion, can at will
Call up thefe fair exemplars of the mind;
Review their features; fcan the fecret laws
Which bind them to each other: and difplay
By forms, or founds, or colours, to the fenfe
Of all the world their latent charms difplay:
Even as in nature's frame (if fuch a word,
If fuch a word, fo bold, may from the lips,
Of man proceed) as in this outward frame
Of things, the great artificer pourtrays.
His own immenfe idea.   Various names,
Thefe among mortals bear, as various figns,
They ufe, and by peculiar organs fpeak
To human fenfe.   There are who by the flight
Of air through tubes with moving ftops diftinct,
Or by extended chords in meafure taught
To vibrate, can affemble powerful founds
Expreffing every temper of the mind
From every caufe, and charming all the foul

With paffion void of care.   Others mean time
The rugged mafs of metal, wood, or ftone
Patiently taming; or with eafier hand   95
Defcribing lines, and with more ample fcope
Uniting colors; can to general fight
Produce thofe permanent and perfect forms,
Thofe characters of heroes and of gods,
Which from the crude materials of the world   100
Their own high minds created.   But the chief
Are poets; eloquent men, who dwell on earth
To clothe whate'er the foul admires or loves
With language and with numbers.   Hence to thefe
A field is open'd wide as nature's fphere;   105
Nay, wider: various as the fudden acts
Of human wit, and vaft as the demands
Of human will.   The bard nor length, nor depth,
Nor place, nor form controuls.   To eyes, to ears,
To every organ of the copious mind,   110
He offereth all its treafures.   Him the hours,
The feafons him obey: and changeful Time
Sees him at will keep meafure with his flight,
At will outftrip it.   To enhance his toil,
He fummoneth from the uttermoft extent   115
Of things which God hath taught him, every form
Auxiliar, every power; and all befide
Excludes imperious.   His prevailing hand
E e.

Gives,

Gives, to corporeal effence, life and fenfe
And every ftately function of the foul,
The foul itfelf to him obfequious lies,
Like matter's paffive heap; and as he wills,
To reafon and affection he affigns
Their juft alliances, their juft degrees:
Whence his peculiar honors; whence the race
Of men who people his delightful world,
Men genuine and according to themfelves,
Tranfcend as far the uncertain fons of earth,
As earth itfelf to his delightful world
The palm of fpotlefs beauty doth refign.

*   *   *   *   *   *   *

O D E S

O N

S E V E R A L   S U B J E C T S.

I N   T W O   B O O K S.

O D E S,

O D E I.

P R E F A C E.

I.

ON yonder verdant hilloc laid,
Where oaks and elms, a friendly fhade,
   O'erlook the falling ftream,
O mafter of the Latin lyre,
Awhile with thee will i retire
   From fummer's noontide beam.

II.

And, lo, within my lonely bower,
The induftrious bee from many a flower
   Collects her balmy dews:
" For me," fhe fings, " the gems are born,
" For me their filken robe adorn,
   " Their fragrant breath diffufe."

III. Sweet

III.

Sweet murmurer! may no rude ftorm
This hofpitable fcene deform,
   Nor check thy gladfome toils;
Still may the buds unfullied fpring,
Still fhowers and funfhine court thy wing
   To thefe ambrofial fpoils.

IV.

Nor fhall my Mufe hereafter fail
Her fellow-labourer thee to hail;
   And lucky be the ftrains!
For long ago did nature frame
Your feafons and your arts the fame,
   Your pleafures and your pains.

V.

Like thee, in lowly, fylvan fcenes,
On river-banks and flowery greens
   My Mufe delighted plays;
Nor through the defart of the air,
Though fwans or eagles triumph there,
   With fond ambition ftrays.

VI. Nor

VI.

Nor where the boding raven chaunts,
Nor near the owl's unhallow'd haunts
    Will she her cares imploy;
But flies from ruins and from tombs,
From superstition's horrid glooms,
    To day-light and to joy.

VII.

Nor will she tempt the barren waste;
Nor deigns the lurking strength to taste
    Of any noxious thing;
But leaves with scorn to envy's use
The insipid nightshade's baneful juice,
    The nettle's sordid sting.

VIII.

From all which nature fairest knows,
The vernal blooms, the summer rose,
    She draws her blameless wealth;
And, when the generous task is done,
She confecrates a double boon,
    To pleasure and to health.

O D E II.

ON THE WINTER-SOLSTICE,

M.D.CC.XL.

I.

THE radiant ruler of the year
At length his wintry goal attains;
Soon to reverfe the long career,
And northward bend his fteady reins.
Now, piercing half Potofi's height,
Prone rufh the fiery floods of light
Ripening the mountain's filver ftores:
While, in fome cavern's horrid fhade,
The panting Indian hides his head,
And oft the approach of eve implores.

II.

But lo, on this deferted coaft
How pale the fun! how thick the air!
Muftering his ftorms, a fordid hoft,
Lo, winter defolates the year.

The.

The fields refign their lateft bloom;
No more the breezes waft perfume,
No more the ftreams in mufic roll:
But fnows fall dark, or rains refound;
And, while great nature mourns around,
Her griefs infect the human foul.

III.

Hence the loud city's bufy throngs
Urge the warm bowl and fplendid fire:
Harmonious dances, feftive fongs
Againft the fpiteful heaven confpire.
Meantime perhaps with tender fears
Some village-dame the curfew hears,
While round the hearth her children play:
At morn their father went abroad;
The moon is funk and deep the road;
She fighs, and wonders at his ftay.

IV.

But thou, my lyre, awake, arife,
And hail the fun's returning force:
Even now he climbs the northern fkies,
And health and hope attend his courfe.
Then louder howl the aërial wafte,
Be earth with keener cold imbrac'd,

Yet

Yet gentle hours advance their wing;
And fancy, mocking winter's might,
With flowers and dews and streaming light
Already decks the newborn spring.

V.

O fountain of the golden day,
Could mortal vows promote thy speed,
How soon before thy vernal ray
Should each unkindly damp recede!
How soon each hovering tempest fly,
Whose stores for mischief arm the sky,
Prompt on our heads to burst amain,
To rend the forest from the steep,
Or, thundering o'er the Baltic deep,
To whelm the merchant's hopes of gain!

VI.

But let not man's unequal views
Presume o'er nature and her laws:
'Tis his with grateful joy to use
The indulgence of the sovran cause;
Secure that health and beauty springs
Through this majestic frame of things,

Beyond

Beyond what he can reach to know;
And that heaven's all-fubduing will,
With good the progeny of ill,
Attempereth every ftate below.

VII.

How pleafing wears the wintry night,
Spent with the old illuftrious dead!
While, by the taper's trembling light,
I feem thofe awful fcenes to tread
Where chiefs or legiflators lie,
Whofe triumphs move before my eye
In arms and antique pomp array'd;
While now i tafte the Ionian fong,
Now bend to Plato's godlike tongue
Refounding through the olive fhade.

VIII.

But fhould fome cheerful, equal friend
Bid leave the ftudious page awhile,
Let mirth on wifdom then attend,
And focial eafe on learned toil.
Then while, at love's uncareful fhrine,
Each dictates to the god of wine

Her name whom all his hopes obey,
What flattering dreams each bosom warm,
While absence, heightening every charm,
Invokes the slow-returning May!

IX.

May, thou delight of heaven and earth,
When will thy genial star arise?
The auspicious morn, which gives thee birth,
Shall bring Eudora to my eyes.
Within her sylvan haunt behold,
As in the happy garden old,
She moves like that primeval fair:
Thither, ye silver-sounding lyres,
Ye tender smiles, ye chaste desires,
Fond hope and mutual faith, repair.

X.

And if believing love can read
His better omens in her eye,
Then shall my fears, o charming maid,
And every pain of absence die:
Then shall my jocund harp, attun'd
To thy true ear, with sweeter sound

Pursue

Purfue the free Horatian fong :
Old Tyne fhall liften to my tale,
And echo, down the bordering vale,
The liquid melody prolong.

O D E III.

TO A FRIEND, UNSUCCESSFUL IN LOVE.

I.

Indeed, my Phædria, if to find
That wealth can female wifhes gain
Had e'er difturb'd your thoughtful mind,
Or coft one ferious moment's pain,
I fhould have faid that all the rules,
You learn'd of moralifts and fchools,
Were very ufelefs, very vain.

II.

Yet i perhaps miftake the cafe——
Say, though with this heroic air,
Like one that holds a nobler chace,
You try the tender lofs to bear,
Does not your heart renounce your tongue?
Seems not my cenfure ftrangely wrong
To count it fuch a flight affair?

III.

When Hefper gilds the fhaded fky,
Oft as you feek the well-known grove,
Methinks i fee you caft your eye
Back to the morning fcenes of love:
Each pleafing word you heard her fay,
Her gentle look, her graceful way,
Again your ftruggling fancy move.

IV.

Then tell me, is your foul intire?
Does wifdom calmly hold her throne?
Then can you queftion each defire,
Bid this remain, and that begone?
No tear half-ftarting from your eye?
No kindling blufh you know not why?
No ftealing figh, nor ftifled groan?

V. Away

V.

Away with this unmanly mood!
See where the hoary churl appears,
Whofe hand hath feiz'd the favorite good
Which you referv'd for happier years:
While, fide by fide, the blufhing maid
Shrinks from his vifage, half-afraid,
Spite of the fickly joy fhe wears.

VI.

Ye guardian powers of love and fame,
This chafte, harmonious pair behold;
And thus reward the generous flame
Of all who barter vows for gold.
O bloom of youth, o tender charms
Well-buried in a dotard's arms!
O equal price of beauty fold!

VII.

Ceafe then to gaze with looks of love:
Bid her adieu, the venal fair:
Unworthy fhe your blifs to prove;
Then wherefore fhould fhe prove your care?
No: lay your myrtle garland down;
And let awhile the willow's crown
With luckier omens bind your hair.

VIII.

'O juſt eſcap'd the faithleſs main,
Though driven unwilling on the land;
To guide your favor'd ſteps again,
Behold your better genius ſtand:
Where truth revolves her page divine,
Where virtue leads to honor's ſhrine,
Behold, he lifts his awful hand.

IX.

Fix but on theſe your ruling aim,
And time, the fire of manly care,
Will fancy's dazzling colors tame
A ſoberer dreſs will beauty wear:
Then ſhall eſteem by knowledge led
Inthrone within your heart and head
Some happier love, ſome truer fair.

O D E

O D E IV.

A F F E C T E D I N D I F F E R E N C E.

T O T H E S A M E.

I.

YES: you contemn the perjur'd maid
Who all your favorite hopes betray'd:
Nor, though her heart ſhould home return,
Her tuneful tongue it's falſehood mourn,
Her winning eyes your faith implore,
Would you her hand receive again,
Or once diſſemble your diſdain,
Or liſten to the ſyren's theme,
Or ſtoop to love : ſince now eſteem
And confidence, and friendſhip, is no more.

II.

Yet tell me, Phædria, tell me why,
When ſummoning your pride you try
To meet her looks with cool neglect,
Or croſs her walk with ſlight reſpect,

G g

For

(For ſo is falſchood beſt repaid)
Whence do your cheeks indignant glow?
Why is your ſtruggling tongue ſo ſlow?
What means that darkneſs on your brow?
As if with all her broken vow
You meant the fair apoſtate to upbraid?

O D E V.

AGAINST SUSPICION.

I.

OH fly! 'tis dire Suſpicion's mien;
And, meditating plagues unſeen,
    The ſorcereſs hither bends:
Behold her torch in gall imbrued:
Behold——her garment drops with blood
    Of lovers and of friends.

II. Fly

II.

Fly far! Already in your eyes
I fee a pale fuffufion rife;
    And foon through every vein,
Soon will her fecret venom fpread,
And all your heart and all your head
    Imbibe the potent ftain.

III.

Then many a demon will fhe raife
To vex your fleep, to haunt your ways;
    While gleams of loft delight
Raife the dark tempeft of the brain,
As lightning fhines acrofs the main
    Through whirlwinds and through night.

IV.

No more can faith or candor move;
But each ingenuous deed of love,
    Which reafon would applaud,
Now, fmiling o'er her dark diftrefs,
Fancy malignant ftrives to drefs
    Like injury and fraud.

V.

Farewell to virtue's peaceful times:
Soon will you ftoop to act the crimes
   Which thus you ftoop to fear:
Guilt follows guilt: and where the train
Begins with wrongs of fuch a ftain,
   What horrors form the rear!

VI.

'Tis thus to work her baleful power,
Sufpicion waits the fullen hour
   Of fretfulnefs and ftrife,
When care the infirmer bofom wrings,
Or Eurus waves his murky wings
   To damp the feats of life.

VII.

But come, forfake the fcene unblefs'd
Which firft beheld your faithful breaft
   To groundlefs fears a prey:
Come, where with my prevailing lyre
The fkies, the ftreams, the groves confpire
   To charm your doubts away.

VIII. Thron'd

VIII.

Thron'd in the fun's defcending car,
What power unfeen diffufeth far
   This tendernefs of mind?
What genius fmiles on yonder flood?
What god, in whifpers from the wood,
   Bids every thought be kind?

IX.

O thou, whate'er thy awful name,
Whofe wifdom our untoward frame
   With focial love reftrains;
Thou, who by fair affection's ties
Giv'ft us to double all our joys
   And half difarm our pains;

X.

Let univerfal candor ftill,
Clear as yon heaven-reflecting rill,
   Preferve my open mind;
Nor this nor that man's crooked ways
One fordid doubt within me raife
   To injure human kind.

O D E VI.

HYMN TO CHEERFULNESS.

HOW thick the shades of evening close !
How pale the sky with weight of snows !
Haste, light the tapers, urge the fire,
And bid the joyless day retire.
———Alas, in vain i try within
To brighten the dejected scene,
While rouz'd by grief these fiery pains
Tear the frail texture of my veins;
While winter's voice, that storms around,
And yon deep death-bell's groaning sound
Renew my mind's oppressive gloom,
Till starting horror shakes the room.

Is there in nature no kind power
To sooth affliction's lonely hour?
To blunt the edge of dire disease,
And teach these wintry shades to please?
Come, Cheerfulness, triumphant fair,
Shine through the hovering cloud of care:

O sweet

O fweet of language, mild of mien,
O virtue's friend and pleafure's queen,
Affwage the flames that burn my breaft,
Compofe my jarring thoughts to reft;
And while thy gracious gifts i feel,
My fong fhall all thy praife reveal.

As once ('twas in Aftræa's reign)
The vernal powers renew'd their train,
It happen'd that immortal Love
Was ranging through the fpheres above,
And downward hither caft his eye
The year's returning pomp to fpy.
He faw the radiant god of day,
Waft in his car the rofy May;
The fragrant Airs and genial Hours
Were fhedding round him dews and flowers;
Before his wheels Aurora pafs'd,
And Hefper's golden lamp was laft.
But, faireft of the blooming throng,
When Health majeftic mov'd along,
Delighted to furvey below
The joys which from her prefence flow,
While earth enliven'd hears her voice,
And fwains, and flocks, and fields rejoice;
Then mighty Love her charms confefs'd,
And foon his vows inclin'd her breaft,

And, known from that aufpicious morn,
The pleafing Cheerfulnefs was born.

   Thou, Cheerfulnefs, by heaven defign'd
To fway the movements of the mind,
Whatever fretful paffion fprings,
Whatever wayward fortune brings
To difarrange the power within,
And ftrain the mufical machine;
Thou, Goddefs, thy attempering hand
Doth each difcordant ftring command,
Refines the foft, and fwells the ftrong;
And, joining nature's general fong,
Through many a varying tone unfolds
The harmony of human fouls.

   Fair guardian of domeftic life,
Kind banifher of homebred ftrife,
Nor fullen lip, nor taunting eye
Deforms the fcene where thou art by:
No fickening hufband damns the hour
Which bound his joys to female power;
No pining mother weeps the cares
Which parents wafte on thanklefs heirs:
The officious daughters pleas'd attend;
The brother adds the name of friend:

By thee with flowers their board is crown'd,
With fongs from thee their walks refound;
And morn with welcome luftre fhines,
And evening unperceiv'd declines.

   Is there a youth, whofe anxious heart
Labors with love's unpitied fmart?
Though now he ftray by rills and bowers,
And weeping wafte the lonely hours,
Or if the nymph her audience deign,
Debafe the ftory of his pain
With flavifh looks, difcolor'd eyes,
And accents faltering into fighs;
Yet thou, aufpicious power, with eafe
Can'ft yield him happier arts to pleafe,
Inform his mien with manlier charms,
Inftruct his tongue with nobler arms,
With more commanding paffion move,
And teach the dignity of love.

   Friend to the Mufe and all her train,
For thee i court the Mufe again:
The Mufe for thee may well exert
Her pomp, her charms, her fondeft art,
Who owes to thee that pleafing fway
Which earth and peopled heaven obey.

H h

Let

Let melancholy's plaintive tongue
Repeat what later bards have fung;
But thine was Homer's ancient might,
And thine victorious Pindar's flight:
Thy hand each Lefbian wreathe attir'd:
Thy lip Sicilian reeds infpir'd:
Thy fpirit lent the glad perfume
Whence yet the flowers of Teos bloom;
Whence yet from Tibur's Sabine vale
Delicious blows the inlivening gale,
While Horace calls thy fportive choir,
Heroes and nymphs, around his lyre.

But fee where yonder penfive fage
(A prey perhaps to fortune's rage,
Perhaps by tender griefs opprefs'd,
Or glooms congenial to his breaft)
Retires in defart fcenes to dwell,
And bids the joylefs world farewell.
Alone he treads the autumnal fhade,
Alone beneath the mountain laid
He fees the nightly damps afcend,
And gathering ftorms aloft impend;
He hears the neighbouring furges roll,
And raging thunders fhake the pole:
Then, ftruck by every object round,
And ftunn'd by every horrid found,

He

He aſks a clue for nature's ways;
But evil haunts him through the maze:
He ſees ten thouſand demons riſe
To wield the empire of the ſkies,
And chance and fate aſſume the rod,
And malice blot the throne of God.
—O thou, whoſe pleaſing power i ſing,
Thy lenient influence hither bring;
Compoſe the ſtorm, diſpell the gloom,
Till nature wear her wonted bloom,
Till fields and ſhades their ſweets exhale,
And muſic ſwell each opening gale:
Then o'er his breaſt thy ſoftneſs pour,
And let him learn the timely hour
To trace the world's benignant laws,
And judge of that preſiding cauſe
Who founds on diſcord beauty's reign,
Converts to pleaſure every pain,
Subdues each hoſtile form to reſt,
And bids the univerſe be bleſs'd.

    O thou, whoſe pleaſing power i ſing,
If right i touch the votive ſtring,
If equal praiſe i yield thy name,
Still govern thou thy poet's flame;
Still with the Muſe my boſom ſhare,
And ſooth to peace intruding care.

H h 2

But

But moſt exert thy pleaſing power
On friendſhip's conſecrated hour;
And while my Sophron points the road
To godlike wiſdom's calm abode,
Or warm in freedom's ancient cauſe
Traceth the ſource of Albion's laws,
Add thou o'er all the generous toil
The light of thy unclouded ſmile.
But, if by fortune's ſtubborn ſway
From him and friendſhip torn away,
I court the Muſe's healing ſpell
For griefs that ſtill with abſence dwell,
Do thou conduct my fancy's dreams
To ſuch indulgent placid themes,
As juſt the ſtruggling breaſt may cheer
And juſt ſuſpend the ſtarting tear,
Yet leave that ſacred ſenſe of woe
Which none but friends and lovers know.

O D E   VII.

ON THE USE OF POETRY.

I.

Not for themfelves did human kind
Contrive the parts by heaven affign'd
    On life's wide fcene to play:
Not Scipio's force, nor Cæfar's fkill
Can conquer glory's arduous hill,
    If fortune clofe the way.

II.

Yet ftill the felf-depending foul,
Though laft and leaft in fortune's roll,
    His proper fphere commands;
And knows what nature's feal beftow'd,
And fees, before the throne of God,
    The rank in which he ftands.

III. Who

III.

Who train'd by laws the future age,
Who refcu'd nations from the rage
    Of partial, factious power,
My heart with diftant homage views;
Content if thou, celeftial Mufe,
    Did'ft rule my natal hour.

IV.

Nor far beneath the hero's feet,
Nor from the legiflator's feat
    Stands far remote the bard.
Though not with public terrors crown'd,
Yet wider fhall his rule be found,
    More lafting his award.

V.

Lycurgus fafhion'd Sparta's fame,
And Pompey to the Roman name
    Gave univerfal fway:
Where are they?—Homer's reverend page
Holds empire to the thirtieth age,
    And tongues and climes obey.

VI. And

VI.

And thus when William's acts divine
No longer shall from Bourbon's line
   Draw one vindictive vow;
When Sidney shall with Cato reft,
And Ruffel move the patriot's breaft
   No more than Brutus now;

VII.

Yet then shall Shakefpeare's powerful art
O'er every paffion, every heart,
   Confirm his awful throne:
Tyrants shall bow before his laws;
And freedom's, glory's, virtue's caufe,
   Their dread affertor own.

O D E   VIII.

ON LEAVING HOLLAND.

I. 1.

FAREWELL to Leyden's lonely bound,
The Belgian Mufe's fober feat;
Where dealing frugal gifts around
To all the favorites at her feet,
She trains the body's bulky frame
For paffive, perfevering toils;
And left, from any prouder aim,
The daring mind fhould fcorn her homely fpoils,
She breathes maternal fogs to damp its reftlefs flame.

I. 2.

Farewell the grave, pacific air,
Where never mountain zephyr blew:
The marfhy levels lank and bare,
Which Pan, which Ceres never knew:

The

The Naiads, with obfcene attire,
Urging in vain their urns to flow;
While round them chaunt the croking choir,
And haply footh fome lover's prudent woe,
Or prompt fome reftive bard and modulate his lyre.

I. 3.

Farewell, ye nymphs, whom fober care of gain
Snatch'd in your cradles from the god of love:
She render'd all his boafted arrows vain;
And all his gifts did he in fpite remove.
Ye too, the flow-ey'd fathers of the land,
With whom dominion fteals from hand to hand,
Unown'd, undignify'd by public choice,
I go where liberty to all is known,
And tells a monarch on his throne,
He reigns not but by her preferving voice.

II. 1.

O my lov'd England, when with thee
Shall i fit down, to part no more?
Far from this pale, difcolor'd fea,
That fleeps upon the reedy fhore,
When fhall i plough thy azure tide?
When on thy hills the flocks admire,
Like mountain fnows; till down their fide
I trace the village and the facred fpire,
While bowers and copfes green the golden flope divide?

I i   II. 2. Ye

II. 2.

Ye nymphs who guard the pathlefs grove,
Ye blue-ey'd fifters of the ftreams,
With whom i wont at morn to rove,
With whom at noon i talk'd in dreams;
O! take me to your haunts again,
The rocky fpring, the greenwood glade;
To guide my lonely footfteps deign,
To prompt my flumbers in the murmuring fhade,
And footh my vacant ear with many an airy ftrain.

II. 3.

And thou, my faithful harp, no longer mourn
Thy drooping mafter's inaufpicious hand:
Now brighter fkies and frefher gales return,
Now fairer maids thy melody demand.
Daughters of Albion, liften to my lyre!
O Phœbus, guardian of the Aonian choir,
Why founds not mine harmonious as thy own,
When all the virgin deities above
     With Venus and with Juno move
In concert round the Olympian father's throne?

III. 1.

Thee too, protectrefs of my lays,
Elate with whofe majeftic call
Above degenerate Latium's praife,
Above the flavifh boaft of Gaul,

I dare

I dare from impious thrones reclaim,
And wanton sloth's ignoble charms,
The honors of a poet's name
To Somers' counsels, or to Hamden's arms,
Thee, freedom, I rejoin, and bless thy genuine flame,

III. 2.

Great citizen of Albion.   Thee
Heroic valour still attends,
And useful science pleas'd to see
How art her studious toil extends.
While truth, diffusing from on high
A lustre unconfin'd as day,
Fills and commands the public eye;
Till, pierc'd and sinking by her powerful ray,
Tame faith and monkish awe, like nightly demons, fly.

III. 3.

Hence the whole land the patriot's ardour shares:
Hence dread religion dwells with social joy;
And holy passions and unsullied cares,
In youth, in age, domestic life imploy.
O fair Britannia, hail!—With partial love
The tribes of men their native seats approve,
Unjust and hostile to each foreign fame:
But when for generous minds and manly laws
A nation holds her prime applause,
There public zeal shall all reproof disclaim.

ODE

O D E   IX.

T O   C U R I O.

M D C C X L I V.

I.

THRICE hath the fpring beheld thy faded fame
Since i exulting grafp'd the tuneful fhell:
Eager through endlefs years to found thy name,
Proud that my memory with thine fhould dwell.
How haft thou ftain'd the fplendor of my choice!
Thofe godlike forms which hover'd round thy voice,
Laws, freedom, glory, whither are they flown?
What can I now of thee to time report,
Save thy fond country made thy impious fport,
Her fortune and her hope the victims of thy own?

II.

There are with eyes unmov'd and recklefs heart
Who faw thee from thy fummit fall thus low,
Who deem'd thy arm extended but to dart
The public vengeance on thy private foe.
But, fpite of every glofs of envious minds,
The owl-ey'd race whom virtue's luftre blinds,

Who

Who fagely prove that each man hath his price,
I ftill believ'd thy aim from blemifh free,
I yet, even yet, believe it, fpite of thee
And all thy painted pleas to greatnefs and to vice.

III.

" Thou didft not dream of liberty decay'd,
" Nor wifh to make her guardian laws more ftrong:
" But the rafh many, firft by thee mifled,
" Bore thee at length unwillingly along."
Rife from your fad abodes, ye curft of old
For faith deferted or for cities fold,
Own here one untry'd, unexampled, deed;
One myftery of fhame from Curio learn,
To beg the infamy he did not earn,
And fcape in guilt's difguife from virtue's offer'd meed.

IV.

For faw we not that dangerous power avow'd
Whom freedom oft hath found her mortal bane,
Whom public wifdom ever ftrove to exclude,
And but with blufhes fuffereth in her train?
Corruption vaunted her bewitching fpoils,
O'er court, o'er fenate, fpread in pomp her toils,
And called herfelf the ftates directing foul:
Till Curio, like a good magician, try'd
With eloquence and reafon at his fide,
By ftrength of holier fpells the inchantrefs to controul.

V. Soon

V.

Soon with thy country's hope thy fame extends:
The refcu'd merchant oft thy words refounds:
Thee and thy caufe the rural hearth defends:
His bowl to thee the grateful failor crowns:
The learn'd reclufe, with awful zeal who read
Of Grecian heroes, Roman patriots dead,
Now with like awe doth living merit fcan:
While he, whom virtue in his bleft retreat
Bade focial eafe and public paffions meet,
Afcends the civil fcene, and knows to be a man.

VI.

At length in view the glorious end appear'd:
We faw thy fpirit thro' the fenate reign;
And freedom's friends thy inftant omen heard
Of laws for which their fathers bled in vain.
Wak'd in the ftrife the public Genius rofe
More keen, more ardent from his long repofe:
Deep through her bounds the city felt his call:
Each crouded haunt was ftirr'd beneath his power,
And murmuring challeng'd the deciding hour
Of that too vaft event, the hope and dread of all.

VII.

O ye good powers who look on human kind,
Inftruct the mighty moments as they rowl;
And watch the fleeting fhapes in Curio's mind,
And fteer his paffions fteady to the goal.

O Alfred,

O Alfred, father of the Englifh name,
O valiant Edward, firft in civil fame,
O William, height of public virtue pure,
Bend from your radiant feats a joyful eye
Behold the fum of all your labors nigh,
Your plans of law complete, your ends of rule fecure.

VIII.

'Twas then—O fhame! O foul from faith eftrang'd!
O Albion oft to flattering vows a prey!
'Twas then—Thy thought what fudden frenzy chang'd?
What rufhing palfy took thy ftrength away?
Is this the man in freedom's caufe approv'd?
The man fo great, fo honour'd, fo belov'd?
Whom the dead envy'd and the living blefs'd?
This patient flave by tinfel bonds allur'd?
This wretched fuitor for a boon abjur'd?
Whom thofe that fear'd him, fcorn; that trufted him, deteft?

IX.

O loft alike to action and repofe!
With all that habit of familiar fame,
Sold to the mockery of relentlefs foes,
And doom'd to exhauft the dregs of life in fhame,
To act with burning brow and throbbing heart
A poor deferter's dull exploded part,

To

To flight the favor thou canft hope no more,
　Renounce the giddy croud, the vulgar wind,
　Charge thy own lightnefs on thy country's mind,
And from her voice appeal to each tame foreign fhore.

X.

But England's fons, to purchafe thence applaufe,
　Shall ne'er the loyalty of flaves pretend,
　By courtly paffions try the public caufe;
Nor to the forms of rule betray the end.
O race erect! by manlieft paffions mov'd,
The labors which to virtue ftand approv'd,
Prompt with a lover's fondnefs to furvey;
Yet, where injuftice works her wilful claim,
Fierce as the flight of Jove's deftroying flame,
Impatient to confront, and dreadful to repay.

XI.

Thefe thy heart owns no longer.　In their room
　See the grave queen of pageants, Honor, dwell
　Couch'd in thy bofom's deep tempeftuous gloom
Like fome grim idol in a forcerer's cell.
Before her rites thy fickening reafon flew,
Divine perfuafion from thy tongue withdrew,
While laughter mock'd, or pity ftole a figh:
Can wit her tender movements rightly frame
Where the prime function of the foul is lame?
Can fancy's feeble fprings the force of truth fupply?

XII. But

XII.

But come: 'tis time: ftrong deftiny impends
To fhut thee from the joys thou haft betray'd :
With princes. fill'd, the folemn fane afcends,
By Infamy, the mindful demon fway'd.
There vengeful vows for guardian laws effac'd,
From nations fetter'd, and from towns laid wafte,
For ever through the fpacious courts refound :
There long pofterity's united groan
And the fad charge of horrors not their own,
Affail the giant chiefs, and prefs them to the ground.

XIII.

In fight old Time, imperious judge, awaits :.
Above revenge, or fear, or pity, juft,
He urgeth onward to thofe guilty gates
The Great, the Sage, the Happy, and Auguft.
And ftill he afks them of the hidden plan
Whence every treaty, every war began,
Evolves their fecrets and their guilt proclaims : ·
And ftill his hands defpoil them on the road
Of each vain wreath by lying bards beftow'd,
And crufh their trophies huge, and rafe their fculptur'd names.

XIV.

Ye mighty fhades, arife, give place, attend : ·
Here his eternal manfion Curio feeks :
—Low doth proud Wentworth to the ftranger bend,
And his dire welcome hardy Clifford fpeaks :

" He comes, whom fate with furer arts prepar'd
" To accomplifh all which we but vainly dar'd;
" Whom o'er the ftubborn herd fhe taught to reign:
" Who footh'd with gaudy dreams their raging power
" Even to it's laft irrevocable hour;
" Then baffled their rude ftrength, and broke them to the chain."

XV.

But ye, whom yet wife liberty infpires,
Whom for her champions o'er the world fhe claims,
(That houfehold godhead whom of old your fires
Sought in the woods of Elbe and bore to Thames)
Drive ye this hoftile omen far away;
Their own fell efforts on her foes repay;
Your wealth, your arts, your fame, be her's alone:
Still gird your fwords to combat on her fide;
Still frame your laws her generous teft to abide;
And win to her defence the altar and the throne.

XVI.

Protect her from yourfelves, ere yet the flood
Of golden luxury, which commerce pours,
Hath fpread that felfifh fiercenefs through your blood,
Which not her lighteft difcipline indures:
Snatch from fantaftic demagogues her caufe:
Dream not of Numa's manners, Plato's laws:
A wifer founder, and a nobler plan,
O fons of Alfred, were for you affign'd:
Bring to that birthright but an equal mind,
And no fublimer lot will fate referve for man.

O D E X.

T O T H E M U S E.

I.

QUEEN of my fongs, harmonious maid,
Ah why haft thou withdrawn thy aid?
Ah why forfaken thus my breaft
With inaufpicious damps opprefs'd?
Where is the dread prophetic heat,
With which my bofom wont to beat?
Where all the bright myfterious dreams
Of haunted groves and tuneful ftreams,
That woo'd my genius to divineft themes?

II.

Say, goddefs, can the feftal board,
Or young Olympia's form ador'd;
Say, can the pomp of promis'd fame
Relume thy faint, thy dying flame?

Or

Or have melodious airs the power
To give one free, poetic hour?
Or, from amid the Elyſian train,
The ſoul of Milton ſhall i gain,
To win thee back with ſome celeſtial ſtrain?

III.

O powerful ſtrain! o ſacred ſoul!
His numbers every ſenſe controul:
And now again my boſom burns;
The Muſe, the Muſe herſelf returns.
Such on the banks of Tyne, confeſs'd,
I hail'd the fair immortal gueſt,
When firſt ſhe ſeal'd me for her own,
Made all her blifsful treaſures known,
And bade me ſwear to follow Her alone.

O D E

ON LOVE, TO A FRIEND.

I.

No, foolifh youth — To virtuous fame
If now thy early hopes be vow'd,
If true ambition's nobler flame
Command thy footfteps from the croud,
Lean not to love's inchanting fnare;
His fongs, his words, his looks beware,
Nor join his votaries, the young and fair.

II.

By thought, by dangers, and by toils,
The wreath of juft renown is worn;
Nor will ambition's awful fpoils
The flowery pomp of eafe adorn:
But love unbends the force of thought;
By love unmanly fears are taught;
And love's reward with gaudy floth is bought.

III. Yet

III.

Yet thou haft read in tuneful lays,
And heard from many a zealous breaft,
The pleafing tale of beauty's praife
In wifdom's lofty language drefs'd;
Of beauty powerful to impart
Each finer fenfe, each comelier art,
And footh and polifh man's ungentle heart.

IV.

If then, from love's deceit fecure,
Thus far alone thy wifhes tend,
Go; fee the white-wing'd evening hour
On Delia's vernal walk defcend:
Go, while the golden light ferene,
The grove, the lawn, the foften'd fcene
Becomes the prefence of the rural queen.

V.

Attend, while that harmonious tongue
Each bofom, each defire commands:
Apollo's lute by Hermes ftrung
And touch'd by chafte Minerva's hands,
Attend. I feel a force divine,
O Delia, win my thoughts to thine;
That half the color of thy life is mine.

VI. Yet

VI.

Yet confcious of the dangerous charm,
Soon would i turn my fteps away;
Nor oft provoke the lovely harm,
Nor lull my reafon's watchful fway.
But thou, my friend—i hear thy fighs:
Alafs, i read thy downcaft eyes;
And thy tongue falters; and thy color flies.

VII.

So foon again to meet the fair?
So penfive all this abfent hour?
—O yet, unlucky youth, beware,
While yet to think is in thy power.
In vain with friendfhip's flattering name
Thy paffion veils its inward fhame;
Friendfhip, the treacherous fuel of thy flame!

VIII.

Once, i remember, new to love,
And dreading his tyrannic chain,
I fought a gentle maid to prove
What peaceful joys in friendfhip reign:
Whence we forfooth might fafely ftand,
And pitying view the lovefick band,
And mock the winged boy's malicious hand.

IX. Thus

IX.

Thus frequent pafs'd the cloudlefs day,
To fmiles and fweet difcourfe refign'd ;
While i exulted to furvey
One generous woman's real mind :
Till friendfhip foon my languid breaft
Each night with unknown cares poffefs'd,
Dafh'd my coy flumbers, or my dreams diftrefs'd.

X.

Fool that i was——And now, even now
While thus i preach the Stoic ftrain,
Unlefs i fhun Olympia's view,
An hour unfays it all again.
O friend !—when love directs her eyes
To pierce where every paffion lies,
Where is the firm, the cautious, or the wife ?

O D E

O D E XII.

TO SIR FRANCIS HENRY DRAKE, BARONET.

I.

BEHOLD; the Balance in the fky
Swift on the wintry fcale inclines :
To earthy caves the Dryads fly,
And the bare paftures Pan refigns.
Late did the farmer's fork o'erfpread
With recent foil the twice-mown mead,
Tainting the bloom which autumn knows :
He whets the rufty coulter now,
He binds his oxen to the plough,
And wide his future harveft throws.

II.

Now, London's bufy confines round,
By Kenfington's imperial towers,
From Highgate's rough defcent profound,
Eflexian heaths, or Kentifh bowers,
Where'er i pafs, i fee approach
Some rural ftatefman's eager coach

L l

Hurried

Hurried by fenatorial cares:
While rural nymphs (alike, within,
Afpiring courtly praife to win)
Debate their drefs, reform their airs.

III.

Say, what can now the country boaft,
O Drake, thy footfteps to detain,
When peevifh winds and gloomy froft
The funfhine of the temper ftain?
Say, are the priefts of Devon grown
Friends to this tolerating throne,
Champions for George's legal right?
Have general freedom, equal law,
Won to the glory of Naffau
Each bold Weffexian fquire and knight?

IV.

I doubt it much; and guefs at leaft
That when the day, which made us free,
Shall next return, that facred feaft
Thou better may'ft obferve with me.
With me the fulphurous treafon old
A far inferior part fhall hold
In that glad day's triumphal ftrain;
And generous William be rever'd,
Nor one untimely accent heard
Of James or his ignoble reign.

V. Then,

V.

Then, while the Gafcon's fragrant wine
With modeft cups our joy fupplies,
We'll truly thank the power divine
Who bade the chief, the patriot rife;
Rife from heroic eafe (the fpoil
Due, for his youth's Herculean toil,
From Belgium to her favior fon)
Rife with the fame unconquer'd zeal
For our Britannia's injur'd weal,
Her laws defac'd, her fhrines o'erthrown.

VI.

He came.   The tyrant from our fhore,
Like a forbidden demon, fled;
And to eternal exile bore
Pontific rage and vaffal dread.
There funk the mouldering Gothic reign:
New years came forth, a liberal train,
Call'd by the people's great decree.
That day, my friend, let bleffings crown:
—Fill, to the demigod's renown
From whom thou haft that thou art free.

VII.

Then, Drake, (for wherefore fhould we part
The public and the private weal?)
In vows to her who fways thy heart,
Fair health, glad fortune, will we deal.

L l 2

Whether

Whether Aglaia's blooming cheek,
Or the soft ornaments that speak
So eloquent in Daphne's smile,
Whether the piercing lights that fly
From the dark heaven of Myrto's eye,
Haply thy fancy then beguile.

VIII.

For so it is. thy stubborn breast,
Though touch'd by many a flighter wound,
Hath no full conquest yet confess'd,
Nor the one fatal charmer found.
While i, a true and loyal swain,
My fair Olympia's gentle reign
Through all the varying seasons own.
Her genius still my bosom warms:
No other maid for me hath charms,
Or i have eyes for her alone.

ODE

O D E XIII.

ON LYRIC POETRY.

I. 1.

ONCE more i join the Thespian choir,
And taste the inspiring fount again :
O parent of the Grecian lyre,
Admit me to thy powerful strain—
And lo, with ease my step invades
The pathless vale and opening shades,
Till now i spy her verdant seat ;
And now at large i drink the sound,
While these her offspring, listening round,
By turns her melody repeat.

I. 2.

I see Anacreon smile and sing,
His silver tresses breathe perfume ;
His cheek displays a second spring
Of roses taught by wine to bloom.
Away, deceitful cares, away,
And let me listen to his lay ;

Let

Let me the wanton pomp injoy,
While in smooth dance the light-wing'd Hours
Lead round his lyre it's patron powers,
Kind laughter and convivial joy.

I. 3.

Broke from the fetters of his native land,
Devoting shame and vengeance to her lords,
With louder impulse and a threatening hand
The * Lesbian patriot smites the founding chords:
　　Ye wretches, ye perfidious train,
　　Ye curs'd of gods and freeborn men,
　　　Ye murderers of the laws,
　　Though now ye glory in your lust,
　Though now ye tread the feeble neck in dust,
Yet Time and righteous Jove will judge your dreadful cause.

II. 1.

But lo, to Sappho's melting airs
Descends the radiant queen of love :
She smiles, and asks what fonder cares
Her suppliant's plaintive measures move :
Why is my faithful maid distress'd ?
Who, Sappho, wounds thy tender breast ?
Say, flies he ?——Soon he shall pursue :
Shuns he thy gifts——He soon shall give :
Slights he thy sorrows ?——He shall grieve,
And soon to all thy wishes bow.

　　　　　　* Alcæus.

II. 2.

But, o Melpomene, for whom
Awakes thy golden fhell again?
What mortal breath fhall e'er prefume
To echo that unbounded ftrain?
Majeftic in the frown of years,
Behold, the * man of Thebes appears:
For fome there are, whofe mighty frame
The hand of Jove at birth indow'd
With hopes that mock the gazing crowd;
As eagles drink the noontide flame,

II. 3.

While the dim raven beats her weary wings,
And clamours far below.—Propitious Mufe,
While i fo late unlock thy purer fprings,
And breathe whate'er thy ancient airs infufe,
  Wilt thou for Albion's fons around
  (Ne'er had'ft thou audience more renown'd)
    Thy charming arts imploy,
  As when the winds from fhore to fhore
Through Greece thy lyre's perfuafive language bore,
Till towns and ifles and feas return'd the vocal joy?

III. 1.

Yet then did pleafure's lawlefs throng,
Oft rufhing forth in loofe attire,
Thy virgin dance, thy graceful fong
Pollute with impious revels dire.

* Pindar.

O fair,

O fair, o chaste, thy echoing shade
May no foul discord here invade:
Nor let thy strings one accent move,
Except what earth's untroubled ear
'Mid all her social tribes may hear,
And heaven's unerring throne approve.

III. 2.

Queen of the lyre, in thy retreat
The fairest flowers of Pindus glow;
The vine aspires to crown thy seat,
And myrtles round thy laurel grow.
Thy strings adapt their varied strain
To every pleasure, every pain,
Which mortal tribes were born to prove;
And strait our passions rise or fall,
As at the wind's imperious call
The ocean swells, the billows move.

III. 3.

When midnight listens o'er the slumbering earth,
Let me, o Muse, thy solemn whispers hear:
When morning sends her fragrant breezes forth,
With airy murmurs touch my opening ear.
    And ever watchful at thy side,
    Let wisdom's awful suffrage guide
        The tenor of thy lay:
To her of old by Jove was given
To judge the various deeds of earth and heaven;
'Twas thine by gentle arts to win us to her sway.

IV. 1.

Oft as, to well-earn'd eafe refign'd,
I quit the maze where fcience toils,
Do thou refrefh my yielding mind
With all thy gay, delufive fpoils.
But, o indulgent, come not nigh
The bufy fteps, the jealous eye
Of wealthy care or gainful age;
Whofe barren fouls thy joys difdain,
And hold as foes to reafon's reign
Whome'er thy lovely works ingage.

IV. 2.

When friendfhip and when letter'd mirth
Haply partake my fimple board,
Then let thy blamelefs hand call forth
The mufic of the Teian chord.
Or if invok'd at fofter hours,
O! feek with me the happy bowers
That hear Olympia's gentle tongue;
To beauty link'd with virtue's train,
To love devoid of jealous pain,
There let the Sapphic lute be ftrung.

IV. 3.

But when from envy and from death to claim
A hero bleeding for his native land;
When to throw incenfe on the veftal flame
Of liberty my genius gives command,

M m

Nor

Nor Theban voice nor Lesbian lyre
From thee, o Muse, do i require ;
     While my presaging mind,
Conscious of powers she never knew,
Astonish'd grasps at things beyond her view,
Nor by another's fate submits to be confin'd.

O D E   XIV.

TO THE HONOURABLE CHARLES TOWNSHEND:

FROM THE COUNTRY.

I.

Say, Townshend, what can London boast
To pay thee for the pleasures lost,
     The health to-day resign'd,
When spring from this her favorite seat
Bade winter hasten his retreat,
     And met the western wind.

II. Oh

II.

Oh knew'ſt thou how the balmy air,
The ſun, the azure heavens prepare
   To heal thy languid frame,
No more would noiſy courts ingage;
In vain would lying faction's rage
   Thy ſacred leiſure claim.

III.

Oft i look'd forth, and oft admir'd;
Till with the ſtudious volume tir'd
   I ſought the open day;
And, ſure, i cry'd, the rural gods
Expect me in their green abodes,
   And chide my tardy lay.

IV.

But ah in vain my reſtleſs feet
Trac'd every ſilent ſhady ſeat
   Which knew their forms of old:
Nor Naiad by her fountain laid,
Nor Wood-nymph tripping through her glade,
   Did now their rites unfold:

M m 2V. Whether

V.

Whether to nurfe fome infant oak
They turn the flowly-tinkling brook
   And catch the pearly fhowers,
Or brufh the mildew from the woods,
Or paint with noontide beams the buds,
   Or breathe on opening flowers.

VI.

Such rites, which they with fpring renew,
The eyes of care can never view;
   And care hath long been mine:
And hence offended with their gueft,
Since grief of love my foul opprefs'd,
   They hide their toils divine.

VII.

But foon fhall thy inlivening tongue
This heart, by dear affliction wrung,
   With noble hope infpire:
Then will the fylvan powers again
Receive me in their genial train,
   And liften to my lyre.

VIII. Beneath

VIII.

Beneath yon Dryad's lonely ſhade
A ruſtic altar ſhall be paid,
  Of turf with laurel fram'd :
And thou the inſcription wilt approve ;
" This for the peace which, loſt by love,
  " By friendſhip was reclaim'd."

O D E   XV.

T O T H E E V E N I N G - S T A R.

I.

To-NIGHT retir'd the queen of heaven
  With young Endymion ſtays :
And now to Heſper is it given
Awhile to rule the vacant ſky,
Till ſhe ſhall to her lamp ſupply
  A ſtream of brighter rays.

II. O Heſper,

II.

O Hefper, while the ftarry throng
   With awe thy path furrounds,
Oh liften to my fuppliant fong,
If haply now the vocal fphere
Can fuffer thy delighted ear
   To ftoop to mortal founds.

III.

So may the bridegroom's genial ftrain
   Thee ftill invoke to fhine :
So may the bride's unmarried train
To Hymen chaunt their flattering vow,
Still that his lucky torch may glow
   With luftre pure as thine.

IV.

Far other vows muft i prefer
   To thy indulgent power.
Alafs, but now i paid my tear
On fair Olympia's virgin tomb :
And lo, from thence, in queft i roam
   Of Philomela's bower.

V. Propitious

V.

Propitious fend thy golden ray,
   Thou pureft light above:
Let no falfe flame feduce to ftray
Where gulph or fteep lie hid for harm:
But lead where mufic's healing charm
   May footh afflicted love.

VI.

To them, by many a grateful fong
   In happier feafons vow'd,
Thefe lawns, Olympia's haunt, belong:
Oft by yon filver ftream we walk'd,
Or fix'd, while Philomela talk'd,
   Beneath yon copfes ftood.

VII.

Nor feldom, where the beachen boughs
   That rooflefs tower invade,
We came while her inchanting Mufe
The radiant moon above us held:
Till by a clamorous owl compell'd
   She fled the folemn fhade.

VIII. But

VIII.

But hark ; i hear her liquid tone.
   Now, Hefper, guide my feet
Down the red marle with mofs o'ergrown,
Through yon wild thicket next the plain,
Whofe hawthorns choke the winding lane
   Which leads to her retreat.

IX.

See the green fpace : on either hand
   Inlarg'd it fpreads around :
See, in the midft fhe takes her ftand,
Where one old oak his awful fhade
Extends o'er half the level mead
   Inclos'd in woods profound.

X.

Hark, how through many a melting note
   She now prolongs her lays :
How fweetly down the void they float !
The breeze their magic path attends :
The ftars fhine out : the foreft bends :
   The wakeful heifers gaze.

XI. Whoe'er

XI.

Whoe'er thou art whom chance may bring
   To this fequefter'd fpot,
If then the plaintive Syren fing,
Oh foftly tread beneath her bower,
And think of heaven's difpofing power,
   Of man's uncertain lot.

XII.

Oh think, o'er all this mortal ftage,
   What mournful fcenes arife :
What ruin waits on kingly rage :
How often virtue dwells with woe :
How many griefs from knowledge flow :
   How fwiftly pleafure flies.

XIII.

O facred bird, let me at eve,
   Thus wandering all alone,
Thy tender counfel oft receive,
Bear witnefs to thy penfive airs,
And pity nature's common cares
   Till i forget my own.

N n   O D E

O D E   XVI.

T O   C A L E B   H A R D I N G E,   M. D.

I.

WITH ſordid floods the wintry * Urn
Hath ſtain'd fair Richmond's level green:
Her naked hill the Dryads mourn,
No longer a poetic ſcene.
No longer there thy raptur'd eye
The beauteous forms of earth or ſky
Surveys as in their Author's mind:
And London ſhelters from the year
Thoſe whom thy ſocial hours to ſhare
    The Attic Muſe deſign'd.

II.

From Hampſtead's airy ſummit me
Her gueſt the city ſhall behold,
What day the people's ſtern decree
To unbelieving kings is told,
When common men (the dread of fame)
Adjudg'd as one of evil name,

* Aquarius.

Before

Before the fun, the anointed head.
Then feek thou too the pious town,
With no unworthy cares to crown
That evening's awful fhade.

III.

Deem not i call thee to deplore
The facred martyr of the day,
By faft and penitential lore
To purge our ancient guilt away.
For this, on humble faith i reft
That ftill our advocate, the prieft,
From heavenly wrath will fave the land ;
Nor afk what rites our pardon gain,
Nor how his potent founds reftrain
The thunderer's lifted hand.

IV.

No, Hardinge: peace to church and ftate !
That evening, let the Mufe give law :
While i anew the theme relate
Which my firft youth inamor'd faw.
Then will i oft explore thy thought,
What to rejeft which Locke hath taught,
What to purfue in Virgil's lay :
Till hope afcends to loftieft things,
Nor envies demagogues or kings
Their frail and vulgar fway.

N n 2

V. O vers'd

V.

O vers'd in all the human frame,
Lead thou where'er my labor lies,
And Englifh fancy's eager flame
To Grecian purity chaftize :
While hand in hand, at wifdom's fhrine,
Beauty with truth i ftrive to join,
And grave affent with glad applaufe ;
To paint the ftory of the foul,
And Plato's vifions to controul
　　By * Verulamian laws.

* Verulam gave one of his titles to Francis Bacon, author of the Novum Organum.

O D E XVII.

ON A SERMON AGAINST GLORY.

MDCCXLVII.

I.

COME then, tell me, fage divine,
Is it an offence to own
That our bofoms e'er incline
Toward immortal glory's throne ?

For

For with me nor pomp, nor pleaſure,
Bourbon's might, Braganza's treaſure,
So can fancy's dream rejoice,
So conciliate reaſon's choice,
As one approving word of her impartial voice.

II.

If to ſpurn at noble praiſe
Be the paſs-port to thy heaven,
Follow thou thoſe gloomy ways;
No ſuch law to me was given,
Nor, i truſt, ſhall i deplore me
Faring like my friends before me;
Nor an holier place deſire
Than Timoleon's arms acquire,
And Tully's curule chair, and Milton's golden lyre.

ODE

O D E   XVIII.

TO THE RIGHT HONOURABLE

FRANCIS EARL OF HUNTINGDON.

MDCCXLVII.

I. 1.

THE wife and great of every clime,
Through all the fpacious walks of Time,
Where'er the Mufe her power difplay'd,
With joy have liften'd and obey'd.
For taught of heaven, the facred Nine
Perfuafive numbers, forms divine,
    To mortal fenfe impart:
They beft the foul with glory fire;
They nobleft counfels, boldeft deeds infpire;
And high o'er Fortune's rage inthrone the fixed heart.

I. 2.

Nor lefs prevailing is their charm
The vengeful bofom to difarm;
To melt the proud with human woe,
And prompt unwilling tears to flow.

Can

Can wealth a power like this afford?
Can Cromwell's arts, or Marlborough's fword,
  An equal empire claim?
No, Haftings.   Thou my words wilt own:
Thy breaft the gifts of every Mufe hath known;
Nor fhall the giver's love difgrace thy noble name.

I. 3.

  The Mufe's awful art,
And the bleft function of the poet's tongue,
  Ne'er fhalt thou blufh to honour; to affert
From all that fcorned vice or flavifh fear hath fung,
  Nor fhall the blandifhment of Tufcan ftrings
Warbling at will in pleafure's myrtle bower;
  Nor fhall the fervile notes to Celtic kings
By flattering minftrels paid in evil hour,
Move thee to fpurn the heavenly Mufe's reign.
  A different ftrain,
  And other themes
From her prophetic fhades and hallow'd ftreams
(Thou well can'ft witnefs) meet the purged ear:
Such, as when Greece to her immortal fhell
Rejoicing liften'd, godlike founds to hear;
  To hear the fweet inftructrefs tell
  (While men and heroes throng'd around)
  How life its nobleft ufe may find,
  How well for freedom be refign'd;
And how, by glory, virtue fhall be crown'd.

II. 1.

Such was the Chian father's ſtrain
To many a kind domeſtic train,
Whoſe pious hearth and genial bowl
Had chear'd the reverend pilgrim's ſoul:
When, every hoſpitable rite
With equal bounty to requite,
  He ſtruck his magic ſtrings;
And pour'd ſpontaneous numbers forth,
And ſeiz'd their ears with tales of ancient worth,
And fill'd their muſing hearts with vaſt heroic things.

II. 2.

Now oft, where happy ſpirits dwell,
Where yet he tunes his charming ſhell,
Oft near him, with applauding hands,
The genius of his country ſtands.
To liſtening gods he makes him known,
That man divine, by whom were ſown
  The ſeeds of Grecian fame:
Who firſt the race with freedom fir'd;
From whom Lycurgus Sparta's ſons inſpir'd;
From whom Platæan palms and Cyprian trophies came.

II. 3.

  O nobleſt, happieſt age!
When Ariſtides rul'd, and Cimon fought;
When all the generous fruits of Homer's page
Exulting Pindar ſaw to full perfection bought.

O Pindar,

O Pindar, oft fhalt thou be hail'd of me :
Not that Apollo fed thee from his fhrine ;
Not that thy lips drank fweetnefs from the bee ;
Nor yet that, ftudious of thy notes divine,
Pan danc'd their meafure with the fylvan throng :
   But that thy fong
   Was proud to unfold
What thy bafe rulers trembled to behold ;
Amid corrupted Thebes was proud to tell
The deeds of Athens and the Perfian fhame :
Hence on thy head their impious vengeance fell.
  But thou, o faithful to thy fame,
  The Mufe's law did'ft rightly know ;
  That who would animate his lays,
  And other minds to virtue raife,
Muft feel his own with all her fpirit glow.
   III. 1.
  Are there, approv'd of later times,
  Whofe verfe adorn'd a * tyrant's crimes ?
  Who faw majeftic Rome betray'd,
  And lent the imperial ruffian aid ?
  Alas ! not one polluted bard,
  No, not the ftrains that Mincius heard,
   Or Tibur's hills reply'd,
  Dare to the Mufe's ear afpire ;
Save that, inftructed by the Grecian lyre,
With freedom's ancient notes their fhameful tafk they hide.
   * Octavianus Cæfar.
   O o   III. 2. Mark

III. 2.

Mark, how the dread Pantheon ſtands,

Amid the domes of modern hands:

Amid the toys of idle ſtate,

How ſimply, how ſeverely great!

Then turn, and, while each weſtern clime

Preſents her tuneful ſons to Time,

So mark thou Milton's name;

And add, " Thus differs from the throng

" The ſpirit which inform'd thy awful ſong,

" Which bade thy potent voice protect thy country's fame."

III. 3.

Yet hence barbaric zeal

His memory with unholy rage purſues;

While from theſe arduous cares of public weal

She bids each bard begone, and reſt him with his Muſe.

O fool! to think the man, whoſe ample mind

Muſt graſp at all that yonder ſtars ſurvey;

Muſt join the nobleſt forms of every kind,

The world's moſt perfect image to diſplay,

Can e'er his country's majeſty behold,

Unmov'd or cold!

O fool! to deem

That he, whoſe thought muſt viſit every theme,

Whoſe

Whose heart muſt every ſtrong emotion know
Inſpir'd by nature, or by fortune taught;
That he, if haply ſome preſumptuous foe,
    With falſe ignoble ſcience fraught,
    Shall ſpurn at freedom's faithful band;
    That he their dear defence will ſhun,
    Or hide their glories from the ſun,
Or deal their vengeance with a woman's hand!

IV. 1.

 I care not that in Arno's plain,
    Or on the ſportive banks of Seine,
    From public themes the Muſe's quire
    Content with poliſh'd eaſe retire.
    Where prieſts the ſtudious head command,
    Where tyrants bow the warlike hand
            To vile ambition's aim,
    Say, what can public themes afford,
Save venal honors to an hateful lord,
Reſerv'd for angry heaven and ſcorn'd of honeſt fame?

IV. 2.

    But here, where freedom's equal throne
    To all her valiant ſons is known;
    Where all are conſcious of her cares,
    And each the power, that rules him, ſhares;
                O o 2   Here

Here let the bard, whose daftard tongue
Leaves public arguments unfung,
Bid public praife farewell :
Let him to fitter climes remove,
Far from the hero's and the patriot's love,
And lull myfterious monks to flumber in their cell.

IV.　3.

O Haftings, not to all.
Can ruling heaven the fame endowments lend :.
Yet ftill doth nature to her offspring call,.
That to one general weal their different powers they bend,.
Unenvious.　Thus alone, though ftrains divine
Inform the bofom of the Mufe's fon ;.
Though with new honors the patrician's line
Advance from age to age ; yet thus alone.
They win the fuffrage of impartial fame..

The poet's name
He beft fhall prove,.
Whofe lays the foul with nobleft paffions move.
But thee, o progeny of heroes old,
Thee to feverer toils thy fate requires :·
The fate which form'd thee in a chofen mould,
The grateful country of thy fires,.
Thee to fublimer paths demand ;
Sublimer than thy fires could trace,.
Or thy own Edward teach his race,
Though Gaul's proud genius fank beneath his hand.

V. 1.

From rich domains and subject farms,
They led the rustic youth to arms;
And kings their stern atchievements fear'd;
While private strife their banners rear'd.
But loftier scenes to thee are shown,
Where empire's wide-establish'd throne.
    No private master fills:
Where, long foretold, the People reigns:
Where each a vassal's humble heart disdains;
And judgeth what he sees; and, as he judgeth, wills.

V. 2.

Here be it thine to calm and guide
The swelling democratic tide;
To watch the state's uncertain frame,
And baffle faction's partial aim:
But chiefly, with determin'd zeal,
To quell that servile band, who kneel
    To freedom's banish'd foes;
That monster, which is daily found
Expert and bold thy country's peace to wound;
Yet dreads to handle arms, nor manly counsel knows.

V. 3. 'Tis

V. 3.

'Tis higheſt heaven's command,
That guilty aims ſhould ſordid paths purſue;
That what enſnares the heart ſhould maim the hand,
And virtue's worthleſs foes be falſe to glory too.
But look on freedom.　ſee, through every age,
What labours, perils, griefs, hath ſhe diſdain'd!
What arms, what regal pride, what prieſtly rage,
Have her dread offspring conquer'd or ſuſtain'd!
For Albion well have conquer'd.　Let the ſtrains
　　　　Of happy ſwains,
　　　　Which now reſound
Where Scarſdale's cliffs the ſwelling paſtures bound,
Bear witneſs.　there, oft let the farmer hail
The ſacred orchard which imbowers his gate,
And ſhew to ſtrangers paſſing down the vale,
　　Where Candiſh, Booth, and Oſborne ſate;
　　When burſting from their country's chain,
　　Even in the midſt of deadly harms,
　　Of papal ſnares and lawleſs arms,
They plann'd for freedom this her nobleſt reign.

VI. 2.

　　This reign, theſe laws, this public care,
　　Which Naſſau gave us all to ſhare,
　　Had ne'er adorn'd the Engliſh name,
　　Could fear have ſilenc'd freedom's claim.

But

But fear in vain attempts to bind
Thofe lofty efforts of the mind
    Which focial good infpires;
Where men, for this, affault a throne,
Each adds the common welfare to his own;
And each unconquer'd heart the ftrength of all acquires.

VI. 2.

Say, was it thus, when late we view'd
Our fields in civil blood imbru'd?
When fortune crown'd the barbarous hoft,
And half the aftonifh'd ifle was loft?
Did one of all that vaunting train,
Who dare affront a peaceful reign,
    Durft one in arms appear?
Durft one in counfels pledge his life?
Stake his luxurious fortunes in the ftrife?
Or lend his boafted name his vagrant friends to chear?

VI. 3.

    Yet, Haftings, thefe are they
Who challenge to themfelves thy country's love;
The true; the conftant: who alone can weigh,
What glory fhould demand, or liberty approve!
But let their works declare them. Thy free powers,
The generous powers of thy prevailing mind,
Not for the tafks of their confederate hours,
Lewd brawls and lurking flander, were defign'd.

Be

Be thou thy own approver. Honeſt praiſe
        Oft nobly ſways
        Ingenuous youth :
But, ſought from cowards and the lying mouth,
Praiſe is reproach. Eternal God alone
For mortals fixeth that ſublime award.
He, from the faithful records of his throne,
   Bids the hiſtorian and the bard
   Diſpoſe of honor and of ſcorn ;
   Diſcern the patriot from the ſlave ;
   And write the good, the wiſe, the brave,
For leſſons to the multitude unborn.

THE END OF BOOK THE FIRST.

O D E S,

ODES, BOOK THE SECOND.

O D E I.

THE REMONSTRANCE OF SHAKESPEARE:

Suppofed to have been fpoken at the Theatre Royal, while the
French Comedians were acting by Subfcription.

M D C C X L I X.

IF, yet regardful of your native land,
Old Shakefpeare's tongue you deign to underftand,
Lo, from the blifsful bowers where heaven rewards
Inftructive fages and unblemifh'd bards,
I come, the ancient founder of the ftage,
Intent to learn, in this difcerning age,
What form of wit your fancies have imbrac'd,
And whither tends your elegance of tafte,
That thus at length our homely toils you fpurn,
That thus to foreign fcenes you proudly turn,

P p

That

That from my brow the laurel wreath you claim
To crown the rivals of your country's fame.
    What, though the footsteps of my devious Muse
The measur'd walks of Grecian art refuse?
Or though the franknefs of my hardy style
Mock the nice touches of the critic's file?
Yet, what my age and climate held to view,
Impartial i survey'd and fearlefs drew.
And fay, ye skillful in the human heart,
Who know to prize a poet's noblest part,
What age, what clime, could e'er an ampler field
For lofty thought, for daring fancy, yield?
I faw this England break the shameful bands
Forg'd for the fouls of men by facred hands:
I faw each groaning realm her aid implore;
Her fons the heroes of each warlike shore;
Her naval standard (the dire Spaniard's bane)
Obey'd through all the circuit of the main.
Then too great commerce, for a late-found world,
Around your coast her eager fails unfurl'd:
New hopes, new paffions, thence the bofom fir'd;
New plans, new arts, the genius thence infpir'd;
Thence every fcene, which private fortune knows,
In ftronger life, with bolder fpirit, rofe.

Difgrac'd

Difgrac'd i this full profpect which i drew?
My colours languid, or my ftrokes untrue?
Have not your fages, warriors, fwains, and kings,
Confefs'd the living draught of men and things?
What other bard in any clime appears
Alike the mafter of your fmiles and tears?
Yet have i deign'd your audience to intice
With wretched bribes to luxury and vice?
Or have my various fcenes a purpofe known
Which freedom, virtue, glory, might not own?

Such from the firft was my dramatic plan;
It fhould be your's to crown what i began:
And now that England fpurns her Gothic chain,
And equal laws and focial fcience reign,
I thought, Now furely fhall my zealous eyes
View nobler bards and jufter critics rife,
Intent with learned labour to refine
The copious ore of Albion's native mine,
Our ftately Mufe more graceful airs to teach,
And form her tongue to more attractive fpeech,
Till rival nations liften at her feet,
And own her polifh'd as they own'd her great.

But do you thus my favorite hopes fullfil?
Is France at laft the ftandard of your fkill?

P p 2

Alas

Alas for you! that so betray a mind
Of art unconscious and to beauty blind.
Say; does her language your ambition raise,
Her barren, trivial, unharmonious phrase,
Which fetters eloquence to scantiest bounds,
And maims the cadence of poetic sounds?
Say; does your humble admiration chuse
The gentle prattle of her Comic Muse,
While wits, plain-dealers, fops, and fools appear,
Charg'd to say nought but what the king may hear?
Or rather melt your sympathizing hearts
Won by her tragic scene's romantic arts,
Where old and young declaim on soft desire,
And heroes never, but for love, expire?
    No.   Though the charms of novelty, awhile,
Perhaps too fondly win your thoughtless smile,
Yet not for you design'd indulgent fate
The modes or manners of the Bourbon state.
And ill your minds my partial judgment reads,
And many an augury my hope misleads,
If the fair maids of yonder blooming train
To their light courtship would an audience deign,
Or those chaste matrons a Parisian wife
Chuse for the model of domestic life;

Or

Or if one youth of all that generous band,
The ſtrength and ſplendor of their native land,
Would yield his portion of his country's fame,
And quit old freedom's patrimonial claim,
With lying ſmiles oppreſſion's pomp to ſee,
And judge of glory by a king's decree.
    O bleſt at home with juſtly-envied laws,
O long the chiefs of Europe's general cauſe,
Whom heaven hath choſen at each dangerous hour
To check the inroads of barbaric power,
The rights of trampled nations to reclaim,
And guard the ſocial world from bonds and ſhame ;
Oh let not luxury's fantaſtic charms
Thus give the lye to your heroic arms :
Nor for the ornaments of life imbrace
Diſhoneſt leſſons from that vaunting race,
Whom fate's dread laws (for, in eternal fate
Deſpotic rule was heir to freedom's hate)
Whom in each warlike, each commercial part,
In civil counſel, and in pleaſing art,
The judge of earth predeſtin'd for your foes,
And made it fame and virtue to oppoſe.

ODE

O D E II.

T O S L E E P.

I.

THOU silent power, whose welcome sway
Charms every anxious thought away ;
In whose divine oblivion drown'd,
Sore pain and weary toil grow mild,
Love is with kinder looks beguil'd,
And grief forgets her fondly-cherish'd wound ;
Oh whither haft thou flown, indulgent god ?
God of kind shadows and of healing dews,
Whom dost thou touch with thy Lethæan rod ?
Around whose temples now thy opiate airs diffuse ?

II.

Lo, midnight from her starry reign
Looks awful down on earth and main.
The tuneful birds lie hush'd in sleep,
With all that crop the verdant food,
With all that skim the cryftal flood,
Or haunt the caverns of the rocky steep.
No rushing winds disturb the tufted bowers ;
No wakeful found the moon-light valley knows,
Save where the brook its liquid murmur pours,
And lulls the waving scene to more profound repose.

III. Oh

III.

Oh let not me alone complain,
Alone invoke thy power in vain!
Defcend, propitious, on my eyes;
Not from the couch that bears a crown,
Not from the courtly ftatefman's down,
Nor where the mifer and his treafure lies:
Bring not the fhapes that break the murderer's reft,
Nor thofe the hireling foldier loves to fee,
Nor thofe which haunt the bigot's gloomy breaft:
Far be their guilty nights, and far their dreams from me!

IV.

Nor yet thofe awful forms prefent,
For chiefs and heroes only meant:
The figur'd brafs, the choral fong,
The refcued people's glad applaufe,
The liftening fenate, and the laws
Fix'd by the counfels of * Timoleon's tongue,
Are fcenes too grand for fortune's private ways;
And though they fhine in youth's ingenuous view,
The fober gainful arts of modern days
To fuch romantic thoughts have bid a long adieu.

* After Timoleon had delivered Syracufe from the tyranny of Dionyfius, the people on every important deliberation fent for him into the public affembly, afked his advice, and voted according to it. PLUTARCH.

V.

I aſk not, god of dreams, thy care
To baniſh Love's preſentments fair:
Nor roſy cheek nor radiant eye
Can arm him with ſuch ſtrong command
That the young ſorcerer's fatal hand
Should round my ſoul his pleaſing fetters tie.
Nor yet the courtier's hope, the giving ſmile
(A lighter phantom, and a baſer chain)
Did e'er in ſlumber my proud lyre beguile
To lend the pomp of thrones her ill-according ſtrain.

VI.

But, Morpheus, on thy balmy wing
Such honorable viſions bring,
As ſooth'd great Milton's injur'd age,
When in prophetic dreams he ſaw
The race unborn with pious awe
Imbibe each virtue from his heavenly page:
Or ſuch as Mead's benignant fancy knows
When health's deep treaſures, by his art explor'd,
Have ſav'd the infant from an orphan's woes,
Or to the trembling ſire his age's hope reſtor'd.

O D E

O D E   III.

TO THE CUCKOW.

I.

O ruftic herald of the fpring,
At length in yonder woody vale
Faft by the brook i hear thee fing;
And, ftudious of thy homely tale,
Amid the vefpers of the grove,
Amid the chaunting choir of love,
   Thy fage refponfes hail.

II.

The time has been when i have frown'd
To hear thy voice the woods invade;
And while thy folemn accent drown'd
Some fweeter poet of the fhade,
Thus, thought i, thus the fons of care
Some conftant youth or generous fair
   With dull advice upbraid.

Q q

III. I faid,

III.

I faid, " While Philomela's fong
" Proclaims the paffion of the grove,
" It ill befeems a cuckow's tongue
" Her charming language to reprove"——
Alas, how much a lover's ear
Hates all the fober truth to hear,
　　The fober truth of love !

IV.

When hearts are in each other blefs'd,
When nought but lofty faith can rule
The nymph's and fwain's confenting breaft,
How cuckow-like in Cupid's fchool,
With ftore of grave prudential faws
On fortune's power and cuftom's laws,
　　Appears each friendly fool !

V.

Yet think betimes, ye gentle train
Whom love and hope and fancy fway,
Who every harfher care difdain,
Who by the morning judge the day,
Think that, in April's faireft hours,
To warbling fhades and painted flowers
　　The cuckow joins his lay.

O D E

O D E   IV.

T O

THE HONOURABLE CHARLES TOWNSHEND
IN THE COUNTRY.
M D C C L.

I. 1.

HOW oft shall i survey

This humble roof, the lawn, the greenwood shade,

The vale with sheaves o'erspread,

The glassy brook, the flocks which round thee stray?

When will thy cheerful mind

Of these have utter'd all her dear esteem?

Or, tell me, dost thou deem

No more to join in glory's toilsome race,

But here content imbrace

That happy leisure which thou had'st resign'd?

I. 2.

Alas, ye happy hours,

When books and youthful sport the soul could share,

Ere one ambitious care

Of civil life had aw'd her simpler powers;

Oft as your winged train

Revisit here my friend in white array,

Oh fail not to display

Q q 2

Each

Each fairer scene where i perchance had part,
    That so his generous heart
The abode of even friendship may remain.

I. 3.

For not imprudent of my loss to come,
I saw from contemplation's quiet cell
His feet ascending to another home
Where public praise and envied greatness dwell.
    But shall we therefore, o my lyre
    Reprove ambition's best desire?
        Extinguish glory's flame?
    Far other was the task injoin'd
When to my hand thy strings were first assign'd:
Far other faith belongs to friendship's honor'd name.

II. 1.

    Thee, Townshend, not the arms
Of slumbering ease, nor pleasure's rosy chain,
    Were destin'd to detain:
No, nor bright science, nor the Muse's charms.
    For them high heaven prepares
Their proper votaries, an humbler band:
    And ne'er would Spenser's hand
Have deign'd to strike the warbling Tuscan shell,
    Nor Harrington to tell
What habit an immortal city wears,

II. 2. Had

II. 2.

Had this been born to fhield
The caufe which Cromwell's impious hand betray'd,
Or that, like Vere, difplay'd
His redcrofs banner o'er the Belgian field.
Yet where the will divine
Hath fhut thofe loftieft paths, it next remains,
With reafon clad in ftrains
Of harmony, felected minds to infpire,
And virtue's living fire
To feed and eternize in hearts like thine.

II. 3.

For never fhall the herd, whom envy fways,
So quell my purpofe or my tongue controul,
That i fhould fear illuftrious worth to praife,
Becaufe it's mafter's friendfhip mov'd my foul.
Yet, if this undiffembling ftrain
Should now perhaps thine ear detain
With any pleafing found,
Remember thou that righteous fame
From hoary age a ftrict account will claim
Of each aufpicious palm with which thy youth was crown'd.

III. 1. Nor

III. 1.

Nor obvious is the way
Where heaven expects thee, nor the traveller leads,
   Through flowers or fragrant meads,
Or groves that hark to Philomela's lay.
   The impartial laws of fate
To nobler virtues wed feverer cares.
   Is there a man who fhares
The fummit next where heavenly natures dwell?
   Afk him (for he can tell,
What ftorms beat round that rough laborious height.

III. 2.

Ye heroes, who of old
Did generous England freedom's throne ordain;
   From Alfred's parent reign
To Naffau, great deliverer, wife and bold;
   I know your perils hard,
Your wounds, your painful marches, wintry feas,
   The night eftrang'd from eafe,
The day by cowardice and falfehood vex'd,
   The head with doubt perplex'd,
The indignant heart difdaining the reward

III. 3. Which

III. 3.

Which envy hardly grants.   But, o renown,
O praife from judging heaven and virtuous men,
If thus they purchas'd thy divineft crown,
Say, who fhall hefitate? or who complain?
    And now they fit on thrones above:
    And when among the gods they move
      Before the fovran mind,
    " Lo, thefe," he faith, " lo, thefe are they
" Who to the laws of mine eternal fway
" From violence and fear afferted human kind."

IV. 1.

    Thus honor'd while the train
Of legiflators in his prefence dwell;
    If i may aught foretell,
The ftatefman fhall the fecond palm obtain.
    For dreadful deeds of arms
Let vulgar bards, with undifcerning praife,
    More glittering trophies raife:
But wifeft heaven what deeds may chiefly move
    To favor and to love?
What, fave wide bleffings, or averted harms?

IV. 2. No1

IV. 2.

Nor to the imbattled field
Shall thefe achievements of the peaceful gown
The green immortal crown
Of valor, or the fongs of conqueft, yield.
Not Fairfax wildly bold,
While bare of creft he hew'd his fatal way,
Through Nafefby's firm array,
To heavier dangers did his breaft oppofe
Than Pym's free virtue chofe,
When the proud force of Strafford he controul'd.

IV. 3.

But what is man at enmity with truth?
What were the fruits of Wentworth's copious mind
When (blighted all the promife of his youth)
The patriot in a tyrant's league had join'd?
Let Ireland's loud-lamenting plains,
Let Tyne's and Humber's trampled fwain
Let menac'd London tell
How impious guile made wifdom bafe;
How generous zeal to cruel rage gave place;
And how unblefs'd he liv'd and how difhonor'd fell.

V. 1. Thence

V. 1.

Thence never hath the Mufe
Around his tomb Pierian rofes flung:
   Nor fhall one poet's tongue
His name for mufic's pleafing labor chufe.
   And fure, when nature kind
Hath deck'd fome favor'd breaft above the throng,
   That man with grievous wrong
Affronts and wounds his genius, if he bends
   To guilt's ignoble ends
The functions of his ill-fubmitting mind.

V. 2.

For worthy of the wife
Nothing can feem but virtue; nor earth yield
   Their fame an equal field,
Save where impartial freedom gives the prize.
   There Somers fix'd his name,
Inroll'd the next to William. there fhall Time
   To every wondering clime
Point out that Somers, who from faction's croud,
   The flanderous and the loud,
Could fair affent and modeft reverence claim.

V. 3. Nor

V. 3.

Nor aught did laws or focial arts acquire,
Nor this majeftic weal of Albion's land
Did aught accomplifh, or to aught afpire,
Without his guidance, his fuperior hand.
   And rightly fhall the Mufe's care
   Wreaths like her own for him prepare,
     Whofe mind's inamor'd aim
   Could forms of civil beauty draw
Sublime as ever fage or poet faw,
Yet ftill to life's rude fcene the proud ideas tame.

VI. 1.

   Let none profane be near !
The Mufe was never foreign to his breaft :
   On power's grave feat confefs'd,
Still to her voice he bent a lover's ear.
   And if the bleffed know
Their ancient cares, even now the unfading groves,
   Where haply Milton roves
With Spenfer, hear the inchanted echos round
   Through fartheft heaven refound
Wife Somers, guardian of their fame below.

VI. 3. He

VI. 2.

He knew, the patriot knew,
That letters and the Mufes powerful art
Exalt the ingenuous heart,
And brighten every form of juft and true.
They lend a nobler fway
To civil wifdom, than corruption's lure
Could ever yet procure :
They too from envy's pale malignant light
Conduct her forth to fight
Cloath'd in the faireft colors of the day.

VI. 3.

O Townfhend, thus may Time, the judge fevere,
Inftruct my happy tongue of thee to tell :
And when i fpeak of one to freedom dear
For planning wifely and for acting well,
Of one whom glory loves to own,
Who ftill by liberal means alone
Hath liberal ends purfu'd ;
Then, for the guerdon of my lay,
" This man with faithful friendfhip," will i fay,
" From youth to honor'd age my arts and me hath view'd."

ODE

O D E   V.

ON LOVE OF PRAISE.

I.

OF all the fprings within the mind
   Which prompt her fteps in fortune's maze,
From none more pleafing aid we find
   Than from the genuine love of praife.

II.

Nor any partial, private end
   Such reverence to the public bears;
Nor any paffion, virtue's friend,
   So like to virtue's felf appears.

III.

For who in glory can delight
   Without delight in glorious deeds?
What man a charming voice can flight,
   Who courts the echo that fucceeds?

IV. But

IV.

But not the echo on the voice
   More, than on virtue praiſe, depends;
To which, of courſe, it's real price
   The judgment of the praiſer lends.

V.

If praiſe then with religious awe
   From the ſole perfect judge be ſought,
A nobler aim, a purer law
   Nor prieſt, nor bard, nor ſage hath taught.

VI.

With which in character the ſame
   Tho' in an humbler ſphere it lies,
I count that ſoul of human fame,
   The ſuffrage of the good and wiſe.

ODE

O D E VI.

TO WILLIAM HALL, ESQUIRE:

WITH THE WORKS OF CHAULIEU.

I.

ATTEND to Chaulieu's wanton lyre;
While, fluent as the sky-lark sings
When first the morn allures it's wings,
The epicure his theme pursues:
And tell me if, among the choir
Whose music charms the banks of Seine,
So full, so free, so rich a strain
E'er dictated the warbling Muse.

II.

Yet, Hall, while thy judicious ear
Admires the well-dissembled art
That can such harmony impart
To the lame pace of Gallic rhymes;

While

While wit from affectation clear,
Bright images, and paffions true,
Recall to thy affenting view
The envied bards of nobler times;

III.

Say, is not oft his doctrine wrong?
This prieft of pleafure, who afpires
To lead us to her facred fires,
Knows he the ritual of her fhrine?
Say (her fweet influence to thy fong
So may the goddefs ftill afford)
Doth fhe confent to be ador'd
With fhamelefs love and frantic wine?

IV.

Nor Cato, nor Chryfippus here
Need we in high indignant phrafe
From their Elyfian quiet raife;
But pleafure's oracle alone
Confult; attentive, not fevere.
O pleafure, we blafpheme not thee;
Nor emulate the rigid knee
Which bends but at the Stoic throne.

V.

We own had fate to man affign'd
Nor fenfe, nor wifh but what obey
Or Venus foft or Bacchus gay,
Then might our bard's voluptuous creed
Moft aptly govern human kind :
Unlefs perchance what he hath fung
Of tortur'd joints and nerves unftrung,
Some wrangling heretic fhould plead.

VI.

But now with all thefe proud defires
For dauntlefs truth and and honeft fame ;
With that ftrong mafter of our frame,
The inexorable judge within,
What can be done ? Alas, ye fires
Of love ; alas, ye rofy fmiles,
Ye nectar'd cups from happier foils,
—Ye have no bribe his grace to win.

O D E

O D E   VII.

TO THE RIGHT REVEREND
BENJAMIN LORD BISHOP OF WINCHESTER.
M D C C L I V.

I. 1.

FOR toils which patriots have endur'd,
For treason quell'd and laws secur'd,
In every nation Time displays
The palm of honourable praise.
Envy may rail ; and faction fierce
May strive : but what, alas, can those
(Though bold, yet blind and sordid foes)
To gratitude and love oppose,
To faithful story and persuasive verse ?

I. 2.

O nurse of freedom, Albion, say,
Thou tamer of despotic sway,
What man, among thy sons around,
Thus heir to glory hast thou found ?
What page, in all thy annals bright,
Hast thou with purer joy survey'd

S s

Than

Than that where truth, by Hoadly's aid,

Shines through impofture's folemn.fhade,

Through kingly and through facerdotal night?

I. 3.

To him the Teacher blefs'd,

Who fent religion, from the palmy field

By Jordan, like the morn to cheer the weft,

And lifted up the veil which heaven from earth conceal'd,

To Hoadly thus his mandate he addrefs'd:

" Go thou, and refcue my difhonor'd law

" From hands rapacious and from tongues impure:

" Let not my peaceful name be made a lure

" Fell perfecution's mortal fnares to aid:

" Let not my words be impious chains to draw

" The freeborn foul in more than brutal awe,

" To faith without affent, allegiance unrepaid."

II. 1.

No cold or unperforming hand

Was arm'd by heaven with this command.

The world foon felt it: and, on high,

To William's ear with welcome joy

Did Locke among the bleft unfold

The rifing hope of Hoadly's name,

Godolphin then confirm'd the fame;

And Somers, when from earth he came,

And generous Stanhope the fair fequel told.

II. 2. Then

II. 2.

Then drew the lawgivers around,
(Sires of the Grecian name renown'd)
And liftening afk'd, and wondering knew,
What private force could thus fubdue
The vulgar and the great combin'd;
Could war with facred folly wage;
Could a whole nation difengage
From the dread bonds of many an age,
And to new habits mould the public mind.

II. 3.

For not a conqueror's fword,
Nor the ftrong powers to civil founders known,
Were his: but truth by faithful fearch explor'd,
And focial fenfe, like feed, in genial plenty fown.
Wherever it took root, the foul (reftor'd
To freedom) freedom too for others fought.
Not monkifh craft the tyrant's claim divine,
Not regal zeal the bigot's cruel fhrine
Could longer guard from reafon's warfare fage;
Not the wild rabble to fedition wrought,
Nor fynods by the papal Genius taught,
Nor St. John's fpirit loofe, nor Atterbury's rage.

III. 1.

But where fhall recompence be found?
Or how fuch arduous merit crown'd?
For look on life's laborious fcene :
What rugged fpaces lie between
Adventurous virtue's early toils
And her triumphal throne ! The fhade
Of death, mean time, does oft invade
Her progrefs ; nor, to us difplay'd,
Wears the bright heroine her expected fpoils.

III. 2.

Yet born to conquer is her power :
—O Hoadly, if that favourite hour
On earth arrive, with thankful awe
We own juft heaven's indulgent law,
And proudly thy fuccefs behold ;
We attend thy reverend length of days
With benediction and with praife,
And hail Thee in our public ways
Like fome great fpirit fam'd in ages old.

III. 3.

While thus our vows prolong
Thy fteps on earth, and when by us refign'd
Thou join'ft thy feniors, that heroic throng
Who refcu'd or preferv'd the rights of human kind,
O ! not unworthy may thy Albion's tongue

Thee

Thee ftill, her friend and benefactor, name:
O! never, Hoadly, in thy country's eyes,
May impious gold, or pleafure's gaudy prize,
Make public virtue, public freedom, vile;
Nor our own manners tempt us to difclaim
That heritage, our nobleft wealth and fame,
Which Thou haft kept intire from force and factious guile.

O D E   VIII.

I.

IF rightly tuneful bards decide,
　If it be fix'd in love's decrees,
That beauty ought not to be tried
　But by its native power to pleafe,
Then tell me, youths and lovers, tell,
What fair can Amoret excell?

II.

Behold that bright unfullied fmile,
　And wifdom fpeaking in her mien:
Yet (fhe fo artlefs all the while,
　So little ftudious to be feen)

We

We nought but inftant gladnefs know,
Nor think to whom the gift we owe.

III.

But neither mufic, nor the powers
    Of youth and mirth and frolick cheer,
Add half that funfhine to the hours,
    Or make life's profpect half fo clear,
As memory brings it to the eye
From fcenes where Amoret was by.

IV.

Yet not a fatirift could there
    Or fault or indifcretion find;
Nor any prouder fage declare
    One virtue, pictur'd in his mind,
Whofe form with lovelier colours glows
Than Amoret's demeanor fhows.

V.

This fure is beauty's happieft part:
    This gives the moft unbounded fway:
This fhall inchant the fubject heart
    When rofe and lily fade away;
And fhe be ftill, in fpite of time,
Sweet Amoret in all her prime.

O D E

O D E IX.

AT STUDY.

I.

WHITHER did my fancy ſtray?
By what magic drawn away
  Have I left my ſtudious theme?
From this philoſophic page,
From the problems of the ſage,
  Wandering thro' a pleaſing dream?

II.

'Tis in vain alas! i find,
Much in vain, my zealous mind
  Would to learned wiſdom's throne
Dedicate each thoughtful hour:
Nature bids a ſofter power
  Claim ſome minutes for his own.

III.

Let the bufy or the wife
View him with contemptuous eyes;
   Love is native to the heart:
Guide its wifhes as you will;
Without Love you'll find it ftill
   Void in one effential part.

IV.

Me though no peculiar fair
Touches with a lover's care;
   Though the pride of my defire
Afks immortal friendfhip's name,
Afks the palm of honeft fame,
   And the old heroic lyre;

IV.

Though the day have fmoothly gone,
Or to letter'd leifure known,
   Or in focial duty fpent;
Yet at eve my lonely breaft
Seeks in vain for perfect reft;
   Languifhes for true content.

O D E

O D E X.

T O
THOMAS EDWARDS, ESQUIRE:
ON THE LATE EDITION OF
MR. POPE'S WORKS.
MDCCLI.

I.

BELIEVE me, Edwards, to reſtrain
The licence of a railer's tongue
Is what but ſeldom men obtain
By ſenſe or wit, by proſe or ſong:
A taſk for more Herculean powers,
Nor ſuited to the ſacred hours
Of leiſure in the Muſe's bowers.

II.

In bowers where laurel weds with palm,
The Muſe, the blameleſs queen, reſides:
Fair fame attends, and wiſdom calm
Her eloquence harmonious guides:
While, ſhut for ever from her gate,
Oft trying, ſtill repining, wait
Fierce envy and calumnious hate.

III.

Who then from her delightful bounds
Would ſtep one moment forth to heed
What impotent and ſavage ſounds
From their unhappy mouths proceed ?
No : rather Spenſer's lyre again
Prepare, and let thy pious ſtrain
For Pope's diſhonor'd ſhade complain.

IV.

Tell how diſpleas'd was every bard,
When lately in the Elyſian grove
They of his Muſe's guardian heard,
His delegate to fame above ;
And what with one accord they ſaid
Of wit in drooping age miſled,
And Warburton's officious aid :

V.

How Virgil mourn'd the ſordid fate
To that melodious lyre aſſign'd
Beneath a tutor who ſo late
With Midas and his rout combin'd
By ſpiteful clamor to confound
That very lyre's enchanting ſound,
Though liſtening realms admir'd around :

VI. How

VI.

How Horace own'd he thought the fire
Of his friend Pope's fatiric line
Did farther fuel fcarce require
From fuch a militant divine:
How Milton fcorn'd the fophift vain
Who durft approach his hallow'd ftrain
With unwafh'd hands and lips profane.

VII.

Then Shakefpear debonnair and mild
Brought that ftrange comment forth to view;
Conceits more deep, he faid and fmil'd,
Than his own fools or madmen knew:
But thank'd a generous friend above,
Who did with free adventurous love
Such pageants from his tomb remove.

VIII.

And if to Pope, in equal need,
The fame kind office thou would'ft pay,
Then, Edwards, all the band decreed
That future bards with frequent lay
Should call on thy aufpicious name,
From each abfurd intruder's claim
To keep inviolate their fame.

T t 2

O D E

O D E   XI.

T O   T H E

C O U N T R Y   G E N T L E M E N
O F   E N G L A N D.

M DCC LVIII.

I.

WHITHER is Europe's ancient fpirit fled?
Where are thofe valiant tenants of her fhore,
Who from the warrior bow the ftrong dart fped,
Or with firm hand the rapid pole-ax bore?
Freeman and foldier was their common name.
Who late with reapers to the furrow came,
Now in the front of battle charg'd the foe:
Who taught the fteer the wintry plough to indure,
Now in full councils check'd incroaching power,
And gave the guardian laws their majefty to know.

II. But

II.

But who are ye ? from Ebro's loitering fons
To Tiber's pageants, to the fports of Seine ;
From Rhine's frail palaces to Danube's thrones
And cities looking on the Cimbric main,
Ye loft, ye felf-deferted ? whofe proud lords
Have baffled your tame hands, and given your fwords
To flavifh ruffians, hir'd for their command :
Thefe, at fome greedy monk's or harlot's nod,
See rifled nations crouch beneath their rod :
Thefe are the public will, the reafon of the land.

III.

Thou, heedlefs Albion, what, alas, the while
Doft thou prefume ?   O inexpert in arms,
Yet vain of freedom, how doft thou beguile,
With dreams of hope, thefe near and loud alarms ?
Thy fplendid home, thy plan of laws renown'd,
The praife and envy of the nations round,
What care haft thou to guard from fortune's fway ?
Amid the ftorms of war, how foon may all
The lofty pile from its foundations fall,
Of ages the proud toil, the ruin of a day !

IV.

No : thou art rich, thy ſtreams and fertile vales
Add induſtry's wiſe gifts to nature's ſtore :
And every port is crouded with thy ſails,
And every wave throws treaſure on thy ſhore.
What boots it ? If luxurious plenty charm
Thy ſelfiſh heart from glory, if thy arm
Shrink at the frowns of danger and of pain,
Thoſe gifts, that treaſure is no longer thine.
Oh rather far be poor.   Thy gold will ſhine
Tempting the eye of force, and deck thee to thy bane.

V.

But what hath force or war to do with thee ?
Girt by the azure tide and thron'd ſublime
Amid thy floating bulwarks, thou canſt ſee,
With ſcorn, the fury of each hoſtile clime
Daſh'd ere it reach thee.   Sacred from the foe
Are thy fair fields. athwart thy guardian prow
No bold invader's foot ſhall tempt the ſtrand—
Yet ſay, my country, will the waves and wind
Obey thee ? Haſt thou all thy hopes reſign'd
To the ſky's fickle faith ? the pilot's wavering hand ?

VI. For

VI.

For oh may neither fear nor ftronger love
(Love, by thy virtuous princes nobly won)
Thee, laft of many wretched nations, move,
With mighty armies ftation'd round the throne
To truft thy fafety.   Then, farewell the claims
Of freedom ! Her proud records to the flames
Then bear, an offering at ambition's fhrine ;
Whate'er thy ancient patriots dar'd demand
From furious John's, or faithlefs Charles's hand,
Or what great William feal'd for his adopted line.

VII.

But if thy fons be worthy of their name,
If liberal laws with liberal hearts they prize,
Let them from conqueft, and from fervile fhame
In war's glad fchool their own protectors rife.
Ye chiefly, heirs of Albion's cultur'd plains,
Ye leaders of her bold and faithful fwains,
Now not unequal to your birth be found :
The public voice bids arm your rural ftate,
Paternal hamlets for your enfigns wait,
And grange and fold prepare to pour their youth around.

VIII. Why

VIII.

Why are ye tardy? what inglorious care
Detains you from their head, your native poft?
Who moft their country's fame and fortune fhare,
'Tis .theirs to fhare her toils, her perils moft.
Each man his tafk in focial life fuftains.
With partial labours, with domeftic gains
Let others dwell: to you indulgent heaven
By counfel and by arms the public caufe
To ferve for public love and love's applaufe,
The firft imployment far, the nobleft hire, hath given.

IX.

Have ye not heard of Lacedæmon's fame?
Of Attic chiefs in freedom's war divine?
Of Rome's dread generals? the Valerian name?
The Fabian fons? the Scipios, matchlefs line?
Your lot was theirs. the farmer and the fwain
Met his lov'd patron's fummons from the plain;
The legions gather'd; the bright eagles flew:
Barbarian monarchs in the triumph mourn'd;
The conquerors to their houfhold gods return'd,
And fed Calabrian flocks, and fteer'd the Sabine plough.

X. Shall

X.

Shall then this glory of the antique age,
This pride of men, be loft among mankind?
Shall war's heroic arts no more ingage
The unbought hand, the unfubjected mind?
Doth valour to the race no more belong?
No more with fcorn of violence and wrong
Doth forming nature now her fons infpire,
That, like fome myftery to few reveal'd,
The fkill of arms abafh'd and aw'd they yield,
And from their own defence with hopelefs hearts retire?

XI.

O fhame to human life, to human laws!
The loofe adventurer, hireling of a day,
Who his fell fword without affection draws,
Whofe God, whofe country, is a tyrant's pay,
This man the leffons of the field can learn;
Can every palm, which decks a warrior, earn,
And every pledge of conqueft: while in vain,
To guard your altars, your paternal lands,
Are focial arms held out to your free hands:
Too arduous is the lore; too irkfome were the pain.

U uXII. Meantime

XII.

Meantime by pleasure's lying tales allur'd,
From the bright sun and living breeze ye stray;
And deep in London's gloomy haunts immur'd,
Brood o'er your fortune's, freedom's, health's decay.
O blind of choice and to yourselves untrue!
The young grove shoots, their bloom the fields renew,
The manfion asks its lord, the swains their friend;
While he doth riot's orgies haply share,
Or tempt the gamester's dark, destroying snare,
Or at some courtly shrine with slavish incense bend.

XIII.

And yet full oft your anxious tongues complain
That lawless tumult prompts the rustic throng;
That the rude village-inmates now disdain
Those homely ties which rul'd their fathers long.
Alas, your fathers did by other arts
Draw those kind ties around their simple hearts,
And led in other paths their ductile will;
By succour, faithful counsel, courteous cheer,
Won them the ancient manners to revere,
To prize their country's peace and heaven's due rites fulfill.

XIV. But

XIV.

But mark rhe judgement of experienc'd Time,
   Tutor of nations.   Doth light difcord tear
A ftate? and impotent fedition's crime?
   The powers of warlike prudence dwell not there;
   The powers who to command and to obey,
   Inftruct the valiant.   There would civil fway
The rifing race to manly concord tame?
   Oft let the marfhal'd field their fteps unite,
   And in glad fplendor bring before their fight
One common caufe and one hereditary fame.

XV.

Nor yet be aw'd, nor yet your tafk difown,
   Though war's proud votaries look on fevere;
   Though fecrets, taught erewhile to them alone,
They deem profan'd by your intruding ear.
   Let them in vain, your martial hope to quell,
   Of new refinements, fiercer weapons tell,
And mock the old fimplicity, in vain:
   To the time's warfare, fimple or refin'd,
   The time itfelf adapts the warrior's mind;
And equal prowefs ftill fhall equal palms obtain.

XVI. Say

XVI.

Say then ; if England's youth, in earlier days,
On glory's field with well-train'd armies vy'd,
Why shall they now renounce that generous praife ?
Why dread the foreign mercenary's pride ?
Though Valois brav'd young Edward's gentle hand,
And Albret rush'd on Henry's way-worn band,
With Europe's chofen fons in arms renown'd,
Yet not on Vere's bold archers long they look'd,
Nor Audley's fquires nor Mowbray's yeomen brook'd :
They faw their ftandard fall, and left their monarch bound.

XVII.

Such were the laurels which your fathers won ;
Such glory's dictates in their dauntlefs breaft :
— Is there no voice that fpeaks to every fon ?
No nobler, holier call to You addrefs'd ?
O ! by majeftic freedom, righteous laws,
By heavenly truth's, by manly reafon's caufe,
Awake ; attend ; be indolent no more :
By friendfhip, focial peace, domeftic love,
Rife ; arm ; your country's living fafety prove ;
And train her valiant youth, and watch around her fhore.

O D E

O D E   XII.

ON RECOVERING FROM A FIT OF SICKNESS,
IN THE COUNTRY.
M D C C L V I I I.

I.

THY verdant scenes, O Goulder's hill,
Once more i seek, a languid gueft:
With throbbing temples and with burden'd breaft
Once more i climb thy fteep aerial way.
O faithful cure of oft-returning ill,
   Now call thy fprightly breezes round,
   Diffolve this rigid cough profound,
And bid the fprings of life with gentler movement play.

II.

   How gladly 'mid the dews of dawn
   My weary lungs thy healing gale,
The balmy weft or the frefh north, inhale!
How gladly, while my mufing footfteps rove
Round the cool orchard or the funny lawn,
   Awak'd i ftop, and look to find
   What fhrub perfumes the pleafant wind,
Or what wild fongfter charms the Dryads of the grove.

III. Now,

III.

Now, ere the morning walk is done,
The diſtant voice of health i hear
Welcome as beauty's to the lover's ear.
" Droop not, nor doubt of my return," ſhe cries;
" Here will i, 'mid the radiant calm of noon,
　" Meet thee beneath yon cheſnut bower,
　" And lenient on thy boſom pour
" That indolence divine which lulls the earth and ſkies."

IV.

The goddeſs promis'd not in vain.
I found her at my favorite time.
Nor wiſh'd to breathe in any ſofter clime,
While (half-reclin'd, half-ſlumbering as i lay)
She hover'd o'er me.　Then, among her train
　Of nymphs and zephyrs, to my view
　Thy gracious form appear'd anew,
Then firſt, o heavenly Muſe, unſeen for many a day.

V.

In that ſoft pomp the tuneful maid
Shone like the golden ſtar of love.
I ſaw her hand in careleſs meaſures move;
I heard ſweet preludes dancing on her lyre,
While my whole frame the ſacred ſound obey'd.
　New ſunſhine o'er my fancy ſprings,
　New colours clothe external things,
And the laſt glooms of pain and ſickly plaint retire.

VI. O

VI.

O Goulder's hill, by thee reftor'd
Once more to this inliven'd hand,
My harp, which late refounded o'er the land
The voice of glory, folemn and fevere,
My Dorian harp fhall now with mild accord
To thee her joyful tribute pay,
And fend a lefs-ambitious lay
Of friendfhip and of love to greet thy mafter's ear.

VII.

For when within thy fhady feat
Firft from the fultry town he chofe,
And the tir'd fenate's cares, his wifh'd repofe,
Then waft thou mine; to me a happier home
For focial leifure : where my welcome feet,
Eftrang'd from all the intangling ways
In which the reftlefs vulgar ftrays,
Through nature's fimple paths with ancient faith might roam.

VIII.

And while around his fylvan fcene
My Dyfon led the white-wing'd hours,
Oft from the Athenian Academic bowers
Their fages came : oft heard our lingering walk
The Mantuan mufic warbling o'er the green :
And oft did Tully's reverend fhade,
Though much for liberty afraid,
With us of letter'd eafe or virtuous glory talk.

IX. But

IX.

But other guefts were on their way,

And reach'd erelong this favor'd grove;

Even the celeftial progeny of Jove,

Bright Venus, with her all-fubduing fon,

Whofe golden fhaft moft willingly obey

The beft and wifeft.   As they came,

Glad Hymen wav'd his genial flame,

And fang their happy gifts, and prais'd their fpotlefs throne.

X.

I faw when through yon feftive gate

He led along his chofen maid,

And to my friend with fmiles prefenting faid;

" Receive that faireft wealth which heaven affign'd

" To human fortune.   Did thy lonely ftate

" One wifh, one utmoft hope confefs?

" Behold, fhe comes, to adorn and blefs:

" Comes, worthy of thy heart, and equal to thy mind."

O D E

O D E   XIII.

TO THE AUTHOR OF MEMOIRS OF THE HOUSE OF BRANDENBURGH:
M D C C L I.

I.

THE men renown'd as chiefs of human race,
And born to lead in counfels or in arms,
Have feldom turn'd their feet from glory's chace
To dwell with books or court the Mufe's charms.
Yet, to our eyes if haply time hath brought
Some genuine tranfcript of their calmer thought,
There ftill we own the wife, the great, or good ;
And Cæfar there and Xenophon are feen,
As clear in fpirit and fublime of mien,
As on Pharfalian plains, or by the Affyrian flood.

II.

Say thou too, Frederic, was not this thy aim ?
Thy vigils could the ftudent's lamp ingage,
Except for this ? except that future fame
Might read thy genius in the faithful page ?

X x

That

That if hereafter envy shall presume
With words irreverent to inscribe thy tomb,
And baser weeds upon thy palms to fling,
That hence posterity may try thy reign,
Assert thy treaties, and thy wars explain,
And view in native lights the hero and the king.

III.

O evil foresight and pernicious care!
Wilt thou indeed abide by this appeal?
Shall we the lessons of thy pen compare
With private honor or with public zeal?
Whence then at things divine those darts of scorn?
Why are the woes, which virtuous men have borne
For sacred truth, a prey to laughter given?
What fiend, what foe of nature urg'd thy arm
The Almighty of his scepter to disarm?
To push this earth adrift and leave it loose from heaven?

IV.

Ye godlike shades of legislators old,
Ye who made Rome victorious, Athens wise,
Ye first of mortals with the bless'd inroll'd,
Say did not horror in your bosoms rise,
When thus by impious vanity impell'd
A magistrate, a monarch, ye beheld

Affronting

Affronting civil order's holieft bands ?
Thofe bands which ye fo labor'd to improve ?
Thofe hopes and fears of juftice from above,
Which tam'd the favage world to your divine commands ?

O D E XIV.

THE COMPLAINT.

I.

AWAY! Away!
Tempt me no more, infidious love :
Thy foothing fway
Long did my youthful bofom prove :
At length thy treafon is difcern'd,
At length fome dear-bought caution carn'd :
Away! nor hope my riper age to move.

II.

1 know, i fee
Her merit.   Needs it now be fhewn,
Alas, to me ?
How often, to myfelf unknown,
The graceful, gentle, virtuous maid
Have i admir'd! How often faid,
What joy to call a heart like her's one's own !

X x 2   III. But,

III.

But, flattering god,
O squanderer of content and eafe,.
In thy abode
Will care's rude leffon learn to pleafe ?
O fay, deceiver, haft thou won,
Proud fortune to attend thy throne,
Or plac'd thy friends above her ftern decrees ?

O D E XV.

ON DOMESTIC MANNERS.
[UNFINISHED.]

I.

MEEK honor, female fhame,
O! whither, fweeteft offspring of the fky,
From Albion doft thou fly ;
Of Albion's daughters once the favorite fame ?
O beauty's only friend,
Who giv'ft her pleafing reverence to infpire ;
Who felfifh, bold defire
Doft to efteem and dear affection turn ;
Alas, of thee forlorn
What joy, what praife, what hope can life pretend ?

II. Behold ;

II.

Behold; our youths in vain
Concerning nuptial happinefs inquire:
   Our maids no more afpire
The arts of bafhful Hymen to attain;
   But with triumphant eyes
And cheeks impaffive, as they move along,
   Afk homage of the throng.
The lover fwears that in a harlot's arms
   Are found the felf-fame charms,
And worthlefs and deferted lives and dies.

III.

Behold; unblefs'd at home,
The father of the cheerlefs houfehold mourns:
   The night in vain returns,
For love and glad content at diftance roam;
   While fhe, in whom his mind
Seeks refuge from the day's dull tafk of cares,
   To meet him fhe prepares,
Through noife and fpleen and all the gamefter's art,
   A liftlefs, harrafs'd heart,
Where not one tender thought can welcome find.

IV. 'Twas

IV.

'Twas thus, along the fhore
Of Thames, Britannia's guardian Genius heard,
From many a tongue preferr'd,
Of ftrife and grief the fond invective lore:
At which the queen divine
Indignant, with her adamantine fpear
Like thunder founding near,
Smote the red crofs upon her filver fhield,
And thus her wrath reveal'd.
(I watch'd her awful words and made them mine.)

*   *   *   *   *

THE END OF BOOK THE SECOND.

NOTES

N O T E S

ON THE

TWO BOOKS OF ODES.

B. I. Ode XVIII. Stanza II. 2.] *Lycurgus* the *Lacedæmonian* lawgiver brought into *Greece* from *Asia Minor* the first complete copy of *Homer's* works.—At *Platæa* was fought the decisive battle between the *Persian* army and the united militia of *Greece* under *Pausanias* and *Ariflides.*—*Cimon* the *Athenian* erected a trophy in *Cyprus* for two great victories gained on the same day over the *Persians* by sea and land. *Diodorus Siculus* has preserved the inscription which the *Athenians* affixed to the confecrated spoils, after this great success; in which it is very remarkable, that the greatness of the occasion has raised the manner of expression above the usual simplicity and modefty of all other ancient inscriptions. It is this:

ΕΞ. ΟΥ. Γ'. ΕΥΡΩΠΗΝ. ΑΣΙΑΣ. ΔΙΧΑ. ΠΟΝΤΟΣ. ΕΝΕΙΜΕ.
ΚΑΙ. ΠΟΛΕΑΣ. ΘΝΗΤΩΝ. ΘΟΥΡΟΣ. ΑΡΗΣ. ΕΠΕΧΕΙ.
ΟΥΔΕΝ. ΠΩ. ΤΟΙΟΥΤΟΝ. ΕΠΙΧΘΟΝΙΩΝ. ΓΕΝΕΤ'. ΑΝΔΡΩΝ.
ΕΡΓΟΝ. ΕΝ. ΗΠΕΙΡΩΙ. ΚΑΙ. ΚΑΤΑ. ΠΟΝΤΟΝ. ΑΜΑ.
ΟΙΔΕ. ΓΑΡ. ΕΝ. ΚΥΠΡΩΙ. ΜΗΔΟΥΣ. ΠΟΛΛΟΥΣ. ΟΛΕΣΑΝΤΕΣ.
ΦΟΙΝΙΚΩΝ. ΕΚΑΤΟΝ. ΝΑΥΣ. ΕΛΟΝ. ΕΝ. ΠΕΛΑΓΕΙ.
ΑΝΔΡΩΝ. ΠΛΗΘΟΥΣΑΣ. ΜΕΓΑ. Δ'. ΕΣΤΕΝΕΝ. ΑΣΙΣ. ΥΠ'. ΑΥΤΩΝ.
ΠΛΗΓΕΙΣ'. ΑΜΦΟΤΕΡΑΙΣ. ΧΕΡΣΙ. ΚΡΑΤΕΙ. ΠΟΛΕΜΟΥ.

The following tranflation is almost literal:

> Since first the sea from *Asia's* hostile coast
> Divided *Europe*, and the god of war
> Assail'd imperious cities; never yet,
> At once among the waves and on the shore,
> Hath such a labour been atchiev'd by men
> Who earth inhabit. They, whose arms the *Medes*
> In *Cyprus* felt pernicious, they, the same,
> Have won from skilful *Tyre* an hundred ships
> Crouded with warriors. *Asia* groans, in both
> Her hands fore smitten, by the might of war

Stanza II. 3.] *Pindar* was cotemporary with *Aristides* and *Cimon*, in whom the glory of ancient *Greece* was at its height. When *Xerxes* invaded *Greece*, *Pindar* was true to the common interest of his country; though his fellow citizens, the *Thebans*, had sold themselves to the *Persian* king. In one of his odes he expresses the great distress and anxiety of his mind, occasioned by the vast preparations of *Xerxes* against *Greece*. (*Isthm.* 8.) In another he celebrates the victories of *Salamis*, *Platæa*, and *Himera*. (*Pyth.* 1.) It will be necessary to add two or three other particulars of his life, real or fabulous, in order to explain what follows in the text concerning him. First then, he was thought to be so great a favourite of *Apollo*, that the priests of that deity allotted him a constant share of their offerings. It was said of him, as of some other illustrious men, that at his birth a swarm of bees lighted on his lips, and fed him with their honey. It was also a tradition concerning him, that *Pan* was heard to recite his poetry, and seen dancing to one of his hymns on the mountains near *Thebes*. But a real historical fact in his life is, that the *Thebans* imposed a large fine upon him on account of the veneration which he expressed in his poems for that heroic spirit, shewn by the people of *Athens* in defence of the common liberty, which his own fellow citizens had shamefully betrayed. And, as the argument of this ode implies, that *great poetical talents, and high sentiments of liberty, do reciprocally produce and assist each other*, so *Pindar* is perhaps the most exemplary proof of this connection, which occurs in history. The *Thebans* were remarkable, in general, for a slavish disposition through all the fortunes of their common-wealth; at the time of its ruin by *Philip*; and even in its best state, under the administration of *Pelopidas* and *Epaminondas :* and every one knows, they were no less remarkable for great dullness, and want of all genius. That *Pindar* should have equally distinguished himself from the rest of his fellow citizens in both these respects, seems somewhat extraordinary, and is scarce to be accounted for but by the preceding observation.

Stanza III. 3.] Alluding to his *Defence of the people of* England against *Salmasius.* See particularly the manner in which he himself speaks of that undertaking, in the introduction to his reply to *Morus.*

Stanza IV. 3.] *Edward* the Third; from whom descended *Henry Hastings*, third Earl of *Huntingdon*, by the daughter of the Duke of *Clarence*, brother to *Edward* the Fourth.

Stanza V. 3.] At *Whittington*, a village on the edge of *Scarsdale* in *Derbyshire*, the Earls of *Devonshire* and *Danby*, with the Lord *Delamere*, privately concerted the plan of the Revolution. The house in which they met is at present a farmhouse, and the country people distinguish the room where they sat, by the name of *the plotting parlour.*

B. II. Ode VII. Stanza II. 1.] Mr. *Locke* died in 1704, when Mr. *Hoadly* was beginning to distinguish himself in the cause of civil and religious liberty : **Lord**

Godolphin

Godolphin in 1712, when the doctrines of the Jacobite faction were chiefly favoured by those in power: Lord *Somers* in 1716, amid the practices of the nonjuring clergy against the proteſtant eſtabliſhment; and Lord *Stanhope* in 1721, during the controverſy with the lower houſe of convocation.

B. II. Ode X. Stanza V.] During Mr. *Pope's* war with *Theobald*, *Concanen*, and the reſt of their tribe, Mr. *Warburton*, the preſent Lord Biſhop of *Gloucefter*, did with great zeal cultivate their friendſhip; having been introduced, forſooth, at the meetings of that reſpectable confederacy : a favour which he afterwards ſpoke of in very high terms of complacency and thankfulneſs. At the ſame time in his intercourſe with them he treated Mr. *Pope* in a moſt contemptuous manner, and as a writer without genius. Of the truth of theſe aſſertions his Lordſhip can have no doubt, if he recollects his own correſpondence with *Concanen*; a part of which is ſtill in being, and will probably be remembered as long as any of this prelate's writings.

B. II. Ode XIII.] In the year 1751 appeared a very ſplendid edition, in quarto, of *Memoires pour fervir à l'Hiſtoire de la Maifon de Brandebourg, à Berlin & à la Haye*; with a privilege ſigned FEDERIC; the ſame being engraved in imitation of hand-writing. In this edition, among other extraordinary paſſages, are the two following, to which the third ſtanza of this ode more particularly refers :

Page 163.] *Il ſe fit une migration* (the author is ſpeaking of what happened on the revocation of the edict of *Nantes*) *dont on n'avoit guere vu d'exemples dans l'hiſtoire: un peuple entier fortit du royaume par l'eſprit de parti en haine du pape, & pour recevoir fous un autre ciel la communion fous les deux efpeces: quatre cens mille ames ſ'expatrierent ainſi & abandonnerent tous leur biens pour detonner dans d'autres temples les vieux pfeaumes de Clement Marot.*

Page 242.] *La crainte donna le jour à la credulité, & l'amour propre intereſſa bientot le ciel au deſtin des hommes.*

Y y

HYMN

H Y M N

TO THE

N A I A D S.

MDCCXLVI.

A R G U M E N T.

The Nymphs, who preside over springs and rivulets, are addressed at day-break, in honor of their several functions, and of the relations which they bear to the natural and to the moral world. Their origin is deduced from the first allegorical deities, or powers of nature; according to the doctrine of the old mythological poets, concerning the generation of the gods and the rise of things. They are then successively considered, as giving motion to the air and exciting summer-breezes; as nourishing and beautifying the vegetable creation; as contributing to the fullness of navigable rivers, and consequently to the maintenance of commerce; and by that means, to the maritime part of military power. Next is represented their favourable influence upon health, when assisted by rural exercise: which introduces their connection with the art of physic, and the happy effects of mineral medicinal springs. Lastly, they are celebrated for the friendship which the Muses bear them, and for the true inspiration which temperance only can receive: in opposition to the enthusiasm of the more licentious poets.

H Y M N

H Y M N

T O   T H E

N A I A D S.

O'ER yonder eastern hill the twilight pale
Walks forth from darkness; and the God of day,
With bright Astræa seated by his side,
Waits yet to leave the ocean.   Tarry, Nymphs,
Ye Nymphs, ye blue-ey'd progeny of Thames,
Who now the mazes of this rugged heath
Trace with your fleeting steps; who all night long
Repeat, amid the cool and tranquil air,
Your lonely murmurs, tarry: and receive
My offer'd lay.   To pay you homage due,
I leave the gates of sleep; nor shall my lyre
Too far into the splendid hours of morn
Ingage your audience: my observant hand
Shall close the strain ere any sultry beam

Approach

Approach you.　To your fubterranean haunts
Ye then may timely fteal ; to pace with care
The humid fands ; to loofen from the foil
The bubbling fources ; to direct the rills
To meet in wider channels ; or beneath
Some grotto's dripping arch, at height of noon
To flumber, fhelter'd from the burning heaven.

　　Where fhall my fong begin, ye Nymphs ? or end ?
Wide is your praife and copious—Firft of things,
Firft of the lonely powers, ere Time arofe,
Were Love and Chaos.　Love, the fire of Fate ;
Elder than Chaos.　Born of Fate was Time,
Who many fons and many comely births
Devour'd, relentlefs father : 'till the child
Of Rhea drove him from the upper fky,
And quell'd his deadly might.　Then focial reign'd
The kindred powers, Tethys, and reverend Ops,
And fpotlefs Vefta ; while fupreme of fway
Remain'd the cloud-compeller.　From the couch
Of Tethys fprang the fedgy-crowned race,
Who from a thoufand urns, o'er every clime,
Send tribute to their parent ; and from them
Are ye, o Naiads : Arethufa fair,
And tuneful Aganippe ; that fweet name,
Bandufia ; that foft family which dwelt

With

With Syrian Daphne; and the honour'd tribes
Belov'd of Pæon.   Liſten to my ſtrain,
Daughters of Tethys: liſten to your praiſe.
     You, Nymphs, the winged offspring, which of old
Aurora to divine Aſtræus bore,
Owns; and your aid beſeecheth.   When the might
Of Hyperion, from his noontide throne,
Unbends their languid pinions, aid from you
They aſk: Favonius and the mild South-weſt
From you relief implore.   Your ſallying ſtreams
Freſh vigour to their weary wings impart.
Again they fly, diſporting; from the mead
Half ripen'd and the tender blades of corn,
To ſweep the noxious mildew; or diſpel
Contagious ſteams, which oft the parched earth
Breathes on her fainting ſons.   From noon to eve,
Along the river and the paved brook,
Aſcend the cheerful breezes: hail'd of bards
Who, faſt by learned Cam, the Æolian lyre
Sollicit; nor unwelcome to the youth
Who on the heights of Tibur, all inclin'd
O'er ruſhing Anio, with a pious hand
The reverend ſcene delineates, broken fanes,
Or tombs, or pillar'd aqueducts, the pomp
Of ancient Time; and haply, while he ſcans

The

The ruins, with a filent tear revolves
The fame and foitune of imperious Rome.
    You too, o Nymphs, and your unenvious aid
The rural powers confefs; and ftill prepare
For you their choiceft treafures.   Pan commands,
Oft as the Delian king with Sirius holds
The central heavens, the father of the grove
Commands his Dryads over your abodes
To fpread their deepeft umbrage.   well the god
Remembereth how indulgent ye fupplied
Your genial dews to nurfe them in their prime.
    Pales, the pafture's queen, where'er ye ftray,
Purfues your fteps, delighted; and the path
With living verdure clothes.   Around your haunts
The laughing Chloris, with profufeft hand,
Throws wide her blooms, her odors.   Still with you
Pomona feeks to dwell: and o'er the lawns,
And o'er the vale of Richmond, where with Thames
Ye love to wander, Amalthea pours
Well-pleas'd the wealth of that Ammonian horn,
Her dower; unmindful of the fragrant ifles
Nyfæan or Atlantic.   Nor can'ft thou,
(Albeit oft, ungrateful, thou doft mock
The beverage of the fober Naiad's urn,
O Bromius, o Lenæan) nor can'ft thou

Difown

Difown the powers whofe bounty, ill repaid,
With nectar feeds thy tendrils.   Yet from me,
Yet, blamelefs Nymphs, from my delighted lyre,
Accept the rites your bounty well may claim;
Nor heed the fcoffings of the Edonian band.

    For better praife awaits you.   Thames, your fire,
As down the verdant flope your duteous rills
Defcend, the tribute ftately Thames receives,
Delighted; and your piety applauds;
And bids his copious tide roll on fecure,
For faithful are his daughters; and with words
Aufpicious gratulates the bark which, now
His banks forfaking, her adventurous wings
Yields to the breeze, with Albion's happy gifts
Extremeft ifles to blefs.   And oft at morn,
When Hermes, from Olympus bent o'er earth
To bear the words of Jove, on yonder hill
Stoops lightly-failing; oft intent your fprings
He views: and waving o'er fome new-born ftream
His bleft pacific wand, " And yet," he cries,
" Yet," cries the fon of Maia, " though reclufe
" And filent be your ftores, from you, fair Nymphs,
" Flows wealth and kind fociety to men.
" By you my function and my honor'd name
" Do i poffefs; while o'er the Bœtic vale,

Z z

" Or

" Or through the towers of Memphis, or the palms
" By sacred Ganges water'd, i conduct
" The English merchant : with the buxom fleece
" Of fertile Ariconium while i clothe
" Sarmatian kings ; or to the houshold gods
" Of Syria, from the bleak Cornubian shore,
" Dispense the mineral treasure which of old
" Sidonian pilots sought, when this fair land
" Was yet unconscious of those generous arts
" Which wise Phœnicia from their native clime
" Transplanted to a more indulgent heaven."
    Such are the words of Hermes : such the praise,
O Naiads, which from tongues cœlestial waits
Your bounteous deeds.   From bounty issueth power :
And those who, sedulous in prudent works,
Relieve the wants of nature, Jove repays
With noble wealth, and his own seat on earth,
Fit judgements to pronounce, and curb the might
Of wicked men.   Your kind unfailing urns
Not vainly to the hospitable arts
Of Hermes yield their store.   For, o ye Nymphs,
Hath he not won the unconquerable queen
Of arms to court your friendship ? You she owns
The fair associates who extend her sway
Wide o'er the mighty deep ; and grateful things

Of

Of you she uttereth, oft as from the shore
Of Thames, or Medway's vale, or the green banks
Of Vecta, she her thundering navy leads
To Calpe's foaming channel, or the rough
Cantabrian surge; her auspices divine
Imparting to the senate and the prince
Of Albion, to dismay barbaric kings,
The Iberian, or the Celt.   The pride of kings
Was ever scorn'd by Pallas: and of old
Rejoic'd the virgin, from the brazen prow
Of Athens o'er Ægina's gloomy surge,
To drive her clouds and storms; o'erwhelming all
The Persian's promis'd glory, when the realms
Of Indus and the soft Ionian clime,
When Libya's torrid champain and the rocks
Of cold Imaüs join'd their servile bands,
To sweep the sons of liberty from earth.
In vain: Minerva on the bounding prow
Of Athens stood, and with the thunder's voice
Denounc'd her terrors on their impious heads,
And shook her burning ægis.   Xerxes saw:
From Heracléum, on the mountain's height
Thron'd in his golden car, he knew the sign
Cœlestial; felt unrighteous hope forsake
His faultering heart, and turn'd his face with shame.

Z z 2

Hail,

Hail, ye who fhare the ftern Minerva's power;
Who arm the hand of liberty for war:
And give to the renown'd Britannic name
To awe contending monarchs: yet benign,
Yet mild of nature: to the works of peace
More prone, and lenient of the many ills
Which wait on human life.   Your gentle aid
Hygeia well can witnefs; fhe who faves,
From poifonous cates and cups of pleafing bane,
The wretch devoted to the intangling fnares
Of Bacchus and of Comus.   Him fhe leads
To Cynthia's lonely haunts.   To fpread the toils,
To beat the coverts, with the jovial horn
At dawn of day to fummon the loud hounds,
She calls the lingering fluggard from his dreams:
And where his breaft may drink the mountain breeze,
And where the fervor of the funny vale
May beat upon his brow, through devious paths
Beckons his rapid courfer.   Nor when eafe,
Cool eafe and welcome flumbers have becalm'd
His eager bofom, does the queen of health
Her pleafing care withhold.   His decent board
She guards, prefiding; and the frugal powers
With joy fedate leads in: and while the brown
Ennæan dame with Pan prefents her ftores;

While

While changing ſtill, and comely in the change,
Vertumnus and the Hours before him ſpread
The garden's banquet; you to crown his feaſt,
To crown his feaſt, o Naiads, you the fair
Hygeia calls: and from your ſhelving feats,
And groves of poplar, plenteous cups ye bring,
To ſlake his veins: 'till ſoon a purer tide
Flows down thoſe loaded channels; waſheth off
The dregs of luxury, the lurking ſeeds
Of crude diſeaſe; and through the abodes of life
Sends vigour, fends repoſe.   Hail, Naiads: hail,
Who give, to labour, health; to ſtooping age,
The joys which youth had ſquander'd.   Oft your urns
Will i invoke; and frequent in your praiſe,
Abaſh the frantic Thyrſus with my ſong.

   For not eſtrang'd from your benignant arts
Is he, the god, to whoſe myſterious ſhrine
My youth was ſacred, and my votive cares
Belong; the learned Pæon.   Oft when all
His cordial treaſures he hath fearch'd in vain;
When herbs, and potent trees, and drops of balm
Rich with the genial influence of the ſun,
(To rouſe dark fancy from her plantive dreams,
To brace the nervelefs arm, with food to win
Sick appetite, or huſh the unquiet breaſt

Which

Which pines with silent paffion) he in vain
Hath prov'd ; to your deep manfions he defcends.
Your gates of humid rock, your dim arcades,
He entereth ; where impurpled veins of ore
Gleam on the roof; where through the rigid mine
Your trickling rills infinuate.   There the god
From your indulgent hands the ftreaming bowl
Wafts to his pale-ey'd fuppliants ; wafts the feeds
Metallic and the elemental falts
Wafh'd from the pregnant glebe.   They drink : and foon
Flies pain ; flies inaufpicious care : and foon
The focial haunt or unfrequented fhade
Hears Io, Io Pæan ; as of old,
When Python fell.   And, o propitious Nymphs,
Oft as for haplefs mortals i implore
Your falutary fprings, through every urn
Oh fhed your healing treafures.   With the firft
And fineft breath, which from the genial ftrife
Of mineral fermentation fprings, like light
O'er the frefh morning's vapours, luftrate then
The fountain, and inform the rifing wave.

    My lyre fhall pay your bounty.   Scorn not ye
That humble tribute.   Though a mortal hand
Excite the ftrings to utterance, yet for themes
Not unregarded of cœleftial powers,

1 frame

I frame their language; and the Mufes deign
To guide the pious tenor of my lay.
The Mufes (facred be their gifts divine)
In early days did to my wondering fenfe
Their fecrets oft reveal: oft my rais'd ear
In flumber felt their mufic: oft at noon
Or hour of funfet, by fome lonely ftream,
In field or fhady grove, they taught me words
Of power from death and envy to preferve
The good man's name. whence yet with grateful mind,
And offerings unprofan'd by ruder eye,
My vows i fend, my homage, to the feats
Of rocky Cirrha, where with you they dwell:
Where you their chafte companions they admit
Through all the hallow'd fcene: where oft intent,
And leaning o'er Caftalia's moffy verge,
They mark the cadence of your confluent urns,
How tuneful, yielding gratefulleft repofe
To their conforted meafure: 'till again,
With emulation all the founding choir,
And bright Apollo, leader of the fong,
Their voices through the liquid air exalt,
And fweep their lofty ftrings: thofe powerful ftrings
That charm the mind of gods: that fill the courts
Of wide Olympus with oblivion fweet

Of

Of evils, with immortal reft from cares;
Affuage the terrors of the throne of Jove;
And quench the formidable thunderbolt
Of unrelenting fire.   With flacken'd wings,
While now the folemn concert breathes around,
Incumbent o'er the fceptre of his lord
Sleeps the ftern eagle; by the number'd notes,
Poffefs'd; and fatiate with the melting tone:
Sovereign of birds.   The furious god of war,
His darts forgetting, and the winged wheels
That bear him vengeful o'er the embattled plain,
Relents, and fooths his own fierce heart to eafe,
Moft welcome eafe.   The fire of gods and men,
In that great moment of divine delight,
Looks down on all that live; and whatfoe'er
He loves not, o'er the peopled earth and o'er
The interminated ocean, he beholds
Curs'd with abhorrence by his doom fevere,
And troubled at the found.   Ye, Naiads, ye
With ravifh'd ears the melody attend
Worthy of facred filence.   But the flaves
Of Bacchus with tempeftuous clamours ftrive
To drown the heavenly ftrains; of higheft Jove,
Irreverent; and by mad prefumption fir'd
Their own difcordant raptures to advance.

With

With hoftile emulation.   Down they rufh
From Nyfa's vine-impurpled cliff, the dames
Of Thrace, the Satyrs, and the unruly Fauns,
With old Silenus, reeling through the crowd
Which gambols round him, in convulfions wild
Toffing their limbs, and brandifhing in air
The ivy-mantled thyrfus, or the torch
Through black fmoke flaming, to the Phrygian pipe's
Shrill voice, and to the clafhing cymbals, mix'd
With fhrieks and frantic uproar.   May the gods
From every unpolluted ear avert
Their orgies! If within the feats of men,
Within the walls, the gates, where Pallas holds
The guardian key, if haply there be found
Who loves to mingle with the revel-band
And hearken to their accents; who afpires
From fuch inftructers to inform his breaft
With verfe; let him, fit votarift, implore
Their infpiration.   He perchance the gifts
Of young Lyæus, and the dread exploits,
May fing in apteft numbers: he the fate
Of fober Pentheus, he the Paphian rites,
And naked Mars with Cytherea chain'd,
And ftrong Alcides in the fpinfter's robes,
May celebrate, applauded.   But with you,

A a a

O Naiads,

O Naiads, far from that unhallow'd rout,
Muft dwell the man whoe'er to praifed themes
Invokes the immortal Mufe.   the immortal Mufe
To your calm habitations, to the cave
Corycian or the Delphic mount, will guide
His footfteps; and with your unfullied ftreams
His lips will bathe: whether the eternal lore
Of Themis, or the majefty of Jove,
To mortals he reveal; or teach his lyre
The unenvied guerdon of the patriot's toils,
In thofe unfading iflands of the blefs'd,
Where facred bards abide.   Hail, honor'd Nymphs;
Thrice hail.   for You the Cyrenaïc fhell
Behold, i touch, revering.   To my fongs
Be prefent ye with favorable feet,
And all profaner audience far remove.

                                        NOTES

Page 350. l. 11.   *—Love—*

    Elder than Chaos.] *Hesiod*, in his *Theogony*, gives a different account, and makes Chaos the eldest of beings; though he assigns to Love neither father nor superior; which circumstance is particularly mentioned by *Phædrus*, in *Plato's Banquet*, as being observable not only in *Hesiod*, but in all other writers both of verse and prose: and on the same occasion he cites a line from *Parmenides*, in which Love is expresly stiled the eldest of all the gods. Yet *Aristophanes*, in *The Birds*, affirms, that " Chaos, and Night, and Erebus, and Tartarus, were " first ; and that Love was produced from an egg, which the sable-winged night de- " posited in the immense bosom of Erebus." But it must be observed, that the Love designed by this comic poet was always distinguished from the other, from that original and self-existent being the TO ON or ΑΓΑΘΟΝ of *Plato*, and meant only the ΔΗΜΙΟΥΡΓΟΣ or second person of the old *Græcian* trinity ; to whom is inscribed an hymn among those which pass under the name of *Orpheus*, where he is called *Protogonos*, or the first-begotten, is said to have been born of an egg, and is repre- sented as the principal or origin of all these external appearances of nature. In the fragments of *Orpheus*, collected by *Henry Stephens*, he is named *Phanes*, the disco- verer or discloser; who unfolded the ideas of the supreme intelligence, and ex- posed them to the perception of inferior beings in this visible frame of the world ; as *Macrobius*, and *Proclus*, and *Athenagoras* all agree to interpret the several passages of *Orpheus* which they have preserved.

    But the Love designed in our text, is the one self-existent and infinite mind, whom if the generality of ancient mythologists have not introduced or truly described in accounting for the production of the world and its appearances; yet, to a modern poet, it can be no objection that he hath ventured to differ from them in this par- ticular; though, in other respects, he professeth to imitate their manner and con- form to their opinions. For, in these great points of natural theology, they differ no less remarkably among themselves ; and are perpetually confounding the philo- sophical relations of things with the traditionary circumstances of mythic history:

upon

upon which very account, *Callimachus*, in his hymn to *Jupiter*, declareth his diffent from them concerning even an article of the national creed; adding, that the ancient bards were by no means to be depended on. And yet in the exordium of the old *Argonautic* poem, afcribed to *Orpheus*, it is faid, that " Love, whom mortals " in later times call *Phanes*, was the father of the eternally-begotten Night;" who is generally reprefented by thefe mythological poets, as being herfelf the parent of all things; and who, in the *Indigitamenta*, or *Orphic Hymns*, is faid to be the fame with *Cypris*, or Love itfelf. Moreover, in the body of this *Argonautic* poem, where the perfonated *Orpheus* introduceth himfelf finging to his lyre in reply to *Chiron*, he celebrateth " the obfcure memory of Chaos, and the natures which it contained " within itfelf in a ftate of perpetual viciffitude; how the heaven had its boundary " determined; the generation of the earth; the depth of the ocean; and alfo the " fapient Love, the moft ancient, the felf-fufficient; with all the beings which he " produced when he feparated one thing from another." Which noble paffage is more directly to *Ariftotle's* purpofe in the firft book of his metaphyfics than any of thofe which he has there quoted, to fhew that the ancient poets and mythologifts agreed with *Empedocles*, *Anaxagoras*, and the other more fober philofophers, in that natural anticipation and common notion of mankind concerning the neceffity of mind and reafon to account for the connexion, motion, and good order of the world. For, though neither this poem, nor the hymns which pafs under the fame name, are, it fhould feem, the work of the real *Orpheus*; yet beyond all queftion, they are very ancient. The hymns, more particularly, are allowed to be older than the invafion of *Greece* by *Xerxes*; and were probably a fett of public and folemn forms of devotion: as appears by a paffage in one of them, which *Demofthenes* hath almoft literally cited in his firft oration againft *Ariftogiton*, as the faying of *Orpheus*, the founder of their moft holy myfteries. On this account, they are of higher authority than any other mythological work now extant, the *Theogony* of *Hefiod* himfelf not excepted. The poetry of them is often extremely noble; and the myfterious air which prevails in them, together with its delightful impreffion upon the mind, cannot be better expreffed than in that remarkable defcription with which they infpired the *German* editor *Efchenbach*, when he accidentally met with them at *Leipfic:* " Thefaurum me reperiffe crédidi, fays he, & profecto thefaurum reperi. Incredibile dictu quo me facro horrore afflaverint indigitamenta ifta deorum : nam et tempus ad illorum lectionem eligere cogebar, quod vel folum horrorem incutere animo poteft, nocturnum ; cum enim totam diem confumferim in contemplando urbis fplendore, & in adeundis, quibus fcatet urbs illa, viris doctis; fola nox reftabat, quam *Orpheo* confecrare potui. In abyffum quendam myfteriorum venerandæ antiquitatis defcendere videbar, quotiefcunque filente mundo, folis vigilantibus aftris et luna, μελαινρότας iftos hymnos ad manus fumfi."

l. 11. Chaos.

l. 11. *Chaos.*] The unformed, undigested mass of *Moses* and *Plato:* which *Milton* calls

"The womb of nature."

l. 11. *Love, the sire of Fate.*] Fate is the universal system of natural causes; the work of the Omnipotent Mind, or of Love: so *Minucius Felix:* "Quid enim aliud est fatum, quam quod de unoquoque nostrum deus fatus est." So also *Cicero*, in *The First Book on Divination:* "Fatum autem id appello, quod *Græci* ΕΙΡΜΑΡΜΕΝΗΝ; id est, ordinem seriemque causarum, cum causa causæ nexa rem ex se gignat—ex quo intelligitur, ut fatum sit non id quod superstitiose, sed id quod physice dicitur causa æterna rerum." To the same purpose is the doctrine of *Hierocles*, in that excellent fragment concerning Providence and Destiny. As to the three Fates, or Destinies of the poets, they represented that part of the general system of natural causes which relates to man, and to other mortal beings: for so we are told in the hymn addressed to them among the *Orphic Indigitamenta*, where they are called the daughters of Night (or Love), and, contrary to the vulgar notion, are distinguished by the epithets of gentle, and tender-hearted. According to *Hesiod, Theog.* ver. 904, they were the daughters of *Jupiter* and *Themis:* but in the *Orphic Hymn to Venus*, or Love, that Goddess is directly stiled the mother of Necessity, and is represented, immediately after, as governing the three Destinies, and conducting the whole system of natural causes.

l. 12. *Born of Fate was Time.*] Cronos, Saturn, or Time, was, according to *Apollodorus*, the son of *Cælum* and *Tellus*. But the author of the hymns gives it quite undisguised by mythological language, and calls him plainly the offspring of the earth and the starry heaven; that is, of Fate, as explained in the preceding note.

l. 13. *Who many sons-devour'd.*] The known fable of Saturn devouring his children was certainly meant to imply the dissolution of natural bodies; which are produced and destroyed by Time.

l. 14, 15. *The child of Rhea.*] Jupiter, so called by *Pindar*.

l. 15. *Drove him from the upper sky.*] That *Jupiter* dethroned his father *Saturn*, is recorded by all the mythologists. *Phurnutus*, or *Cornutus*, the author of a little *Greek* treatise on the nature of the gods, informs us, that by *Jupiter* was meant the vegetable soul of the world, which restrained and prevented those uncertain alterations which *Saturn*, or Time, used formerly to cause in the mundane system.

l. 16. *Then social reign'd.*] Our mythology here supposeth, that before the establishment of the vital, vegetative, plastic nature (represented by *Jupiter*), the four elements were in a variable and unsettled condition; but afterwards, well-disposed and at peace among themselves. *Tethys* was the wife of the Ocean; *Ops*, or *Rhea*, the Earth; *Vesta*, the eldest daughter of *Saturn*, Fire; and the cloud-compeller, or Ζεὺς νεφεληγερέτης, the Air: though he also represented the plastic principle of nature, as may be seen in the *Orphic* hymn inscribed to him.

l. 20.

l. 20. *The sedgy-crowned race.*] The river-gods; who, according to *Hesiod's* Theogony, were the sons of *Oceanus* and *Tethys.*

l. 22, 23. *From them, are ye, o Naiads.*] The defcent of the Naiads is lefs certain than moft points of the *Greek* mythology. *Homer*, Odyff. xiii. κεραι Διος. *Virgil*, in *The Eighth Book of the Æneid*, fpeaks as if the Nymphs, or Naiads, were the parents of the rivers: but in this he contradicts the teftimony of *Hefiod*, and evidently departs from the orthodox fyftem, which reprefenteth feveral nymphs as retaining to every fingle river. On the other hand, *Callimachus*, who was very learned in all the fchool-divinity of thofe times, in his hymn to *Delos*, maketh *Peneus*, the great *Theffalian* river-god, the father of his nymphs: and *Ovid*, in *The Fourteenth Book of his Metamorphofes*, mentions the Naiads of *Latium* as the immediate daughters of the neighbouring river-gods. Accordingly, the Naiads of particular rivers are occafionally, both by *Ovid* and *Statius*, called by a patronymic, from the name of the river to which they belong.

P. 351. l. 1. *Syrian Daphne.*] The grove of *Daphne* in Syria, near *Antioch*, was famous for its delightful fountains.

l. 1, 2. *The tribes belov'd by Pæon.*] Mineral and medicinal fprings. *Pæon* was the phyfician of the gods.

l. 4. *The winged offspring.*] The Winds; who, according to *Hefiod* and *Apollodorus*, were the fons of *Aftræus* and *Aurora*.

l. 7. *Hyperion.*] A fon of *Cælum* and *Tellus*, and father of the Sun, who is thence called, by *Pindar*, *Hyperionides*. But *Hyperion* is put by *Homer* in the fame manner as here, for the Sun himfelf.

l. 10. *Your fallying ftreams.*] The ftate of the atmofphere with refpect to reft and motion is, in feveral ways, affected by rivers and running ftreams; and that more efpecially in hot feafons: firft, they deftroy its equilibrium, by cooling thofe parts of it with which they are in contact; and fecondly, they communicate their own motion: and the air which is thus moved by them, being left heated, is of confequence more elaftic than other parts of the atmofphere, and therefore fitter to preferve and to propagate that motion.

P. 352. l. 6. *Delian king.*] One of the epithets of *Apollo*, or the Sun, in the *Orphic* hymn infcribed to him.

l. 15. *Chloris.*] The ancient *Greek* name for *Flora.*

l. 19. *Amalthea.*] The mother of the firft *Bacchus*, whofe birth and education was written, as *Diodorus Siculus* informs us, in the old *Pelafgic* character, by *Thymætes*, grandfon to *Laomedon*, and contemporary with *Orpheus. Thymætes* had travelled over *Libya* to the country which borders on the weftern ocean; there he faw the ifland of *Nyfa*, and learned from the inhabitants, that " *Ammon*, king " of *Libya*, was married in former ages to *Rhea*, fifter of *Saturn* and the *Titans*: " that he afterwards fell in love with a beautiful virgin whofe name was *Amalthea*;

" had

" had by her a fon, and gave her poffeffion of a neighbouring tract of land, won-
" derfully fertile; which in fhape nearly refembling the horn of an ox, was thence
" called the *Hefperian* horn, and afterwards the horn of *Amalthea:* that fearing
" the jealoufy of *Rhea,* he concealed the young *Bacchus,* with his mother, in the
" ifland of *Nyfa;*" the beauty of which, *Diodorus* defcribes with great dignity and
pomp of ftyle. This fable is one of the nobleft in all the ancient mythology, and
feems to have made a particular impreffion on the imagination of *Milton;* the only
modern poet (unlefs perhaps it be neceffary to except *Spenfer)* who, in thefe myfterious traditions of the poetic ftory, had a heart to feel, and words to exprefs,
the fimple and folitary genius of antiquity. To raife the idea of his *Paradife,* he
prefers it even to

<blockquote>
————" that Nyfean ifle
Girt by the river Triton, where old Cham,
(Whom Gentiles Ammon call, and Libyan Jove)
Hid Amalthea, and her florid fon,
Young Bacchus, from his ftepdame Rhea's eye."
</blockquote>

P. 353. l. 5. *Edonian band.*] The prieftesses and other minifters of *Bacchus;* fo
called from *Edonus,* a mountain of *Thrace,* where his rites were celebrated.

l. 16. *When Hermes.*] *Hermes,* or *Mercury,* was the patron of commerce; in
which benevolent character he is addreffed by the author of the *Indigitamenta,* in
thefe beautiful lines:

<blockquote>
Ερμήυευ ϖαίʃων, κερδέμπορε, λυσιμέριμνε,
Ὁς χηρέσθιυ ἔχης εἰρήνης ὅπλον ἀμέμφες.
</blockquote>

P. 354. l. 7. *Difpenfe the mineral treafure.*] The merchants of *Sidon* and *Tyre*
made frequent voyages to the coaft of *Cornwall,* from whence they carried home
great quantities of tin.

l. 22. *Hath he not won.*] *Mercury,* the patron of commerce, being fo greatly de-
pendent on the good offices of the Naiads, in return obtains for them the friendfhip
of *Minerva,* the goddefs of war: for military power, at leaft the naval part of it,
hath conftantly followed the eftablifhment of trade; which exemplifies the preceding
obfervation, that " from bounty iffueth power."

P. 355. l. 4, 5. *Calpe—Cantabrian furge.*] *Gibraltar* and *The Bay of Bifcay.*

l. 11. *Ægina's gloomy furge.*] Near this ifland, the *Athenians* obtained the victory of *Salamis,* over the *Perfian* navy.

l. 21. *Xerxes faw.*] This circumftance is recorded in that paffage, perhaps the
moft fplendid among all the remains of ancient hiftory, where *Plutarch,* in his *Life
of Themiftocles,* defcribes the fea-fights of *Artemifium* and *Salamis.*

P. 357. l. 15. *Thyrfus.*] A ftaff, or fpear, wreathed round with ivy: of conftant ufe in the bacchanalian myfteries.

P. 358.

P. 358. l. 13. *Io, Pæan.*] An exclamation of victory and triumph, derived from *Apollo's* encounter with *Python.*

P. 359. l. 13. *Cirrha.*] One of the summits of *Parnassus,* and sacred to *Apollo.* Near it were several fountains, said to be frequented by the Muses. *Nysa,* the other eminence of the same mountain, was dedicated to *Bacchus.*

l. 24. *Charm the mind of gods.*] This whole passage, concerning the effects of sacred music among the gods, is taken from *Pindar's* first *Pythian* ode.

P. 361. l. 8. *Phrygian pipe's.*] The *Phrygian* music was fantastic and turbulent, and fit to excite disorderly passions.

l. 13, 14. *The gates where Pallas holds*

   The guardian key.] It was the office of *Minerva* to be the guardian of walled cities; whence she was named ΠΟΛΙΑΣ & ΠΟΛΙΟΥΧΟΣ, and had her statues placed in their gates, being supposed to keep the keys; and on that account stiled ΚΛΗΔΟΥΧΟΣ.

l. 21, 22. *Fate of sober Pentheus.*] *Pentheus* was torn in pieces by the bacchanalian priests and women, for despising their mysteries.

P. 362. l. 4, 5. *The cave Corycian.*] Of this cave *Pausanias,* in his *Tenth Book,* gives the following description: " Between *Delphi* and the eminences of *Parnassus,* " is a road to the grotto of *Corycium,* which has its name from the nymph *Corycia,* " and is by far the most remarkable which I have seen. One may walk a great way " into it without a torch. 'Tis of a considerable height, and hath several springs " within it; and yet a much greater quantity of water distills from the shell and " roof, so as to be continually dropping on the ground. The people round *Par-* " *nassus* hold it sacred to the *Corycian* nymphs and to *Pan.*"

l. 5. *Delphic mount.*] *Delphi,* the seat and oracle of *Apollo,* had a mountainous and rocky situation, on the skirts of *Parnassus.*

l. 13. *Cyrenaïc shell.*] *Cyrene* was the native country of *Callimachus,* whose hymns are the most remarkable example of that mythological passion which is assumed in the preceding poem, and have always afforded particular pleasure to the author of it, by reason of the mysterious solemnity with which they affect the mind. On this account he was induced to attempt somewhat in the same manner; solely by way of exercise: the manner itself being now almost intirely abandoned in poetry. And as the meer genealogy, or the personal adventures of heathen gods, could have been but little interesting to a modern reader; it was therefore thought proper to select some convenient part of the history of nature, and to employ these ancient divinities as it is probable they were first employed; to wit, in personifying natural causes, and in representing the mutual agreement or opposition of the corporeal and moral powers of the world: which hath been accounted the very highest office of poetry.

INSCRIP-

INSCRIPTIONS.

INSCRIPTIONS.

I.

FOR A GROTTO.

To me, whom in their lays the shepherds call
Actæa, daughter of the neighbouring stream,
This cave belongs.   The fig-tree and the vine,
Which o'er the rocky entrance downward shoot,
Were plac'd by Glycon.   He with cowslips pale,
Primrose, and purple lychnis, deck'd the green
Before my threshold, and my shelving walls
With honeyfuckle cover'd.   Here at noon,
Lull'd by the murmur of my rifing fount,
I flumber: here my cluftering fruits i tend';
Or from the humid flowers, at break of day,
Fresh garlands weave, and chace from all my bounds
Each thing impure or noxious.   Enter-in,
O ftranger, undifmay'd.   nor bat, nor toad
Here lurks: and if thy breaft of blameless thoughts
Approve thee, not unwelcome fhalt thou tread
My quiet manfion: chiefly, if thy name
Wife Pallas and the immortal mufes own.

II.

FOR A STATUE OF CHAUCER
AT WOODSTOCK.

SUCH was old Chaucer. such the placid mien
Of him who firſt with harmony inform'd
The language of our fathers.   Here he dwelt
For many a cheerful day..   theſe ancient walls
Have often heard him, while his legends blithe
He ſang; of love, or knighthood, or the wiles
Of homely life : through each eſtate and age,
The faſhions and the follies of the world
With cunning hand portraying.   Though perchance
From Blenheim's towers, o ſtranger, thou art come
Glowing with Churchill's trophies; yet in vain
Doſt thou applaud them, if thy breaſt be cold
To him, this other hero; who, in times
Dark and untaught, began with charming verſe
To tame the rudeneſs of his native land.

III. WHO-

III.

WHOE'ER thou art whofe path in fummer lies
Through yonder village, turn thee where the grove
Of branching oaks a rural palace old
Imbofoms. there dwells Albert, generous lord
Of all the harveft round. and onward thence
A low plain chapel fronts the morning light
Faft by a filent riv'let. Humbly walk,
O ftranger, o'er the confecrated ground;
And on that verdant hilloc, which thou fee'ft
Befet with ofiers, let thy pious hand
Sprinkle frefh water from the brook and ftrew
Sweet-fmelling flowers. for there doth Edmund reft,
The learned fhepherd; for each rural art
Fam'd, and for fongs harmonious, and the woes
Of ill-requited love. The faithlefs pride
Of fair Matilda fank him to the grave
In manhood's prime. But foon did righteous heaven
With tears, with fharp remorfe, and pining care,
Avenge her falfhood. nor could all the gold
And nuptial pomp, which lur'd her plighted faith

From

From Edmund to a loftier hufband's home,
Relieve her breaking heart, or turn afide
The ftrokes of death.   Go, traveller; relate
The mournful ftory.   haply fome fair maid
May hold it in remembrance, and be taught
That riches cannot pay for truth or love..

IV.

O YOUTHS and virgins : o declining eld :·
O pale misfortune's flaves : o ye who dwell
Unknown with humble quiet; ye who wait
In courts, or fill the golden feat of kings :·
O fons of fport and pleafure :· o thou wretch·
That weep'ft for jealous love, or the fore wounds.
Of confcious guilt, or death's rapacious hand
Which left thee void of hope : o ye who roam
In exile; ye who through the embattled field
Seek bright renown ; or who for nobler palms
Contend, the leaders of a public caufe ;
Approach : behold this marble.   Know ye not

The

The features? Hath not oft his faithful tongue
Told you the fashion of your own estate,
The secrets of your bosom? Here then, round
His monument with reverence while ye stand,
Say to each other: " This was Shakespear's form ;
" Who walk'd in every path of human life,
" Felt every passion ; and to all mankind
" Doth now, will ever, that experience yield
" Which his own genius only could acquire."

V.

GVLIELMVS III. FORTIS, PIVS, LIBERATOR, CVM INEVNTE AETATE
PATRIAE LABENTI ADFVISSET SALVS IPSE VNICA ; CVM MOX
ITIDEM REIPVBLICAE BRITANNICAE VINDEX RENVNCIATVS ESSET
ATQVE STATOR ; TVM DENIQVE AD ID SE NATVM RECOGNOVIT
ET REGEM FACTVM, VT CVRARET NE DOMINO IMPOTENTI
CEDERENT PAX, FIDES, FORTVNA, GENERIS HVMANI.
AVCTORI PVBLICAE FELICITATIS P. G. A. M. A.

VI. FOR

FOR A COLUMN AT RUNNYMEDE.

T H O U, who the verdant plain doſt traverſe here,
While Thames among his willows from thy view
Retires ; o ſtranger, ſtay thee, and the ſcene
Around contemplate well.   This is the place
Where England's ancient barons, clad in arms
And ſtern with conqueſt, from their tyrant king
(Then render'd tame) did challenge and ſecure
The charter of thy freedom.   Paſs not on
Till thou haſt bleſs'd their memory, and paid
Thoſe thanks which God appointed the reward
Of public virtue. and if chance thy home
Salute thee with a father's honour'd name,
Go, call thy ſons : inſtruct them what a debt
They owe their anceſtors ; and make them ſwear
To pay it, by tranſmitting down intire
Thoſe ſacred rights to which themſelves were born.

THE WOOD NYMPH.

APPROACH in filence. 'tis no vulgar tale
Which i, the Dryad of this hoary oak,
Pronounce to mortal ears.   The fecond age
Now hafteneth to its period, fince i rofe
On this fair lawn.   The groves of yonder vale
Are, all, my offspring: and each Nymph, who guards
The copfes and the furrow'd fields beyond,
Obeys me.   Many changes have i feen
In human things, and many awful deeds
Of juftice, when the ruling hand of Jove
Againft the tyrants of the land, againft
The unhallow'd fons of luxury and guile,
Was arm'd for retribution.   Thus at length
Expert in laws divine, i know the paths
Of wifdom, and erroneous folly's end
Have oft prefag'd: and now well-pleas'd i wait
Each evening till a noble youth, who loves
My fhade, awhile releas'd from public cares,
Yon peaceful gate fhall enter, and fit down
Beneath my branches.   Then his mufing mind
I prompt, unfeen; and place before his view

C c c

Sincereft

Sincereſt forms of good; and move his heart
With the dread bounties of the ſire ſupreme
Of gods and men, with freedom's generous deeds,
The lofty voice of glory and the faith
Of ſacred friendſhip.   Stranger, i have told
My function.   If within thy boſom dwell
Aught which may challenge praiſe, thou wilt not leave
Unhonor'd my abode, nor ſhall i hear
A·ſparing benediction from thy tongue.

VIII.

Y E powers unſeen, to whom, the bards of Greece
Erected altars; ye who to the mind
More lofty views unfold, and prompt the heart
With more divine emotions; if erewhile
Not quite unpleaſing have my votive rites
Of you been deem'd when oft this lonely ſeat
To you i conſecrated; then vouchſafe
Here with your inſtant energy to crown
My happy ſolitude.   It is the hour
When moſt i love to invoke you, and have felt
Moſt frequent your glad miniſtry divine.
The air is calm: the ſun's unveiled orb

Shines

Shines in the middle heaven.   the harveft round
Stands quiet, and among the golden fheaves
The reapers lie reclin'd.   the neighbouring groves
Are mute ; nor even a linnet's random ftrain
Echoeth amid the filence.   Let me feel
Your influence, ye kind powers.   Aloft in heaven,
Abide ye ? or on thofe tranfparent clouds
Pafs, ye from hill to hill ? or on the fhades·
Which yonder elms caft o'er the lake below
Do you converfe retir'd ?   From what lov'd haunt
Shall i expect you ?   Let me once more feel
Your influence, o ye kind infpiring powers :
And i will guard it well, nor fhall a thought
Rife in my mind, nor fhall a paffion move
Acrofs my bofom unobferv'd, unftor'd
By faithful memory.   and then at fome
More active moment,· will i call them forth
Anew ; and join them in majeftic forms,
And give them utterance in harmonious ftrains ;
That all mankind fhall wonder at your fway.

M E tho' in life's fequefter'd vale
The Almighty fire ordain'd to dwell,
Remote from glory's toilfome ways,
And the great fcenes of public praife ;
Yet let me ftill with grateful pride
Remember how my infant frame
He temper'd with prophetic flame,
And early mufic to my tongue fupply'd.

'Twas then my future fate he weigh'd,
And, This be thy concern, he faid,
At once with Paffion's keen alarms,
And Beauty's pleafurable charms,
And facred Truth's eternal light,
To move the various mind of Man ;
Till under one unblemifh'd plan,
His Reafon, Fancy, and his Heart unite.

THE END.

www.ingramcontent.com/pod-product-compliance
Lightning Source LLC
Chambersburg PA
CBHW032149110726
47902CB00003B/755